MISGUIDED

Dave McVeigh
Jim Bolone

NOTE

Some of what you are about to read is based on the actual history of Northern Michigan. The rest of it is made up.

PROLOGUE

Instamatic Island

2007

Opening Night

"Keep it together," Jack McGuinn whispered to himself. His voice, not quite quivering, hissed out, snake-like. He glanced around, bewildered, hoping nobody noticed, as he preferred not to appear insane in public. Jack was nearing fifty, but a devilish sparkle in his eyes made him look younger.

Tonight, he felt fifty.

He was in stunned disbelief as he stood alone, smack dab in the middle of his own art gallery. Gone was his usual uniform of black jeans and a black v-neck T-shirt, a simple, signature look that allowed him to blend anonymously into the shadows of any photo shoot. He had even combed his unruly brown hair into a state of reluctant neatness. Clean khakis and a cotton buttoned-down shirt added a sheen of polish but made him feel foolish. He felt like a Midwest salesman reluctantly dragged to a weekend baby shower by his wife.

Jack's job as a photographer had him squaring off against some of the harshest, most terrifying critics on earth: Corporate America. These were the brand architects, the gatekeepers of the image, their cold eyes missing nothing. Waiting on the verdict from the head of marketing at General Motors as he scrutinized shots of the new Chevy Blazer, or the editor of Vogue Magazine as she silently inspected a photo spread of the latest two-piece swimwear was pressure that either forged you or destroyed you. And he'd risen to the top.

Tonight should've been a cakewalk.

So why was his beer bottle slowly slipping through his fingers? It wasn't the condensation on the bottle. It was the sweat on his palm.

The location was Market Street, Mackinac Island, on the opening night of his photography studio, Rogues' Gallery. He may have been suffering from a colossal, jaw-locking attack of opening night jitters, but at least he was sure about one thing: the gallery's name.

He loved it.

Was he a gallery owner? The very idea felt absurd. But the space buzzed with an enthusiastic crowd of locals and tourists. *It just might work.*

For the fiftieth time, he scanned the walls covered with his photographs, many snapped during his misspent youth on the island with a Kodak Instamatic camera he'd carried with him since he was nine. That's why he labeled the show *Instamatic Island,* a catchy name not quite as satisfying as Rogues' Gallery but serviceable.

In many ways, the *Instamatic Island* show recreated a colossal scrapbook of his life over the last 35 years, all tastefully framed and mounted. Maybe that was the root cause of his apprehension. What he intended as a touching tribute to a place he loved—Mackinac Island—might be the most narcissistic display of ego in the island's history. The line felt razor-thin. Another wave of knee-weakening unease crested as he recalled a critique from a brilliant, smart-assy professor at the Rhode Island School of Design, where he had studied for a few years in his twenties.

"It's good work, Jack. But it's still too *Look, ma! No hands!*" Still too cocky, he'd meant. Too sure of itself. Riding a bike with no hands was showing off. A hard crash to the pavement was sure to follow. Blood would flow.

Was tonight's opening still too *Look, ma! No hands?*

Too late now.

He drowned the queasy concept with a sip of beer. Amid the chatter and clinking of glasses, he focused on the calming strains of the cello across the room—a sound he adored. It was the sound of his wife, Erin, a professional cello player with the Detroit Symphony Orchestra. But today, he loved it even more because his daughter Sara played the instrument. Only twelve, already remarkably skilled, she played away in a corner of the gallery, clad in a frilly dress. Erin stood close to her in a matching outfit— they liked to do that—her intense blue eyes tracking Sara's every chord change. Sara played "Just Like Heaven" by *The Cure.* No doubt, Erin's idea. She had a knack for injecting a touch of subversive, Black Irish rebellion into every cello-worthy event, a trick she'd passed to her daughter.

When Jack met Erin in the summer of 1989, eighteen years earlier, she was playing a stunningly beautiful rendi- tion of "Seek and Destroy" by *Metallica* on the front porch of Grand Hotel. Jack, working as a dockporter, was riding past the hotel with a massive load of luggage in his bike's basket. He was probably the only person who picked up on her sexy, heavy-metal act of defiance at a hotel venerated for decorum, champagne cocktails, and the subdued strains of *The Four Seasons* by Vivaldi. He fell hard for her. Literally. The bungee cord hook barely missed his left nostril when the bike went end-over-end.

Erin floated over and put a comforting hand on Jack's back. While he sparked twitchy nerve-ends, Erin glowed like a campfire. She had been the driving force behind Rogue's Gallery, pushing her husband to unearth the art buried deep in his photos and leave behind the corporate gigs that filled their bank account—but not his soul. It was long overdue. Erin had seen the potential in him long before he had, all the way back to the summer they first met.

A gaggle of Jack's old buddies, many former dock-porters themselves, closed in on her and Jack. Erin had that way. She was Dublin born and bred and carried her who-gives-a-rip spirit as naturally as her lilting accent. She also happened to be drop-dead beautiful, which, for Jack's pals, was an added bonus.

"Hello boyos," she smiled, arms wide as she greeted her husband's cronies like family. They'd all been there that fateful summer of 1989 when she and Jack first collided, scattering love, desire, and betrayal all over Main Street like dumped suitcases.

Smitty, Jack's friend since they were boys, pointed toward one of Jack's photographs. He looked fantastically out of place in an ill-fitting suit that somehow managed to swallow his stocky frame. With short-cropped, salt-and-pepper hair and sharp Native American features, Smitty looked like a blend of a Chippewa warrior and a slimmer Don Rickles, the famous insult comic from the Sinatra era.

"Tell us about this one, Jacky," he said, stroking his chin in an exaggerated mimicry of a pretentious art critic. "I'm fascinated by the intersecting lines and the streaks of light. And ... that blurry, blobby thing." Smitty thrust a bottle of Coors to Jack's face like a microphone. "What was your inspiration?"

Jack's gaze followed Smitty's to the photograph—a striking black-and-white image of the Arnold Line ferry dock. The summer sun had drenched the day in an intense, almost blinding glare, and the effect in black-and-white was undeniably dramatic. Jack McGuinn was talented, even at a young age.

Jack shook his head. "I have no memory of taking that one. I was hungover after closing Horn's Bar the night before. I needed to burn the rest of the roll before the ferry was unloaded. Benjamin's Photo Shop had a two-for-one special on prints, so I snapped it. Truthfully, I'm not sure I even looked through the viewfinder."

AJ, another former porter, fifty-ish, handsome and lean with jet-black Italian hair, leaned in close. His ensemble contrasted with Smitty's, a sleek hipster blazer over a T-shirt touting the eighties band English Beat. "See, now that story would make me want to buy it. It's the *story* that makes it valuable."

Smitty joined in. "True. Otherwise, it's just a *dock*. Who gives a crap about … *a dock?*" He looked at the photo again and squinted. "But I guess it's sorta … grrr, what's the word?" He snapped his fingers frantically.

"Overpriced?" asked AJ.

"Definitely that. *Artsy!* That's the word!"

AJ gave the photo another scan. "You're right, Smitty. It's also a tad bit, dare I say … *fartsy.*"

Smitty nodded, still fake snooty. "One might even classify it as … a*rtsy-fartsy.*"

Smitty gave Jack a brotherly punch on the shoulder, and Jack suddenly felt like he might survive the night. His friends' total lack of respect for his talent was one of the many reasons he wanted them around. Their brutal mockery was the oxygen he needed, saving him from artistic hyperventilation. Other old-school dockporters from the eighties wandered the gallery, drinks in hand, good-naturedly critiquing Jack's work. Foster, Jack's original mentor, laughed with two other 'dock dogs'—Spengler and Superfly—standing in front of a stunning photo of a younger Erin in a rowboat, undoubtedly passing some scandalous detail about the shot.

These boys knew all the stories.

Jack exhaled and smiled. His racing pulse slowed down, almost—but not quite—back to normal. Together, this rabid pack of scoundrels might pull Jack through his low-grade existential meltdown.

The front door jingled. A whip-thin, ancient man in a wheelchair, guided by a woman clad in a light blue nurse's uniform, rolled in. The man's wild, unruly gray hair sprouted from a head like the wax *Phantom of the Opera* figure at the Haunted Theater on Main Street. He raised his left hand, and the rolling chair halted. His long arm suggested he might be tall if he could stand. He took charge of the chair and swiveled to survey the thirty or forty photographs like a film director inspecting an establishing shot. He smiled, and at least a decade dropped away from his face.

He wheeled his chair closer to one photograph, a teenage Jack and three other older guys tricked out in Fort Mackinac guide costumes: blue coats, tricorn hats, and muskets in hand. They stood tall and struck cocky military poses. Despite their faux serious stances, a collective twinkle sparkled. Trouble. A laugh about to break. A whiff of something's up. Their smiles hid capers. Antics. Maybe a mission or two. The old man's eyes danced across the photo.

Jack walked over. "Do you have any questions?"

He turned to Jack and smiled, revealing enormous, horsey teeth. He pointed at the guide photo. "Tell me about this one." His voice cracked, and he coughed hard to clear his throat, which activated a series of deeper hacks.

Jack waited for the fit to subside, then spoke. "This is probably the least artistic of anything here, but for some reason, I hung it on the wall anyway."

"You're some tough negotiator, son," smiled the old man. "Welcome to my side."

"I took it in the summer of 1984. Well, I sorta took it. I set it up. That's me in the middle when I worked as a guide for a summer at Fort Mackinac. I hear now they call them *interpreters*."

Jack took a few steps closer and tapped his finger on the glass. "This tall one is Bert Shively. Rollie Shartz is the heavy guy. This character with the shit-eating grin is Myles Fordham." Jack grew oddly quiet. He hadn't thought of the guides in … how long? Decades, it seemed. But that summer, they were brothers.

The man's eyes didn't leave the photo. "Every picture tells a story, eh?"

"You got that right, sir. And this one's a novel. A ticket-taker at Fort Mackinac actually took the shot. College girl. Really beautiful. Way out of my league." Jack turned away. *What was her name again?* Hard to believe he'd forgotten. There was a phase that summer when her name would flicker across the inside of his eyelids like a neon sign each time he faded off to sleep.

"This was right after we'd finished a reenactment show. Maybe our best show ever."

"There's something in your faces." He leaned closer to the photo. "You look like you're up to no damn good."

If he only knew.

"It was a wild summer. But if you look around this

place," Jack said, "you'll see a lot of wild summers. Somehow, between it all, I managed to sneak in a little art, even if I had no idea that's what I was doing at the time." His voice conveyed a hint of wonder as if seeing his work for the first time.

"You know, I always found that's how the best things happen," the old man said. "Seems artists find their stride amid chaos." His voice sounded paper-thin and coarse. "No second-guessing, just rolling with the punches, letting the story tell itself. The minute you try to control things, it all unravels. All hell breaks loose."

He glanced up at his nurse with a smile. "Jesus, Edna! Pretty profound stuff. Where was I when I needed me?" She smiled back at him. Kind eyes. They had history. He gestured to the photo. "So, any chance the list price includes the story behind it?"

"Only if you're a serious buyer," said Jack, half-joking. He crouched low so the old man could hear him over the din. "There's a lot to tell. Like I said, it was the summer of 1984. I didn't expect to have the guide job at all. See, I kinda—"

"—wait!" The old man signaled. "Stop. The last thing you need right now is to get trapped, yapping to some ancient invalid on your big night. Go make some more money. This deal's closed. I'll be on the island for a few more days." For reasons he couldn't pinpoint, Jack wanted to continue the story, but the old man had a point. It wasn't the ideal time to get stuck in a stop-and-go traffic jam on Memory Lane.

"How about this," Jack said. "I'll prepare the photo for you, wrap it up for shipping, and deliver it tomorrow. Marquette Park, anytime after noon. It's a tradition—me, the family, and some of the fellas get together in the park. Tell a few stories from the old days."

The man grinned. "Deal. Although that doesn't sound like a delivery to me. You're making me work for it." He gestured to Edna. "Okay, you're making *Edna* work for it since she's the one who has to wheel my rotting carcass through the park."

"I'll tell you the whole story behind the photo. Straight, no chaser. What's your go-to lunch?" Jack asked, already planning a picnic menu.

"Leave the sandwiches to us," the old man said. "But do me a favor: Bring me a six-pack of your favorite beer. The doctor said remove all fun from my life if I plan on sticking around another five years, but I'll take the fun. Five more years of crapping in a diaper sounds just *awful.*" He flashed a nod at Edna. She nodded back, skillfully pivoting the wheelchair, and they made their way to the exit.

As they neared the door, he called back. "Consider the soldier-boy photo claimed at the going price, kid. If I find out you sold it to someone else, I'll have Edna here beat your ass. She knows jujee … jee … jilla …" He looked up at her. "What's it called again?"

"Jujitsu!" she shot back, pretending to slap him on the top of his head. "But I never said I knew jujitsu!"

"Quiet, woman! I'm trying to put the fear of God into the kid," he said as they rolled through the front door and out into the island night.

The next day at noon, Jack, Erin, Sarah, and their son John, who was fifteen, sprawled out on a ratty but service-able blanket in Marquette Park. Foster, another of Jack's ride-or-die dockporter buddies, along with AJ, tossed a fris-

bee, their outdated jokes drowned out by the cries of seagulls. Smitty, clad in a garish green Adidas tracksuit, was
passed out, his labored snores barely audible over ferry
horns echoing through the marina. The previous night's
excesses had left a mark, and recovery was slower than in
the old days. Each muffled, staggered hitch in Smitty's
snore pattern caused John and Sarah to erupt in a fresh
round of hysterics.

Jack sold seventeen photos the night before—a huge
success—but more importantly, he reconnected with island
friends he hadn't seen in years. He'd been back many times
since the summers of his wild youth, but for some reason,
last night felt like coming home for the first time.

Jack spotted the old man across the park, pushed in his
wheelchair by Edna through the thick grass.

"Here he comes. Right on time," Jack said, removing a
hair-of-the-dog beer from a bag and repositioning the
framed photograph wrapped in brown paper. "It's story
time."

"Here we go, kids. Another Jack McGuinn story," said
Erin, squinting toward the approaching figures. She
reclined on the blanket and sighed, her jet-black hair splay-
ing. "Oi! Me fookin' head hurts," she said in an exaggerated Irish brogue and began to cackle. "What a night. This
island is absolutely *mental*."

They devoured the sandwiches the old man had
promised. Edna meticulously set up an umbrella over her
boss and joined them on the blanket. She graciously
accepted a beer from Erin and cracked it open. Her boss
gazed out at the marina and the straits behind it, observing

as a freighter glided between Mackinac and Round Island. He tapped a pretty decent rhythm on the side of his can.

"I've been thinking. I'm pretty sure I overpaid for that photo, kid," the old man said, finally breaking the silence but never looking at Jack.

Jack shook his head good-naturedly. "Negative. You paid the asking price."

"Right. The asking price. But in my world, the *asking price* is overpaying." He sighed. "Okay, fine. A deal's a deal. Let's get this show started." They all watched, amused, as he meticulously manipulated the controls of his chair like Captain Kirk heading into a battle with the Klingons. The chair hummed in small, controlled bursts and reclined him into a new position. He stretched his long arms as if reaching for something. He dropped the empty beer can into the grass and leaned back, placing his arms behind his head.

"This is just *perfect,*" he said, content with his new, improved position. "Start from the beginning. Don't leave anything out." Jack nodded, ready.

More or less, the story went like this ...

CHAPTER 1

The Busboy

1984

All that sweet luggage pouring off the ferries.

And here I was.

A friggin' busboy.

Amid the clatter of dirty forks and the buzz of tourists, I found myself elbow-deep in the sticky aftermath of another chaotic lunchtime rush at the Fort Mackinac Tea Room, an outdoor cafe perched 150 feet above the sparkling blue Straits of Mackinac. A particularly nasty table lay before me, its surface a gravy-spattered mess of napkins, half-eaten meals, and overturned glasses. Ahead, a lineup of six more tables awaited, stretching off into the horizon like a row of Oklahoma mobile homes after a late summer twister.

My gaze shifted from the nauseating display of leftover meals down to the ferry boat docks jutting into the expanse of Mackinac Island's crescent harbor. The crisscrossing, rolling ferries mocked me, each vessel overflowing with overnight tourists sporting fat wallets, good moods, and not one lipstick-smudged coffee cup I'd have to touch with my bare hands.

All that sweet luggage pouring off the ferries.

And here I was.

A friggin' busboy.

Was I repeating myself?

Yes. Yes, I was.

As I wrestled with the remnants of a decimated kiddy meal and cold, ketchup-soaked fries, I may have mumbled, "Any day now," to the universe at large.

"Any day now, I'm gonna be standing on that dock like a gladiator, wearing khaki cargo shorts, a golf shirt with a name tag, and some sweet-ass Ray-Ban knock-offs, loading suitcases into James's wire basket. This is the summer it happens."

James was the name of my dockporter bike.

I know. It's all very weird.

"A buck a bag. No more schlepping plastic bus tubs full of dishes. No more smelly dish rags and soap-puckered fingers. Nope. It's Hartmann and Louis Vuitton suitcases stacked high with tips. This is the summer it happens."

Yep. I was talking to myself.

A gentle voice sliced through my whiney soliloquy. "Keep dreaming, Jack," it teased, a gentle breeze carrying the words to my ears. *Wait.* Had one of God's sweet angels floated down to the Tea Room to screw with my head? I spun around, the dish rag tucked into my apron flipping outward like a matador's soggy cape.

Maya, the matriarch of the waitstaff, stood two feet behind me. Large. In charge. Her ballpoint pen danced across her checkpad as she finalized an order for a four-top.

"You've been perfecting that song for two summers straight—the *I'm-Not-a-Dockporter-Yet Blues.* You need help, boy. Should I call the waaaah-haaaa-ambulance?" She rotated her fists in front of her eyes, imitating the exaggerated wails of a toddler denied candy.

Coming from anyone else, I'd be halfway to a rage quit. But Maya rocked.

I just shrugged. "Everyone needs a hobby, Maya. Mine is complaining."

She nodded with a knowing smile. "You're still hoping Trina LaFromme's your ticket outta here?"

"Yup." I nodded. "She's finally hiring a dockporter for the WibHo." The WibHo was island lingo for the Waterview Inn and Boarding House. "And she's probably too broke to pay a legal adult."

"Well, don't that just make you the perfect candidate." She looked me over. "Young, dumb, and affordable. So what's the problem?"

My shoulders sagged. "I was supposed to hear back from her last week about the job. Still nada."

"And here you are, drowning in dirty dishes, wearing knickers, dad socks, and a poofy shirt." She cackled.

It was all true. Fort Mackinac was a historical attraction and required even the lowliest busboys to wear colonial garb. My daily outfit landed somewhere on the spectrum between peasant and piss-boy.

Big Jack, my dad, hooked me up with the gig when I was thirteen. At the time, it was exciting. Stepping into the working world opened the doors to a place called freedom. Build up the ol' resume for my future dockporter career. Earn some cash. Splurge on Tastee Freeze soft-serve when the urge hit. Stash away some greenbacks for tinted windows on my '81 Oldsmobile Omega. Yet, two and a half summers down the line, I was still shackled to the Tea Room, my dream of hauling luggage drifting away like an unmoored dinghy.

Maya's gaze softened. "Give it time." She pointed down to the harbor. "Those dockporters have years on you. You're sixteen."

"I'm almost seventeen."

"That's exactly what I said. Sixteen. Maybe it wouldn't hurt to wait a few more summers. Pack on some pounds before you start wrestling those suitcases," she said, puffing out her chest and widening her stance in a comical display of bulk. "You know, counterbalance."

She pointed at the cold remains of a hotdog in my bus tub. "Eat that hotdog. I dare you."

I shook her off. "No, see, you don't get it. I'm ready. I've ridden big loads. Five summers back, I hauled a huge load of baggage to the set of *Somewhere in Time*. Practically saved the entire production. It was extremely windy, and they were shooting the big scene on the beach with—"

"—and boom! There it is! The legendary 'Paperboy Saves the Movie' tale. Scrappy Jack rides Superman's wardrobe to the set on an oversized dockporter bike. The crowd goes wild! Jane Seymour asks for his phone number. And now you've added wind!" She shook her head. "Honestly, that load of crap gets taller every time you tell it, kid. But riding one load when you were eleven years old doesn't put you in the Hall of Fame."

"It's not a load of crap … and I was almost twelve."

"That's what I said. *Eleven*."

"Anyway, age is just a number. Listen, if I can manage this beast," I said, nodding toward the overflowing bus tub as I hoisted it up to my waist, "then I can handle anythi—"

Suddenly, my foot slipped on a pad of melted butter and collided with a chair leg. I stumbled, and the bus tub slipped from my grip, crashing onto the patio floor. A few patrons glanced up from their meals. I looked down in disbelief.

Not a single dish was broken.

"See that? No damage! It's a sign, Maya. Even when I dump, I'm a pro," I said. "I'm telling you, this is my summer."

Maya flashed a maternal smile that bordered on pity and moved away to a newly seated four-top, plastering on her good-ol' gal welcome face. She called back. "Keep your eyes open, kid. Sometimes the best specials aren't on the board."

CHAPTER 2

Getting Home

As much as I detested schlepping dishes for eight hours at the Tea Room, it paled in comparison to the final phase of my day: getting home.

The journey from the Tea Room to Wildcliffe Cottage felt like navigating a surreal mash-up of three classic games: Mouse Trap, Frogger, and Hide 'N Seek. This was all thanks to my fragile teenage ego, which fiercely resisted any chance of being spotted in my splattered colonial costume outside the Fort Mackinac walls.

By anyone.

I'd drawn a fat black line with a mental Sharpie to protect what remained of my dignity. Thus began my secretive daily route. My own personal run-of-shame back home after each shift.

Why didn't I ride my bike? Simple. Avoiding the roads was standard operating procedure, a lesson drilled into me from every World War II movie I'd ever seen. *Always avoid the roads.* The enemy had them mined.

Besides, this way, no smoking-hot college girl in cut-off jeans could zoom past me on her gleaming Schwinn, while

I pedaled home, hair plastered with sweat, leaving a trail of my unique stench in the warm island breeze for her olfactory enjoyment.

So, the routine stayed consistent. When my shift was over, I'd sneak out the fort's rear exit—the North Sally Port—and sprint straight into a convenient grouping of pine trees. After a quick breather, another spastic dash brought me to the deeper woods along the bluff overlooking the harbor. The journey became calmer. Meditative even. I'd move stealthily down narrow, tree-shaded trails unknown to most tourists. If I heard voices, I'd dart toward a large cedar and conceal myself. While it was true that most potential onlookers would be tourists—people I'd never see again. Besides, to them, my attire looked quaint. But I had no interest in appearing *quaint*. I'd been quaint all day. My interest was in getting home, stripping off the costume, hosing myself down in the shower, and resuming my civilian life as a T-shirt and jeans-wearing, unequivocally *un*quaint numbskull.

That was the routine.

I navigated a narrow path, approaching Anne's Tablet, a little-known hideaway I would utilize for my first legitimate romantic outing years later. The clip-clop of horse carriages echoed up from the town below. All clear. I slipped down the cedar-lined trail, feeling the tension start to melt away as I prepared for the final leg back to Wildcliffe.

I caught a calm hit of harbor breeze as it brushed against the limestone cliff. Cutting through the strait between Mackinac and Round Island was the *Stuart J. Cort*, a thousand-foot-long freighter heading southbound, loaded to the gills with iron ore.

I stopped to watch, admiring its size and power. Even from this distance, I could make out the deep, resonant hum of the engines. Across the harbor, the green pines of Round Island stood out against sky and water—a stunning vista I'd dream about during long, gray downstate winters as I waited for our annual return to the island after school let out.

"Well, if it isn't Ichabod Crane running away from the Headless Horseman!"

I whirled around to see Gordon Whitaker, his blinding white teeth gleaming in a broad, shit-eating grin. His arm was casually draped around the shoulder of a blonde girl who had a fashionable backpack strapped over both shoulders. Two graphite tennis rackets with neon strings jutted out.

She flashed an obligatory smile. I'd met her before—Sandy Stortson or Stetson. Maybe Steensman? Something vaguely Viking. She was the daughter of an auto tycoon from downstate who'd just moved into a sprawling cottage on the West Bluff. Gordon had been dating her since the start of summer.

Objectively, she was the prettiest girl I'd ever seen in person—a classic all-American beauty with sun-kissed, golden blonde hair and deep blue eyes as dense and undecipherable as hieroglyphs. She was distant, aloof—at least toward me—and wholly captivated by Gordon's annoying, burgeoning charm.

"Oh, hi there, you two. I was just—"

"—hiding?" Gordon interjected. Sandy lit up and let out an adorable little giggle, catching herself, and covering her adorable little mouth. I stood perfectly still, taking it. Her smile vanished, replaced by a cold detachment. It was as if her joy was chemically activated by Gordon's mockery.

"No. I mean, maybe. I'm not really hiding. I like the

view from here. It's so …" I trailed off, out of crap to shovel.

"… far away from everyone who might see you in that costume?" Gordon finished gleefully. "Listen, pal, there's nothing wrong with your get-up. It's *quaint.*" He turned to Sandy, playing the gentleman. "Right, baby? *Quaint?*"

Her sexy, dead eyes scanned me from head to toe like I was modeling a particularly tragic outfit in a boutique window. "Sure. Totally. Yeah. It's … *quaint.*"

I gazed longingly at Round Island in the distance, wishing I was there instead of here. Far from Gordon's casual jabs and his Viking girlfriend, I could stroll alone through a wooded grotto where my colonial stench would offend nobody but the beavers.

Gordon's gaze turned scrutinizing. "Wait, Jack. I thought you were a dockporter now. Three summers, and you're still trapped in the Tea Room? What's the problem?"

I shrugged. Maintaining my composure, especially in front of Sandy Stortson-Viking, had become critical. But why was I trying to impress her? Other than her cold appraisal of my outfit, she'd barely acknowledged me, and I'd been standing three feet away.

"No problem. It's all looking good," I lied. "I just need to iron out a few details with Trina from the WibHo. From what I can tell, we're good to go. Maybe after one more week at the Tea Room, I'll be on the docks. Riding the big loads." I nodded, knowing how full of crap it all sounded. Still, I kept going. "Yupper. Any day now. I'll be rolling in the cash."

Yupper? I'd never said *yupper* in my life. Not once.

Gordon nodded, but his mild smirk told me he wasn't buying any of it. He turned to Sandy. "Jack's been eyeing the dockporter job at the Waterview Inn and Boarding House—they call it the 'WibHo'—for years."

Sandy nodded and let loose a world-weary "Awesome." I'd met her three times, and besides today's curveball word—"quaint"—she mostly said "awesome."

"I swear I remember you saying the same thing to me last summer right about this time. That you were almost ready to close a deal with Trina to be a dockporter. Am I remembering that right?" Gordon could slip an insult into a perfectly reasonable-sounding question so casually you wouldn't realize you'd been sliced until you were already bleeding.

"Na. I mean. Well, yeah. I might've. But I wasn't big enough last year. Or the year before. But this summer, I've been ... ummm ..."

Good God, get me to Round Island.

"What? Lifting weights?" Gordon eyed my physique doubtfully.

"Not really lifting weights, but I've been practicing with luggage. I stack old suitcases full of rocks in James's basket. You remember James, my bike."

Wonderful. Now even the Viking temptress knows I named my bike.

"Jack named his dockporter bike *James*," Gordon told Sandy, pretending it was a detail she needed to hear. Cutting me again. Damn, he was good.

"Awesome," she said, taking a few wary steps back. It was only at that moment that I realized that naming your bike is not normal.

"And I'm getting good with bungee cords," I barreled on. "I can load up double wings with just one cord."

Sandy now looked at me as if I was speaking in tongues. Gordon nodded, his work done. His attention turned elsewhere, most likely to Sandy's long, tan legs on the tennis court. "Well, I'd love to stand around and sniff your apron, buddy, but Sandy and I are going to play a few sets. She wants to learn how to hit a top-spin backhand. Whatta ya think, baby?"

She displayed her perfect teeth. "Awesome." This time she meant it.

"Good luck with the new job, buddy," said Gordon. He may just as well have said *good luck in the NBA draft, buddy.* And off they went.

A momentary wave of sadness washed over me as I watched Gordon and Sandy vanish down the trail. At one time, Gordon had been one of my best friends. There were summers when all I did was hang out with him and Smitty, the third member of our triumvirate. We'd skip stones, scam fudge, and bowl at the tiny lane at Stonecliffe. Gordon even helped load the wardrobe cases on that insane, windy day I rode to the *Somewhere in Time* set five years earlier.

Yes, that really happened.

They'd been my partners in other escapades too, not all strictly legal, but always for the greater good. Along the way, we'd spin wild dreams of conquering Mount Everest, pulling off heists in Bolivia like a modern-day Butch and Sundance, or living it up as Bond-esque spies in Monte Carlo (wherever that was). Our most frequent fantasy was forming a band to rival *Rush* or *The Police*, never mind our collective lack of musical talent.

But as Cap Riley, the grizzled captain of the ferry *Straits of Mackinac II*, liked to say, "If you want to hear God laugh, tell him your plans." His weathered face would crinkle as if he'd learned this lesson the hard way.

We never did start that band.

Gordon was no longer the innocent, fun-loving kid I once knew. That part of him had vanished like fog on a summer morning. His parents' nasty divorce had carved deeper scars than he'd ever admit, transforming his lazy, good-natured jabs into razor-sharp sarcasm that cut anyone who came too close. Even Smitty, who usually couldn't tell (or care) when he was being insulted, backed away. "Gordo's turned into a real jerk," he'd said, in that crystal-clear delivery only Smitty could manage.

I crumpled the unpleasantries into a mental wad and tossed them aside, taking one last look at the lake. The huge ship was now a tiny line, steaming toward the Mackinac Bridge in the distance.

Three more winding stretches lay ahead on my covert trek. Soon, I'd be back at Wildcliffe, scrubbing off the residue of fifty-plus meals and the grimy reality of losing a friend to the confusing haze of growing up.

CHAPTER 3

Gramp's Bike

The quiet of Wildcliffe was heavy, a silence that left a ringing in your ears—all except for the melodies trickling from the record player in Gramps' upstairs bedroom. Old songs from the 1940s. He'd been playing them a lot lately. I sprawled across the kitchen table, head on outstretched arm. Beth sat across from me, gnawing on her pen while flipping through what looked like a stack of order forms. I'd been sitting across from her for ten minutes.

It was time to say something.

"Whatcha doin'?" Not exactly profound, but enough to stir the pot. I was bored.

Beth had a hint of mild irritation and concern on her face. She let out a sigh as the pen slipped from her lips.

"What am I doing? *Being annoyed.* That's what I'm doing," she said. "These T-shirt order forms read like Hungarian gibberish. I hate numbers."

"I hear ya," I said. I didn't.

My eyes settled on the mood ring shoved on my left index finger. I'd picked it up at Sally's Gifts earlier in the week. At the moment, it was green, which meant "average and calm" according to the tiny booklet that came with it.

"Whaddya know? I'm average and calm. This mood ring actually works."

She glanced up, flashed the tiniest hint of a smirk, then went back to her paperwork. "It should say 'below average and mentally unbalanced.'"

"Hilarious. Really. You should put that on a T-shirt."

"I just might."

"Who's down there!?" Gramps' gravelly voice cascaded down the stairs.

"Me and Jack," Beth called back.

Gramps strolled into the kitchen. An unlit cigar was stuffed in his mouth, giving him the appearance of a grumpy captain despite not being a sailor. He sported his usual University of Michigan block M baseball cap, even though he never went to college.

"Hop to it, worms. I need some help in the barn," he announced.

Beth and I shared a glance. "Is this a quick one? I'm doing some inventory for the shop." She gestured to her forms. "I'm in a certain headspace right now."

He snorted. "Hm. Certain headspace? How truly modern. Well, it's time to get in a *different* headspace, which starts with getting up off your certain buttspace." He motioned for us to follow him to the barn by way of the back porch.

I hopped up, happy to see him emerge from his room with a mission. That summer, he'd become a bit of an apparition. Gramps was a certifiable island legend, the ceremonial mayor of Mackinac Island—whatever that meant—who ruled not with any actual power but with charm. He was also a survivor, having crashed his fighter plane into the Philippine Sea after taking flak from a

Japanese destroyer in 1944. Eventually, he made it all the way from the South Pacific to northern Michigan in 1955, where he discovered a beat-up, semi-affordable bluff-side cottage on a strange island with no cars and named it Wildcliffe. Once there, he got busy celebrating every day of his life like it was borrowed—which, in his case, was accurate.

But this summer, he was a changed man, often retreating to his room, where the only sounds were the crackles and pops of brittle 78 RPM records.

When he did venture outside, it was to stand guard over a row of geranium pots on the porch. The stubborn splashes of red refused to brighten, no matter how much water he absently let gush into the pots. The hose in his hands weaved an abstract, pointless pattern while his eyes fixed on some distant point beyond Lake Huron.

The geraniums stayed mum, and like any proper Midwestern family, we all ignored the "Gramps Issue." His slow fade probably hurt me the most. I missed being the Chosen One. Gramps, the wisecracker, his cigar dancing between his fingers, saw something special in me. I was sure of it.

Until he didn't.

Gramps pulled a matchstick from his shirt pocket, passed it across the rusted latch on the barn door to spark a flame, and pulsed his cigar to life. I opened the old door, and we walked inside.

The small, weathered barn out back was crammed with nearly forgotten stuff. We rarely ventured in, except to toss more onto the heap. The McGuinns weren't hoarders; we were chronic forgetters. The barn was an impenetrable snarl of neglected games, toys, parts, boxes, bikes, and things that once floated. Big Jack once described it as "where fun goes to die."

"I need you to fetch my bike," he said, the smoke now wreathing his head in swirls. At least three years had passed since we last saw Gramps on his bike, now forgotten in the far corner of the barn, decorated with dust and cobwebs, barely visible through the dusty forest of crap.

"Why that chunk of junk?" Beth asked. "The Schwinn Shop downtown has tons of new models. You should get something from, I dunno, maybe this century?"

"You're cute as a goddamn button, missy," Gramps returned. "But I want *my* bike. The Sears Fleetwood. The gold three-speed." He pointed toward a darkened corner. "It's back there somewhere."

"What's the rush?" I asked him, genuinely curious. Gramps had taken to walking the last few summers, and at seventy-something, we figured his biking days had wound down.

Gramps waved us off, annoyed. "What is this, a deposition? My gym membership at Vic Tanny's ran out, your honor. Just get the bike, please."

After a period of maneuvering, moving, and balancing ourselves between the years of filthy stuff, we finally located Gramp's bike. The rims and fenders were pitted, and the tires were flat and cracked. I wheeled it carefully toward the door while Beth cleared a path, punting aside a deflated football that looked like a giant brown prune.

Gramps studied the rig, puffing contemplatively. "Think she's still got some life in her?"

"I'm not sure. The thing looks pretty beat up," I said, squinting to envision him riding the relic without side-swiping a Clydesdale and causing a stampede on Main Street.

Gramps absently extended his right hand and pointed his index finger at Beth. "Pull," he said. Equally absently, she did, and he broke wind like a trombone blasting an E flat.

"Ewww!"

"You enjoy my tune?" Gramps said. "I can play it again if you'd like. Next time with feeling."

Beth waved away toxic vapors and staggered a few steps. *"Seriously?* Like we need the stench of old man fart in this place!"

"That's not old man fart, little lady! It's French cologne. I call it *Eau de-Doo-Dah-Day.* Very expensive. You can only get it in Paris." Beth gagged, as if she'd been gassed in a Belgian trench during the Great War.

"Gramps, that is SO EFFING *GROSS!*"

"Aw, come on, Beth. That gag used to crack you up." His eyes never left the bike.

I turned away from the hazy stench, eyes watering.

Gramps, proud of his air biscuit, smirked. But something else flickered. A sort of reverent curiosity. He ran his fingers over the bike's aged, cracked leather seat. I couldn't shake the theory that his flatulence was strategic. A nasty blast of tear gas to clear the zone and steal a few uninterrupted moments with his long-lost rig.

"You really planning to ride it again?" I called from a safe corner of the barn. He took a thoughtful drag from his cigar, the smoke coiling around him as he placed a sturdy hand on the grip. He didn't answer me. But in the darkness of the barn, I thought I made out the tiniest of tiny smiles.

CHAPTER 4

On the Dock

It was my day off, and I was on the Arnold Line dock, hunched over James, the dockporter bike I'd rescued from obscurity during the wild summer of 1979 when the movie people came to town. The old Schwinn had undergone five years of renovation and fine-tuning under my watch, but I'd only hauled luggage in the battered basket once.

At first glance, the bike was nothing special: a run-of-the-mill Schwinn Heavy-Duti with more than a few years on it. The rusted steel basket was decked out with age-cracked key fobs from every island hotel. The bike had been around the block, lugging bags, probably since before I was born. But I was convinced the rig still had the heart of a steed and deserved to one day ride again.

Today's upgrade included securing a wooden plank to the base of the basket, reinforcing it for the heavy loads of luggage I was sure would come this summer when I began my career as the next Mackinac Island dockporter.

I torqued down hard on a bolt as the soft plywood molded to the wire base of the basket. Through the corner of my straining-with-effort eye, I caught a glimpse of Skip, the nine-year-old island paperboy across the dock. He methodically folded and filled his bike basket with newspapers, tongue peeking out of his mouth, eyes focused downward. I couldn't help but notice that Skip was an unbelievably quick folder. Like machine-quick.

If you had tied me to a chair and let a CIA goon go to town with a rubber hose, I would eventually confess the truth: Skip could out-fold me any day of the week, even in my paperboy prime.

Nevertheless, I couldn't stop myself from launching into coach mode. I approached him, wrench in hand. "You're pretty fast, Skip. But if you'll allow me, I'll show you a trick that works like a charm. Here, let me show—"

Skip lifted an outstretched hand, freezing me cold in mid-sentence. Without missing a beat, he pivoted his scrawny body away from me. He then deftly slipped the foam Walkman headphones resting around his neck up and over his ears, leaving me to stand in the hot sun like a profoundly uninteresting statue.

Finally, he stopped folding and took a deep, sad breath as if preparing to speak to someone who still didn't get it. He squinted up at me. "Look, man, I get it. You were the paperboy way back in the seventies. And that's cool. But see, I've got my own folding system," he said. He broke into a sweet, condescending smile. "How about you just let me do my thing? *My* way." With that, he looked back down, resuming his machine-gun folding cadence.

The nerve of this punk!

I should've turned and walked away. Let the little ingrate fail. Instead, I inhaled a deep, steadying breath and continued. After all, isn't that what mentorship is all about? The Master doesn't need to be loved by the Grasshopper. He needs to be respected. I clamped on a paternalistic grin and shook my head with understanding. "I hear you. But trust me on this. Follow my lead, and I guarantee you'll never shred the peacock."

Skip didn't bother to look up, but he did scoff. "Shred the peacock? What's that even mean?"

Bam-bam-bam.

Three more perfectly folded newspapers dropped into his basket.

Goddamn, this kid was fast. I couldn't even see his fingers as they folded, creased, and tossed. Unconsciously, I looked down and inspected my own hands. Two-day-old mashed corn was wedged under my fingernails. I almost gagged.

"Shredding the peacock?" I said, snapping back. "Oh, I made up that phrase. Shredding the peacock happens when you toss a paper, and the wind catches it. The newspaper separates it mid-air. The idea is that it's like a peacock because the pages are like the feathers, and the wind is sort of like—" His hand shot up again.

"Got it. Cute. Listen, I'm on a tight schedule." He checked his watch and rotated his back to me entirely. I lingered for a moment, secretly hoping for a follow-up question.

Nothing.

Apparently, Skip wasted enough of his precious folding time indulging a washed-up paperboy with useless tips and stupid metaphors. I headed off to finish screwing bolts. If this kid didn't want to learn from a veteran who'd paid his dues in the trade for half a decade, then screw him. I wasn't running some charity clinic.

Amid a loud rubber-on-wood screech, a bicycle skidded, halting inches from my head. It was Foster Dupree, a long-time dockporter at the Windermere Hotel.

"Are you still fiddling with that old rig, Jack?" His voice

had a pitying tone that reminded me too much of Maya's days earlier.

I nodded, masking my leftover humiliation. Skip's spot-on dismissal was an ego sucker punch, leaving a lingering, dull ache I was trying to hide.

Foster was the quintessential dockporter: solidly built, with sun-bleached hair and a pair of wire-rimmed Ray-Bans that had seen better days. Rugged, witty, and unpolished, he was the subject of endless gossip and speculation. Was he really the reluctant heir to a millionaire from Las Vegas? Did he really date Madonna in Ann Arbor before she became famous? Stories swirled around him like dried horse crap in the wind. But to me, he was a dockporter—one of the best—which was much more interesting than gossip.

I first met him years ago, even roping him into a few schemes. He'd always seemed intrigued by my dockporter dream. Who knows why? Boredom? Pity? I'd like to believe he saw some of himself in my scrappy determination, but that was a stretch. The *why* didn't matter. I just liked being around him. Like Gramps, Foster made me feel noticed. It was a rare gift that kept me returning to the docks. Was I a mentor junkie? Could be. That theory also would explain why I was drawn to Myles Fordham.

But we'll get to that later.

"Adding the final touch," I said, proudly indicating the basket mounted on my bike. "Wood reinforcement, just like yours."

Foster just smiled, "Jack McGuinn. Too old to haul papers, too young to haul luggage. Where does that leave him?"

Before I could respond, Skip pulled off his headphones and called over, "Hauling dishes dressed like a fruity pilgrim?'

Foster erupted in laughter, parked his bike, and jogged over to offer the little smartass a fleshy low-five. *"A fruity pilgrim?* That's priceless! Good one, Skip!"

Their giggles echoed across the dock, bounced off the freight shack, and smacked me in the face like a big red kickball. My cheeks flushed. It looked like Foster found a more entertaining sidekick.

"Gotta go, Foster. Catch you tomorrow," said Skip, mounting his bike.

"Always and forever," said Foster.

Skip gave me a tiny head nod of acknowledgment—the barest of bare minimums—and kicked off to deliver the news.

Foster's eyes fixated on the ferry that had just bumped the dock. Like a seasoned hunter in a deer blind, he scrutinized the disembarking travelers in search of a prized redcap load—the eight-point buck of the luggage trade. Untagged bags, not marked for any specific hotel, known as "redcaps," were hotly contested by dockporters. I strolled over and joined his vigil, secretly hoping some tourist cutie might mistake me for a dockporter merely because I stood in the gravitational pull of his confident stance.

As the passengers flowed down the ramp like a raging river, a man I recognized as Trenton Feagler, wearing a dark blue suit and red tie, darted onto the dock. With his brisk stride and smart-looking female assistant at his side, he stood out from the loud, colorful, tacky tourist masses like a mortician at a parade.

Foster's eyes narrowed. "There he is. Captain Deep-dish. He never comes to the island on that huge yacht anymore. Always on the ferry. Very odd." If Foster said something was odd, it was.

"Very odd," he repeated.

The last few summers, island chatter about Feagler floated like pollen. *There goes Feagler,* they'd murmur, voices tinged with intrigue as he weaved through the Main Street masses, always on foot, never on a bike.

Known in Michigan for his outrageous marketing stunts, pizza entrepreneur Trenton Feagler had transformed *"Get a Pizza the Action!"* from a slogan into the unofficial motto for seizing the day in the Great Lake State. His ads featured scantily-clad models in bright green bathing suits stretching mozzarella like some cheese-pulling subset of soft-core porn. They gazed at the camera with a hunger that suggested, without leaving much to the imagination, that they craved more than pizza. His ads, combined with admittedly damn fine pizza—always delivered in under 22 minutes or your money back—made him very, very, *very* rich.

Feagler was long and languid, with an intensity that stretched him even taller. From the ground up, he'd built his cheesy kingdom with nothing but a knack for numbers and raging ambition. He was Michigan's richest man, known not only for pies and stacks of cash but for the influence he peddled with it. In a state known for automation, he was a one-man rumor factory.

He also harbored a seething resentment for Mackinac Island. Despite Feagler's hefty donations to the Allies of Mackinac charity, his attempt to join the Wawashkamo Golf Club—locally known as "Wawa"—was a no-go. In those days, Wawa wasn't exactly a fortress of exclusivity. Hell, Gramps was a board member, and he *hated* golf.

The point is that Wawa didn't have snobbish standards. But the more money he offered, the faster the rejections came. For *years.* The Pizza King had found something he couldn't possess. The snub lit a righteous fire in Feagler's hollowed-out marathoner's gut, burning as hot as one of his pizza ovens.

After the summer of the cold shoulder, Feagler frequently returned to the island, but the "golfer on holiday" look—colorful pants and expensive Hawaiian shirts—was gone. Now, he stalked Main Street in a severe suit, eyes scanning everything. His stunning brunette sidekick, dressed in a sharp blazer that matched his, carried an oversized green handbag that swung confidently from her shoulder.

Rumor had it that Feagler was collecting Michigan historical artifacts with one goal: to create his own tourist haven on nearby Beaver Island, fifty miles west of Mackinac Island. This new destination was to be bigger and better, a living testament to toxic grudges.

A few of the more conspiracy-minded types who drank at the Mustang Bar swore up and down that Feagler was a direct descendant of King Stromberg, the infamous religious leader who proclaimed Beaver Island as his kingdom in 1850. Stromberg met a violent death at the hands of the locals, primarily Irish immigrants, who, having fled Europe, were none-too-thrilled with the concept of a king in the New (ish) World. Some claimed that his head was still firmly lodged in the crown when he was finally dethroned.

I never bought into the Feagler-Stromberg connection rumor. Then again, if KISS could perform without makeup, I suppose anything on God's green earth was possible.

Foster watched as Feagler faded into the crowds heading toward Main Street. "Think he's here to play a quick round at Wawa?"

I didn't laugh. There was something in Feagler's focused stare that reminded me of a scene from a TV show

I loved called *Animal Kingdom*. A vulture eyeing a mouse, dead eyes unblinking, calculating, waits for the exact moment to strike.

"Or maybe he's a guy with too much dough and not enough cents," Foster said. "Get it? *Dough? Cents?* Come on, Jack, lighten up! You look like you saw a ghost!" He elbowed me hard in the sternum, and I staggered backward, grabbing a wood piling seconds before falling off the dock into the lake.

Now, the Arnold Line dock was awash with tourists, luggage, laughter, and confusion. Amid the chaos, I conveniently forgot all about pizza, Wawa, vultures, and mice.

CHAPTER 5

The Bluecoats

Every day at noon, an ear-piercing air-raid siren, lasting precisely thirty seconds, disrupted the peaceful vibe of Mackinac Island. I had long stopped questioning why. We were not under attack. It was not the Battle of Britain. The Nazis were not carpet bombing Windermere Point in preparation for a massive land invasion.

It was just … noon.

I was half-sprawled across an old wood table in the Tea Room break room, forehead resting on the top of my flattened left hand, sweaty right forearm sticking to the splayed metro section of the *Detroit Free Press.* Waiting for the siren to end. A clacking metal fan blew directly at my face, offering a blissful reprieve from the baking heat on the patio seeping through the screen door.

Across from me sat "Squawbait" McGee.

Squawbait was the Tea Room's ageless, laconic dishwasher. Wrapped in his stained apron, his thrashed leather boots rested on the table six inches from my face. He was engrossed in the newest issue of *Motocross Action* magazine.

Nobody could recall a time when Squawbait wasn't firmly entrenched behind his colossal metal dish machine tucked away in the hellish depths of the Tea Room kitchen. His real name was Patrick, but he preferred Squawbait, and no one questioned it. And why would they? Poetic and weird, it rolled off the tongue like a penny spinning on a ceramic countertop. It was fun to say. *Squawbait McGee.*

Try it. You'll agree.

I watched him stare at a garish centerfold of a Yamaha YZ 250 and turn the page, drinking it all in.

"You really like those dirtbikes, don'tcha, Squawbait?" I asked him.

"You figure that one out on your own?" He didn't look up.

"Yeah." Unfazed, I continued. "If you're so into dirt bikes, why do you spend your summers on an island where motorcycles are outlawed? Kinda weird if you ask me."

He flipped a page. "True, but see, I *didn't* ask you."

"True." Properly rebuffed, I scanned the breakroom and shot up straight. It was Jenna Bonner, one of the ticket-takers at the entrance gate. Maya nicknamed her "Jenna Bonnet" behind her back because of the headgear she was required to wear as part of her uniform. Despite the wildly unflattering colonial garb, she somehow still managed to look stunning. Her smooth skin glowed against the fabric, and her large brown eyes sparkled with quiet confidence. Loose strands of chestnut hair framed her face. Even the bonnet, which should have looked ridiculous, worked to her benefit. It was borderline irritating how beautiful people could make anything look good.

She sat alone, reading a *Cider House Rules* paperback and sipping pink lemonade. A sophomore at Indiana University majoring in history, she'd been accepted into the Tri-Delt sorority the previous winter. However, she was having second thoughts about accepting the bid, uncomfortable with the outdated, elitist rituals of the Greek system. She planned to backpack through France and Italy with her best friend Kim next summer and had already purchased her Eurail Pass, which was much cheaper than she expected.

You might wonder how I knew all this.

Simple.

I eavesdropped.

Daily.

I had developed a wildly unrealistic crush on Jenna Bonnet. While it all sounds weird and stalky, I was convinced my homework would pay off someday when I worked up the nerve to actually speak to her. She'd be impressed by my maturity and deep empathy for her struggles, dreams, and aspirations. She'd naturally overlook our five-year age gap. Or, more likely, she'd see me as the sweaty, scrawny teenage creep I was.

Either way, I was ready.

Just as I gathered the guts to pull the pin on my *Boyish Grin* hand grenade, the break room screen door burst open, and four Fort Mackinac guides strutted in.

Wonderful.

The Yale Bluecoats were here. I jammed the pin back in the grenade and stowed it away—no use wasting it today. There'd be other opportunities to display my charm and wit when we were alone together.

They rolled in loud, all four tall and annoyingly good-looking, wearing Continental Army uniforms: blue coats with brass buttons, crisp white linen pants, tall leather boots, and tricorn hats. Their outfits looked almost tailored, as if Hugo Boss had snipped away every excess flap until they resembled Revolutionary War bodysuits.

The tallest Yale Bluecoat, Derek, leaned through the

kitchen door and barked out his order. "Noon sandwiches! Four Fur Trader Dips! And three orders of battlechips, all to go! Plus four lemonades with ice!"

An impossibly gruff voice called back from the bowels of the kitchen. "Sit tight, Yankee Doodle. We've got orders in." Squawbait and I both stared at Derek, waiting for his reaction. He ignored it and struck a hammy pose, his long arm resting on the fireplace's mantle, which hadn't worked since Grover Cleveland was president.

"During the 10 o'clock musket firing, I had the crowd eating out of my hand," Derek said, eyes sparkling. "You guys catch that touch of Stanislavski's method during the climax?"

Devin, his equally tall sidekick, removed his hat dramatically and slicked back his short, blonde hair. "Absolutely. Really effective. I did a little Meisner repetition technique during the spiel about Luther Shively. That little head jerk at the end? All subtext."

I could only assume this was all pretentious actor lingo.

Another Yale Bluecoat, whose name I never bothered to learn, nodded. "I noticed that, Dev! Brilliant emotional recall."

The fourth guy, who seemed to exist solely to agree but never speak, bobbed his head.

Squawbait stifled a low groan behind his magazine as I quietly tried not to puke. Jenna Bonnet looked up from her book, interrupting their actorly little circle jerk. "You guys are *history* majors, right?"

"Yup," they said in unison, thrilled with her attention.

She smiled faintly. "Then why do you speak like theater majors? My roommate at Indiana is an acting student, and she speaks the same way. All that ... *lingo*."

"Well, Jenna," Derek sauntered over. "Dr. Turnbull didn't

hire us just for our historical interest. We have dual majors in history *and* theater." He paused as if explaining a particularly complicated concept to a kindergartner. "It's not just about knowing the dates and events, Jenna. Anyone can memorize facts. The true mastery lies in the *performance*. Bringing history to life requires a certain … well, I guess you could call it *finesse*. An ability to captivate and convey the inner essence of the past. That, Jenna, is what we do." The other Yale Blue-coats nodded along, loving how Derek made them sound: a high-minded troupe of modern Renaissance men.

Squawbait stood up, pushing back his chair with a high-pitched scrape and stuffing his rolled magazine into his back pocket. He turned to me. "I'd rather remove hard-ened corned beef off a plate with a chisel than listen to these blowhards."

And with that, he marched into the kitchen.

Jenna bit back a giggle, her eyes moving away from the Yale Bluecoats and meeting mine. I didn't look away.

Were we having a moment?

Derek cut the tension as he yelled back into the kitchen. "Hey, Chef! How about those sandwiches?"

"Hey, Betsy Ross! How about you come back in ten minutes?" returned the chef's voice. "Go sew some stripes on a flag or some shit!"

Derek shook his head, dismissing the comeback with a contemptuous wave. He turned toward Jenna. "Care to join us at the North Sally Port? The cloud formations are spectacular right now, and the breeze is cool. We'll come back for the food."

She paused, considering the offer. I reached for the *Boyish Grin* grenade again and removed the pin, ready for her to catch my eye for more than three seconds. The timing was perfect. The Yale Bluecoats were exposed, and while I didn't exactly do the exposing, I was friends with the guys who did.

Sort of.

Instead, she slipped a bookmark into her novel. "Ah, why not? It is pretty hot in here." Gathering her belongings, she wordlessly left the break room with the Yale Bluecoats in tow to go look at clouds.

And just like that, my sweet delusion was over.

CHAPTER 6

Meeting Myles

Whoever said, "When one door closes, another opens," had clearly never met Myles Christian Fordham. With Myles, it wasn't about doors opening or closing; it was about getting stuck in a revolving door that spun you around endlessly. He'd stand there, watching and grinning while you screamed, giggled, peed, and barfed, often simultaneously.

The first time I ever saw him, I was elbow-deep in grime at the Tea Room. He'd parked himself at a bluff-side table, feet propped up on the opposite chair, absently flipping through the menu with a wide, satisfied grin as if he wasn't looking at an illustration of a French dip sandwich, but instead remembering the most beautiful woman he'd ever kissed.

Tan and rough-edged, with long, blondish hair and a handlebar mustache, he looked like an out-of-work sailor or a Miami smuggler. He wore torn jeans and a yellow T-shirt that said, *Spooky Pete says Marco Island is for Lovers.* His shoes were worn-out Adidas Stan Smiths. Noticing my glance, he summoned me over with a grand wave as though I were on his personal wait staff. Despite every instinct telling me otherwise, I walked to his table.

"Can I help you?" I asked, straining to sound professional.

"We shall see. You got Lowenbrau in this joint?" he asked, his voice dipping into the kind of low, conspiratorial hush reserved for buying black market machine guns in Beirut. He smelled like Coppertone and Old Spice.

I shifted my weight, cheeks burning. "Um, I'm just the busboy, not a waiter, so…" I trailed off, feeling the heat rise in my face. Truth be told, I wasn't even sure what Lowenbrau was.

"I didn't ask for your job title, Sparky. I'm inquiring about the beer situation. See …" His eyebrows shot up. "I'm real thirsty."

Now I understood. "Dry as a bone. State Park rules. See, because the restaurant is on State land, they have strict—"

"Okay, okay, I get it." He waved a dismissive hand that shut me up. "Skip the history lecture. A simple 'looks like you're out of luck, buddy' would suffice."

Who was this guy?

"Fine. Looks like you're out of luck, buddy." I arched my own eyebrow. "Is there anything else?"

The Tea Room rarely hosted edgy characters sporting handlebar mustaches and demanding imported beer. Mostly, the place was populated with exhausted tourist families desperate for a place to strap their whining children into a highchair for a half-hour while they choked down a sandwich before the next cannon-firing demonstration. This guy did not fit the standard midday rush.

He pointed to the menu. "What's this Redcoat sandwich?"

"It's a turkey sub on rye served with battlechips."

He looked up. "Battlechips?"

"Yeah, it's supposed to sound like battle*ships*—sort of military-themed. But honestly, they're just ridged potato chips."

He sighed and shook his head. "Very creative. I'll take it. And add one of these pink lemonades."

"Like I said," I repeated, a little more sharply this time, "I'm just the busboy."

Leaning back, arms folded, he smiled. "Come on, kid. Just take my order. Ever color outside the lines? Or are you the type who'd ask for a hall pass to fart?"

I felt a surge of irritation rising like a tidal wave. "I do what I have to do," I said, trying to keep my voice steady. The nerve of this guy! Sizing me up as if he had me all figured out. There was a part of me dying to tell him all about the summer of '79. The stuff I got into. Much of it illegal. That would wipe that smug look right off his face.

But I stopped myself. *Why did I care?* I could feel my fists clenching at my sides, the urge to wipe away his smirk growing stronger. I took a deep breath.

"I can be a rebel," I blurted out, immediately wishing I could stuff the words back into my mouth. I felt my face flush. In that outfit, I'd never felt less rebellious in my life.

He seemed to be sizing me up.

"A rebel? *Barney* Rebel, maybe. Heard of him? He was Fred Flintstone's pal. They bowled together. Anyway, about that Redcoat sandwich." He looked toward the server stand and nodded toward Maya, who was cashing out a bill. "Since you're too chickenshit to take my order yourself, pass the word to Flo over there. I'm starving. You two can split my generous tip."

He shut the menu and handed it back with a wink. "Assuming the service is agreeable."

CHAPTER 7

Trina's Verdict

By late afternoon, the Fort's white walls reflected the afternoon sun like a giant mirror, transforming the patio into a human-sized oven. Sweat plastered my shirt to my skin as I swiped at my dripping forehead.

Six tables away, Trina LaFromme, the WibHo's proprietor, sat under an umbrella. She fanned herself with a vibrant purple fan, her eyes fixed on the distant harbor.

I glanced over at the wait stand and caught Maya's eye. She shot me a grin and a sneaky pointing gesture that all but ordered: "Go talk to her!"

I took a deep breath, filling my lungs with precious hot air—it was time to close this deal.

Trina LaFromme seemed to have stepped straight out of a vintage film reel. Draped in a purple feather boa, she exuded the faded glamour of a Copacabana headliner. Born dirt-poor on the island, Trina's life took an extraordinary turn when she was discovered and trained in ballroom dancing. It's still a mystery to me how that happened on Mackinac Island in the 1920s, but somehow, it did.

She rose to semi-fame in the thirties and forties when ballroom dancing was all the rage. Trina traveled the globe with her dashing partner, performing for royalty and celebrities, eventually amassing a small fortune. She lived a life that most could only dream of, an island girl who'd spun and leaped into a fairy tale.

Later, with her career over and her knees and ankles ravaged, Trina was drawn back to the island. The former dancer bought one of the homes where she'd once sold lake trout and salmon as a poor fisherman's daughter. It was a sweet vindication for a time. But as the years rolled on and her cash dwindled, necessity transformed the home on Bogan Lane, just up from the shore road, into a boarding house, then an inn, then both.

She christened it the Waterview Inn and Boarding House, even though catching a glimpse of the lake from the porch demanded the skills of a contortionist. With its creaks and groans, the old house seemed to mirror Trina's weary dancer's bones. Over time, both the house and Trina settled into their roles, the Inn becoming a fixture of the island.

The WibHo's rooms lacked air conditioning, TVs, or phones. The walls, covered in peeling floral-patterned wallpaper, gave the place a sagging, aged look. Eventually, this shabby charm became the defining characteristic of the place. It was also affordable, a rarity on an island where prices began pushing many tourists out.

Trina couldn't compete with the luxury inns—she was always on the edge of broke—so she didn't bother trying. Instead, the WibHo attracted a different crowd: financially strapped but fun. The front porch came to life each night with a motley mix of budget travelers and long-term residents. They gathered there, sharing cigarettes, cigars, cheap beers, and jugs of Gallo wine. What drew me in, however, was more calculated: the WibHo never had a dockporter.

I'd always kept on her radar, subtly dropping hints about the dockporter job at the WibHo over the summers. "Playing the long game," as Gramps would say. It was early in the season, my bike was reinforced, and I was ready to ride.

Trina sat nursing her lemonade, which Maya swore was spiked with gin from a mini-bottle collection she always kept in her purse.

With an overloaded bus tub in my arms, I edged closer. "Ms. LaFromme," I said, fighting to keep my voice from cracking.

Her long black eyelashes fluttered like butterflies, and she turned away from the view. Her eyes landed on me as if for the first time.

"Yes?"

I swallowed, feeling my mouth go dry. "I was wondering about the dockporter position at the WibHo we discussed. I wanted to check in on that. Check to see if it, you know … I mean if you … had thought about a timetable for my, you know, my …" I trailed off because my tongue was now firmly glued with saliva paste to the roof of my mouth. I stared at her lemonade longingly.

Her eyebrows lifted in a gentle arch, and a dreamy smile appeared. "What on *earth* are you talking about, darling?" Trina's voice was low and husky, with a rasp of hard living.

I hesitated, flustered by her response. "What? I mean, we've talked about this before, remember? A few times. Like, maybe … *three?*" I could hear the rising panic in my pinched voice. I needed to get control of myself.

"I have no memory of such conversations." She rattled the ice cubes in her lemonade and shrugged. "I make no apologies for my liquid diet. It makes me happy. But it also causes me to forget conversations." Her light laugh peeled back the years. "It makes me forget most things." She looked me straight in the eye. "But that's precisely the point, isn't it, boy."

Disaster.

Had all my strategic hint-dropping been nothing more than a solo act in the theater of my imagination? For over two summers, I'd been laying down hints as frequently as I set bread baskets on her table. Christ, just last week, we had a conversation about it. She'd nodded, hummed an "I'll get back to you," and even winked like it was a done deal.

"Wait." Her gaze sharpened. "You're the McGuinn boy."

"Yes, ma'am," I managed.

She leaned back, a flicker of something unreadable crossing her face. "Me and your grandfather, we go back."

I waited, the bus tub growing heavier by the second.

And?

"How old are you again?"

"Almost seventeen." I stretched, trying to seem taller. A rivulet of sweat seared my eyes.

"You're too thin. And, to be perfectly frank, you're timid. Trina looked out over the water. "If I'm hiring a dockporter, I need a strapping kid with personality. Someone who can charm people, make them feel at home, and show them this island is more than fudge and horses."

I might as well have been standing on Neptune for all she cared. Her mind was somewhere else. "Maybe they'll meet the love of their life—or at least the love of their night." Trina's eyes gleamed. "The WibHo is a beautiful disaster, darling," she said, her eyes sparkling. "I need more than a dockporter. I need a storyteller. Someone who can make guests believe they're part of a grand adventure."

She let the words "grand adventure" linger. *Graaaaand advennnture.* For a moment, I pictured a young, radiant Trina in cities like Paris, Barcelona, or Venice, living out her own grand adventure. What I did not imagine was getting hired as the dockporter at the WibHo.

She sipped, ice clinking like wind chimes. "Come back next summer."

I took a second for her words to land. *"Next summer?"*

That's the precise moment the handle of the overloaded plastic bus tub snapped with a crack. The tub dropped, slamming into the floor. Dishes and silverware flew in all directions. Forks skittered under tables, plates shattered, and glasses exploded into shards. Diners leaped in their seats, some letting out yelps, others frozen in wide-eyed shock. Conversations died mid-sentence as all eyes turned to the disaster. As the last piece of silverware clattered to a stop, the room fell into stunned silence.

My eyes traveled from the mess at my feet to Trina. She had her hands over her ears as if she'd witnessed a train wreck. She lowered them slowly, and rose gracefully from her seat, sliding a sequined purse over her shoulder. Fiddling with the clasp, she offered me a wan smile.

"Stay in touch, darling."

She drifted away, leaving a trail of fake purple feathers from her boa. One feather caught a gust of wind, fluttering over the Tea Room wall and drifting down toward Marquette Park below.

I watched it flutter, fascinated, surrounded by a mountain of shattered dishes at my feet. Another gust, and the feather, now a purple speck, vanished from sight.

In the distance, I saw a ferry gliding into the Arnold

Line dock, the dockporters already waiting to greet the overnight guests.

Lucky bastards.

I crouched down and began cleaning up the mess.

CHAPTER 8

Pep Talk

"So. How'd it go?"

Maya squatted down next to the heap of broken dishes, helping me scoop them up.

"I don't wanna talk about it."

"That good, huh?" She hesitated for a moment. "Hey, this'll cheer you up. Crazy story."

I was in no mood for gossip. A lady in a purple boa had metaphorically kicked me in the balls and left me picking shards off the floor of the Tea Room. Not the ideal moment for *Storytime with Maya.*

"The Bluecoats are toast," Maya whispered, eyes sparkling. "Dr. Trumbull's golden boys have hit the bricks. Fired. 86'd."

This *was* crazy.

"Why? Dr. Trumbull loved those clowns. What did they do?"

Maya tossed some broken pieces into a fresh tub and lowered her voice to a whisper. "I guess they decided a psychedelic drug trip to 1776 was a good idea. So they munched a heap of magic mushrooms and went full

Revolutionary War. *In their uniforms.* All four paraded downtown and staged a musket-firing-at-midnight reen-actment right out front of Jenna Bonnet's apartment. Ended up shattering her window and nearly burned down the island's oldest lilac tree after some stray gunpowder lit up."

Another broken dish clattered into the tub as she continued.

"So Jenna understandably freaks, calls the cops. Derek, the tall one, thought his name was *Thaddeus Blackburn,* a lieutenant in the Continental Army. So there he was, squaring off with Chief of Police Richter, yelling, 'I outrank you! I outrank you!' Richter called in the big boys from the volunteer fire squad to beat him back to reality. I heard it was a nutty scene."

She shook her head as if she'd seen the entire fiasco projected on the back of her eyeballs, and made a throat-slitting gesture. "So Dr. Trumbull shipped 'em back to Yale drama school or wherever those ridiculous hambones hail from."

Her voice dropped even more. "My theory? It was Squawbait. He hates those guys. He put them up to it. Probably told them it was mild stuff. Organic." She giggled a little too loudly and cupped her mouth. She scooped up a broken coffee cup, and a shard poked her hand.

"Ouch, shit! That hurts." She blew on the tiny cut a few times and continued. "And here's the real twist: the governor's fundraiser is in a week. All the heavy-hitting donors will be there, including Trenton Feagler, that pizza guy. Dr. Trumbull's looking to sweet-talk some funds out of him. *With no guides!* From what I've gathered, he's abso-lutely freaking, scrambling to recruit anyone who can squeeze their fat head into a colonial hat."

She stopped and looked at me as if she'd suddenly

become interested in my head size, which, while being many things, was not fat. Her eyes narrowed.

"I just had an amazing idea. You ought to throw your hat in the ring. I'm no psychic, but I believe in the universe dishing out what's meant to be. The Yale Bluecoats getting the boot the night before you find out your dockporter dream is over? That's more than coincidence; it's a sign."

I shot her a sharp look.

"Sorry. I eavesdropped on your little interview with Trina. That. Was. *Brutal.*"

I dropped a few more plates in the tub. "Then why did you ask me how it went?"

"I dunno. I guess I wanted to see if you'd bring it up."

"It doesn't matter," I said. "I'm barely scraping through high school as it is. They want college history majors for that job. Like, smart people. Those guys were from the Ivy League. I think." I squinted. "Is Yale in the Ivy League?"

She shook her head, grinning. "Sweetie, I can't even *spell* Ivy League." A snarl of dirty utensils landed in the tub. "I get it. Too young and too dumb. But trust me, right now, Dr. Trumbull would hire a garden gnome if it could hold a musket. Just stretch the truth a bit. Make up some crap about history. Read a book. I'm telling you, the man is desperate."

"I've seen what those guides do," I said. "They're actor-types."

"You think dockporters aren't actor-types?" Maya said. "Listen, it's not all about loading up suitcases. It's the show. That's how the good porters make money. *Charm.* Sure, you can haul dishes." She looked doubtfully at the shards and paused. "Generally. But you need to up your people skills. You need a rap. Some showmanship. A schtick. Let Trina see what you've got."

She wiped her hands with a rag, ready to move on. "Look, we're all playing parts here. Do you think I'm naturally *the big ol' gal,* hearty waitress type? It's an act! You nail down a Fort Mackinac guide job, and this summer, you learn the *cheeeeeese.*" She let the word ring out like a song. "Next summer," she reached into her apron and pulled out a fat wad of cash, "you'll earn the *cheddar.* Who knows? Maybe Jenna Bonnet, that ticket-taker you're always drooling over, will finally make eye contact. Firing the big guns, wearing that soldier-boy ensemble? The navy waistcoat, those tight pants, and the hat? Ladies love a man in uniform."

"Serious?"

"As a Redcoat on rye," she said. We both stood.

Her smile dropped, and she suddenly turned serious. "Okay. Pep talk over." She indicated the tub full of broken dishes. "Toss this shit in the dumpster and check out table eleven." She squinted toward the far end of the patio. "Looks like a toddler barfed in the sugar bowl."

CHAPTER 9

The Interview

I hesitated at the entrance to Dr. Trumbull's office in the back of the Officers' Quarters building. The creaky door protested. It smelled like old stuff. Artifacts. Maps. Wood. Dirt. I think they call it "history."

I peeked in. Shadows danced in the dim light, creating an eerie vibe that made me half-expect a decaying Redcoat with rotting eye sockets to stumble out from the dark corners. My eyes adjusted slowly, revealing the source of the shadows—a softly glowing lamp on a cluttered desk. As the room came into focus, I realized it was just a dimly lit office, albeit one stuffed with historical artifacts and books.

Fort Mackinac's renowned superintendent, Dr. Trumbull, emerged behind a desk lamp, peering at me through round glasses. His eyes, magnified at 3.75x, were unnervingly sharp.

"Jack McGuinn?" Dr. Trumbull asked as he stood and beckoned me inside. "Have a seat."

I stepped into what felt like a tiny, unfinished museum. The walls were crowded with intricate Native American beadwork and Revolutionary War sketches depicting the island in various states over the past three hundred years or so. Every available surface was cluttered with trinkets scattered amidst well-thumbed research papers. Shelves buckled under the weight of books, and sketches of battles lay across a table, weighted down by stone artifacts.

Dr. Trumbull eyed me as if sizing me up for a uniform, which, no doubt, he was. He looked every bit the seasoned academic warrior. Khakis fastened with a belt featuring a huge brass turtle buckle. His white short-sleeved shirt, snug over his generous middle, hinted at late-night, carb-powered research binges. His hair, a blend of light brown threaded with wisps of gray, retreated from a forehead lined with years. His face was imposing. Stern. Serious. No other way to say it: he looked smart.

He cleared his throat as he sat behind his desk in a creaking wood chair. "Let's get right to the point. I found myself cleaning house a few days back."

"Oh yeah?" I said, leaning forward, feigning ignorance, secretly eager to hear his version of what I had mentally dubbed *the Great Bluecoat Magic Mushroom Caper.* Unfortunately, his details skewed toward vague.

"Let's just say an unfortunate spectacle unfolded downtown. All four of my guides—men I hand-picked, mind you—had to be relieved of their duties. Now I'm very much under the gun. We have an important event coming up very soon: The Governor's Gala."

He dropped his head. "It's a total catastrophe. I'm a Democrat personally, but I have to say, First Lady Nancy Reagan was right about one thing." He jabbed a finger at me. *"Don't do drugs."*

"Noted, sir." I nodded, biting down hard on my tongue and concentrating on an image of two rotting eyeballs floating in a cup of spoiled milk. It was one of my many go-to laugh suppressors.

He glanced at a cluttered desk calendar. "I need four men to fill the guide spots—and I need them now. Normally, this interview process would take weeks. Even months." Behind his glasses, his eyes drifted upward as if seeking divine intervention from the miniature birch bark canoe mounted and suspended from his office ceiling.

"Those men were from Yale! They're supposed to be the best and the brightest!" Remembering he had an audience, his expression switched back to business mode. "Ever fired a rifle?"

Amazingly, for a red-blooded Michigan boy, I had not. Big Jack and Gramps hunted avidly, but after freezing in a deer blind for three hours until both big toes felt like Popsicled nubs, I retired from stalking wild game.

"Yes, sir. I'm an avid hunter," I lied. "We shoot rifles at the range, too." A big toothy **PR** smile. "Nothing like the smell of gunpowder."

He leaned back and lit a pipe. The flare of the match briefly illuminated diplomas, certificates of appreciation, and a collection of photographs of him posing with a cross-section of Michigan celebrities. A shot of Tiger legend Al Kaline hung next to rocker Alice Cooper. The top Detroit news anchor, Bill Bonds, was directly below Stevie Wonder. I scanned the other portraits: Bob Seger, Gordie Howe, and Soupy Sales. I wouldn't have pegged Dr. Trumbull as a celebrity chaser. For a moment, learning this brainy academic sucked up to famous people like an everyday fanboy took the edge off the interrogation and I relaxed a notch.

"How about fife and drum experience?" he asked.

"Excuse me?" I stammered, shaken from my celebrity daydream.

"Do you play either?"

Fife and drum? What the hell was he talking about?

"Do you mean the guys in the famous painting? The short guy with the bandage on his head and … the other guy?"

"The painting is called 'The Spirit of '76,'" he said, eyes narrowing ever so slightly.

I nodded as if it were obvious. "Of course, a classic. I'm a little rusty on the fife but pretty solid on the drum." I was unsure what a fife was, but I knew it wasn't a drum.

He glanced down at an opened notebook. "You come strongly recommended by Maya. I've known her for years from all my meals at the Tea Room. She says you're very hardworking." Thankfully, he'd moved off the fife and drum portion of the interview. I relaxed.

"So. Where are you attending college?"

"College?" I choked back a snort. *What did Maya tell this guy?* I was barely scraping through eleventh grade at Brighton High School.

He fixed me with a look. "Yes. College. I assume you're in university now?" He squinted, scrutinizing my face. "Although I must say, you look very young."

Where did I go to college? Think! For some reason, the movie *Fast Times at Ridgemont High* popped into my glitching brain. Sean Penn as Spicoli.

"Of course. I love college. I started early."

"Wonderful. A sure sign of an academically gifted student. Where are you taking classes?"

"*FFFFFFF—*" I almost said, *Fast Times at Ridgemont High,* but my mouth froze at the 'F' sound.

"*… FFFFF…*"

Dr. Trumbull looked at me with rising concern.

"*… FFFFFffffff …*" I continued.

"Do you need a glass of water?"

"*FFFFFerris State!*" It exploded from my lips like a Nerf

gun. Why Ferris State? I couldn't locate Ferris State on a map.

"I'm majoring in history and …" I frantically scanned his office, my eyes landing on a shovel mounted on the wall with a plaque that read 'Commemorating the French Lane Dump Dig.'

"Archaeology!" I had almost said architecture. Truthfully, at that moment in my life, I wasn't sure I knew the difference.

It seemed to work. He nodded. "That's perfect. We have an upcoming dig near the blockhouse. The North Sally Port project. It's been on hold, but we hope to complete funding after the Governor's Gala. I could use someone with your passion." His eyes twinkled with what looked like excitement. Or maybe it was the reflection of his desk lamp. "Been on many digs?"

"Sure," I said. Sweat trailed down my ass crack. It tickled, but I didn't dare shift my position. Things were going well. "Loads of digs."

"Then you'll appreciate the nuances of stratigraphy and carbon dating. Perhaps you could share your insights on our findings from the last excavation in the region. It appeared in all the archaeological publications."

I leaned forward, chin on hand, and struck a thoughtful pose.

"Of course, the *stratigraphy* layers. They were super layered. Almost like one of those Sanders Bumpy Cakes. But the carbon dating? I wasn't a fan. It made the whole thing seem, I dunno, kinda … dated."

Ridiculous. I sneaked a cautious look. Was he buying it? The historical walls closed in. Soon, the doors would seal shut, and water would come rushing in. "Of course, I meant that in a more hypothetical sense."

He cleared his throat. "Tell me, what era of history do you find most riveting?"

"Excuse me?"

"What era? You know, the Renaissance, Middle Ages, Bronze Age."

"Wow. Okay. Great question. Hm. Most riveting?" I looked up as if the answer might be scribbled on Dr. Trumbull's birch bark canoe. "Gosh. There are so many eras with their own sort of … rivet. Maybe the Prohibition era? Yeah!" I pointed at him as if it were obvious. "That one! Because a lot was going on back then. No beer. Flappers. Speakeasies. Gangsters. Al Capone. Whatnot."

I let out a long, shaky breath. The office was uncomfortably quiet.

"… extremely riveting."

Dr. Trumbull shook his head like a disappointed tutor. "I see. And what of our island's role during the War of Independence? Surely, as a history major, you have an opinion on King George's policies?"

"King George? God. Who doesn't have an opinion on that guy? But before I go on, I'd love to hear what *you* think about King George's policies."

It was worth a shot.

Dr. Trumbull shook his head. No dice. The earlier twinkle in his eyes was replaced by two enlarged, magnified, slightly terrifying bug eyes boring deep into my rotten, lying soul. "I'd prefer you go first."

"Well, King George? I'd say underrated. As a king, his plate was full, right? I mean, think about it. When you're the king, you're like … the Main Man. Nobody messes with you because you can throw them in a dungeon. But on the flip side, nobody helps you either because … I don't know. What if you get it wrong? Giving a king bad advice would be really … ummmm …"

I was running out of steam.

"... *bad?* So I think King George was highly underrated."

He shook his head. "You do realize that the colonists widely regarded King George as a tyrant? This is basic history. Taxation without representation is tyranny. You surely learned that in high school, much less an esteemed university like *Ferris State.*" He spit out the name as if he were saying *Fathead State.*

I swallowed hard, my facade crumbling faster than the ruins I'd claimed to study. "Right. Of course. He was pretty tyrannical. Like Tyrannosaurus Rex. *Ha-ha.*"

Why did I say that?

I was spewing out whatever Irish stew of words came up. I silently cursed my laziness. Why hadn't I prepared for this interview instead of wasting my prep day with Smitty, flirting with the cute ice cream scooper at the Horse and Buggy Drive-In?

"Which brings us right back to archeology," I said, trying to wrap up my rambling monologue. "Speaking of Tyrannosaurus Rex," I leaned in, trying to appear casual —just a couple of scholars talking shop. "Have you guys ever found dinosaur bones on the island?"

A thick silence enveloped the room. My stomach growled, rebelling against the hotdog and two orders of extra-crispy fries I'd inhaled earlier. Maybe it was time to switch to protein shakes and salads. Amazing, the useless crap you think about when you're drowning in a vat of bullshit. Dr. Trumbull removed his glasses, which were incredibly thick from my angle. He pulled a cloth from his pen pocket and rubbed the right lens.

"Mr. McGuinn, you've wasted my time." He didn't look up when he said the next part.

"Kindly leave."

CHAPTER 10

Wild Style T-Shirts

The chime on the Wild Style door jingled as I stepped inside, but it couldn't drown out the shrieking humiliation of Trina LaFromme's rejection and my disastrous interview with Dr. Trumbull. I needed my big sister's reassurance that everything would be okay. Life would go on. Despite being a skeptic, sarcastic, and cruel realist, she had an uncanny knack for making me feel better.

Beth ruled over Wild Style as her fiefdom. The queen of colors, fabric, and iron-on weirdness. The unfinished wood walls were plastered with posters, art, and racks of colorful printed T-shirts. Wild Style felt like stepping into a kaleidoscope—if kaleidoscopes smelled like heat-steamed fabrics and iron-on decals and had a soundtrack powered by the Grateful Dead's *Europe '72* album.

Beth had taken over the hot press at the tiny shop as a teenager, sparking her passion for T-shirt design. She went rogue, soon cranking out witty, all-caps designs with slogans that predated the wildly popular Frankie Goes to Hollywood 'RELAX' T-shirts. 'YOU'RE ALL NUTS!'

and 'I'M NOT A FUDGIE, I LIVE HERE, AND I DON'T ANSWER QUESTIONS' became instant local favorites. She ended up getting backed by a local businessman and was on her way. Beth was clearly cut from the same cloth as our mom, Ana, who ran the Blue Butterfly Dress Shop a few blocks away on Market Street.

So, to recap:

> Mom designed dresses.
> Beth designed T-shirts.
> Dad sold Oldmobiles.
> Gramps was a Legend.
>
> I was a busboy.

Two hulking iron presses dominated the space where Beth worked her poetic voodoo, but today, she lingered near the window, staring at the vacant storefront across the horse-and-bike-packed Main Street, gnawing on her lower lip. I'd never seen her gnaw on her lower lip.

"Can you believe this shit?" her voice a low growl, finger pointing across the street where workers unloaded a horse-drawn dray filled with crates and boxes. "They're selling those cheap T-shirts with *Mackinac Island* printed on the front, probably cranked out in some sweatshop by Chinese slave labor. No wit! No humor! *A hundred different designs,* the sign says!"

Her eyes never left the store across the street. "I turned down a marine biology scholarship to major in business so that I could run this place. And now I'm staring at an avalanche of cheap, bargain-bin junk that's gonna bury me! Put me out of business! I should be on a research ship in the tropics, tagging dolphins' tails with some sexy, tan scientist who plays the guitar." She turned away from the window. "I'm washed up at twenty-two."

I managed a half-hearted nod, but my mind was surfing the waves of my own recent failures.

"Business," I said absently, my attention snagged by a tie-dye shirt on a hanger with a dancing Grateful Dead bear that said, 'GRIN AND BEAR IT.' I grabbed it and displayed it to Beth. "Maybe it's time to practice what you print."

She rolled her eyes. "Thanks for the sage advice, bro. Really. I think I'm cured." Beth waved me off. "Jesus, you're useless. Your brain's on the ferry docks, waiting for Madame LaFromme to give you that bellboy-on-a-bike gig."

I shook my head. "I heard from her a few days ago. No-go. She didn't even know who I was. Looks like …"

Our conversation was interrupted by a shouting match erupting near the second press iron at the back of the store.

"Yeah, but your idea sucks *balls!*" Beth's gangly, twenty-two-year-old heat press operator, Bert Shively, was locked in a heated argument with a pale, long-haired kid sporting spectacular acne. I recognized him from the Turtle Wizard Arcade, always hogging the *Pole Position* game with a towering stack of quarters by the start button that implied, "Back off. This machine's taken." It was a flagrant breach of arcade etiquette.

Pole Position players were always the worst.

"I toldja, man! The Pac-Man needs to be bigger, and the spaceship should be on fire!" the kid growled.

With his wild hair, John Lennon glasses, and a look of total exasperation, Shively tried to reason with the kid. "The proportions are locked. This is the pre-set design. I can't just—"

"—just make it like I said, *One-Shot* Shively!" the kid sneered.

Shively went rigid, his face draining of color as if he'd seen a ghost.

The kid grinned, smelling blood. "Yeah, I know all about you. Your great-great-great-great grandfather *Luther* Shively gave up Fort Mackinac to the Brits with only one shot during the War of 1812. And it was a warning shot! That's why they call every Shively since *One-Shot Shively.* Now gimme the shirt I want!"

Beth moved toward the punk, but I put a hand out to stop her.

Shively's face drained of color, and he spoke in a low, trembling voice, desperately trying to maintain his composure. "That's a complete historical fallacy."

"Oh, is it a *complete historical fallacy?*" mocked the punk in a dead-accurate imitation of Shively's nerdish intonation.

"My great-great-great-great-grandfather was ... well, he was great. And I plan to prove it." His shoulders slumped. "Someday."

Burt Shively's family owned a sprawling cottage in a neighborhood known as the Annex, just north of the West Bluff. The punk was right about one thing: the Shively family had roots on the island stretching back over 150 years. But those roots were tangled in the legend of Luther Shively's surrender to the British, a stain on their legacy that had never quite faded.

Despite being a quirky clan of brilliant minds— hosting poetry readings, philosophical debates, and the occasional heated Scrabble tournament —the stain of Luther's surrender in 1812 couldn't be washed away. Their rambling cottage should have stood as a testament to their intelligence: four tenured professors and an economist short-listed for the Nobel Prize. But to anyone with even a cursory knowledge of island history, it would always be the house of—

"One-Shot Shively, One-Shot Shively!" the punk taunted in a mocking high-pitched falsetto.

Shively stepped out from behind the counter, wielding a lint roller. "Take it back!"

The spotted runt puffed out his chest defiantly. "I ain't taking shit back. Just make my shirt. I know you'll do it. Do you know *why* I know? Because One-Shot Shivelys ALWAYS give up without a fight!"

Shively, visibly vibrating, clenched his fists. But then he did something truly painful to observe: He gave up. Without a fight.

"Hmm. I guess if I stretched the rocket decal, we could make it work." The punk snorted with laughter, rolling his shoulders like a boxer and grinning like a feral rat.

"Hey you!" Beth erupted, her voice booming. "Get the hell outta my shop, you feeble-brained creep!" The punk spun around, eyes wide with shock. Beth's eyes blazed as she took a step forward. "I mean it! If you ever walk in here again, your greasy little head is going under that iron. I'll have Shively print a T-shirt design out of your FACE!"

She stepped closer. I followed. I'd never seen this side of Beth. And I liked it. "Although come to think of it, I seriously doubt anyone would buy it. You wanna know why?"

The punk looked like a shovel hit him in the gut. He choked out a feeble "Why?"

She was now in his face, her finger jabbing. "Because you're just about the ugliest kid on the island, and nobody would want to wear that roadkill you call a *face* on their *T-shirt.* Now *GO!*" The kid started to sputter.

"You heard my sister. *GO!*"

With what was left of his dignity, he straightened and strode out of the shop, slamming the door behind him.

I smiled at Beth. She smiled back. "That was kind of fun, bro," she said. "We should do it again sometime."

A phone mounted on the wall behind the counter rang, slicing short the moment. Beth picked up. "Wild Style. Beth here." She listened for a moment. "Yeah. He is here." She thrust the receiver at me. "It's Dr. Trumbull from Fort Mackinac." Then she whispered in a low hiss, *"What did you do this time?"*

I took the phone as a knot formed in my stomach. "Hello?"

"Mister McGuinn," a voice cut like a blade, sharp and irritable. "I tried you at the number you left. Your grandfather said you might be at your sister's shop. So, let's dissect that interview, shall we?"

The knot tightened. "Um. Now?"

"Don't worry. It won't take long. You waltzed into my office two days ago and spun a tale so tall it could slam dunk a basketball without jumping. It turns out you're sixteen years old, and your report card's a carnival of mediocrity." I could hear him shuffling some papers. "A 'C' in history, wasn't it?"

Heat crept up my neck. "Yes, sir. How did you—"

"—doesn't matter. Then you told me you could easily handle muskets because you hunt deer with your father and grandfather. Well, I spoke to your grandfather about that."

Of course he did.

"Yes. Lovely man. Very chatty. He says the closest you've ever come to hunting … *is fishing,* and even that's a stretch."

I winced. "I may have embellished that part a bit."

"A bit?"

"I'm sorry, Dr. Trumbull. I guess I just really wanted—"

"Save it!"

I saved it.

"As much as it pains me to say this…" He drew in a deep breath. I braced myself for the worst. Maybe, "I'm reporting you to the authorities." But was it illegal to lie to the superintendent of a fort that hadn't been active since 1895? Maybe the gun story broke some obscure law. A RICO statute? Something like that? I had no idea. My brain spun like a slot machine, cycling through all the potentially illegal crap I'd spewed during the interview, waiting to hit the unlucky combination.

There was another long pause on the other end of the line.

"You're hired."

I blinked. "Hired?"

"I have literally no other options. Be at the South Sally Port at 10:00 a.m. tomorrow. It's a trial run. A week. We'll evaluate your skills and see if you're guide material. If so, you can stay. And don't *ever* mention your age. I'm still unsure what the regulations are, and, frankly, I'm not racing to find out." I could hear a pained sigh through the receiver. "I just need bodies."

"I'll be there!" I said. For good measure, I added, "You won't regret this."

"It's far too late for that." It sounded like he blew his nose. "I already regret it."

After hanging up, I faced Beth's curious gaze.

"Wild. I just got hired to be a guide at Fort Mackinac."

Beth smirked. Wait. *You?*"

A voice shot across the shop. It was Shively. He looked miserable. His eyes narrowed to slits, mouth a tight, white line.

He pointed at me, eyes wide. "Wait. *You?* What do *you* know about history?" Sweat dripped down his furrowed brow, his wild hair drooping pathetically.

I shrugged, trying to look casual. "Honestly? Not much. To tell you the truth, I don't even like it that much. Crazy, right?"

His eyes flared, turning almost red with indignation. The message was clear without words: *No, you illiterate buffoon, it's not "crazy." It's a crime against humanity.*

Without a word, he yanked down the press on the arcade rat's T-shirt with a force that made the whole room shudder. The iron hissed and spit, possessed with heat. He looked down at the shirt, revealing his messy mop of sweaty hair.

Then, as if possessed himself, his head snapped back up. He drew a deep breath of T-shirt fabric steam like a demon inhaling sulfur. When he exhaled, narrow streams of steam curled from his nostrils, snaking to the ceiling.

CHAPTER 11

The New Bluecoats

I craned my neck, looking up the long ramp at the base of Fort Mackinac, a limestone wall climbing eastward to the South Sally Port like the bleached bones of some ancient dragon, angling to a gate that promised something called "history" on the other side. I stood as still as a scarecrow.

A giddy tremor roiled in my gut. Doubt? Excitement? Perhaps the greasy two-for-one taco special from the night before? I stole a look over my right shoulder to catch the ferry easing into the Arnold Line dock, the deck crowded with tourists. Dockporters hovered around carts loaded with suitcases like ants on a discarded Snickers wrapper. Was this ramp leading me away from where I needed to be? Hell, where I *deserved* to be?

Was I swapping luggage for muskets? Was this a surrender or a new battleground?

I took a breath and trudged up the ramp, squeegeeing my forehead with a palm. That's when I saw a tall, sloping figure fifty yards ahead of me. Unmistakable. *Shively.* This morning, his unruly hair, wild on a good day, was downright hypnotic. Each strand danced in the breeze, a symphony of wispy tendrils. He heard my footsteps approaching and looked back over his shoulder.

"Where are you going?" I called ahead.

"Same place as you." He paused to catch his breath. I caught up. "The truth is, when I heard they hired a busboy who's still in high school and couldn't care less about Mackinac Island history—and, in fact, seems *proud* of it—I had to make a call. I figured they'd jump at hiring someone who eats, sleeps, and breathes the subject." He started walking again. "Were you aware I'm a PhD candidate at the University of Michigan with a focus on colonial America?"

"No. Sounds … *riveting,*" I said.

He eyed me suspiciously as we trudged along, clearly trying to decode whether I was being sincere or just a smartass. I exaggerated a grin, and he let it go.

"So, does that mean you've ditched the Wild Style gig? My sister's gonna be crushed."

He nodded. "She was fine with it. For me, it's a chance-of-a-lifetime job." He unconsciously picked up the pace. "Beth said a lobotomized chimp could operate a heat press. She said I should follow my passion." He snorted. "*A lobotomized chimp.* I thought that was pretty funny."

I caught up to him again. "She told me she almost didn't hire you because you're so smart that you're dumb."

Shively shrugged. "I prefer 'idiot savant.' I like your sister. She's sharp. I'll miss the T-shirt shop. But that place …" He pointed up toward the white Fort blockhouse above us and stopped again.

"That's where I belong."

His face tightened. "The historical record has twisted my great-great-great-great-grandfather, Luther Shively, into a laughingstock. A coward. He was the commander of the American battalion in 1812, and for decades—*decades* —Fort guides have repeated the same damnable lie: that Luther Shively surrendered the fort after just one warning shot."

Damnable lie? I'd only ever heard that line on TV. He took a breath and looked around as if waking up from a fever dream. A flush of embarrassment visibly crept up his long neck. He'd been caught preaching. Again.

"Well, anyway, I'm setting the record straight this summer." Then, as if a switch flipped, his expression softened. A cloud passed, and he stepped aside, gesturing almost meekly.

"After you."

Dr. Trumbull greeted us at the South Sally Port stairway not with open arms but by checking his watch and rubbing his right lens with a cloth. He stood in his requisite khakis and a crisply pressed, short-sleeved Oxford shirt, this time light blue. His eyes thankfully appeared smaller than during our first meeting. His expression eased at the sight of Shively, as if the budding scholar's credentials lent some legitimacy to his own panicked hiring spree. Nearby, two other figures leaned casually against a wall, partially concealed by shadows.

"Burt Shively and Jack McGuinn, meet Myles Fordham and Roland Shartz." He cleared his throat. "Myles has a history degree from Flagler College—he tells me it's in Florida. Roland is an undergraduate in the Writers' Workshop at the University of Iowa. We exchanged the requisite waves and half-nods.

"Sorry. Did you say *Shartz?*" I asked, wondering if I was the only one stifling a laugh.

Shartz shrugged. "I know. It's gross. Call me Rollie," he said, his grin broad. Chunky, he was squeezed into seer-sucker Bermuda shorts and a tight white Izod polo shirt, the hem creeping up to expose a patch of peach-toned skin. Despite the cloudy skies, he wore Wayfarer sunglasses that somehow complemented his short, strawberry-red hair. "*Roll*-ie," he said. "As in *Rollie-pollie.*"

I froze when I got a clearer look at the second guy. Undoubtedly, it was the same smart-ass pirate who'd ordered beer at the Tea Room. He'd gotten a haircut since our first meeting, but the wide grin and handlebar mustache still ruled his face. Decked out in a checkered cowboy shirt and faded jeans, he caught my eye and winked.

"Hey! If it isn't the skittish busboy. Barney Rebel. Ever dig up that Lowenbrau I asked for?" He elbowed Rollie. "Last time I saw this young buck, he was wearing knickers and looked like he'd been dunked in French's Mustard by the school bully."

Rollie laughed, even though he had no clue what Myles was talking about.

Dr. Trumbull rechecked his watch and shot us the wary glance of an outgunned substitute teacher. "Alright, gentle-men. Follow me." We climbed the final steps of the ramp, passing under a weathered wooden sign that creaked: Fort Mackinac 1780-1895. The parade ground stretched out, an expanse of grass nestled between the Fort's buildings. Dr. Trumbull stopped and swept his arm. "This is the parade ground, where we hold many of our reenact-ments," he said. Tourists meandered across the grounds, seeking refuge from the summer sun under the canopies of centuries-old trees.

"Great! Will there be floats?" said Myles. "Like an inflatable Kermit the Frog? Maybe Snoopy? Can't forget the Shriners! Those tiny little cars. Those funky hats." Myles turned to me. "How about it, busboy? What's your favorite part of a parade?"

I shrugged, stifling a smile, but Myles was impossible to resist. "I dunno. Flag girls, maybe?"

"Flag girls, he says!" Myles crowed as if I'd confirmed some universal truth. "The classic choice for a desperate dish-wrangler swimming in the hormonal whitewater."

Dr. Trumbull's face remained as impassive as a statue, his patience dwindling. "This is a parade ground of a rather different nature. This field is where—"

"—soldiers mastered discipline," Shively interjected. "These grounds are steeped in the tradition of order. Where the rigors of military were drilled into the men before they faced the horror of battle and the—"

"Easy there!" Myles interrupted. "What is this, a funeral oration?" He began addressing an invisible audience. "We gather here to honor Lieutenant Yorick. Alas, I knew him well. A brave soul felled by a fifty caliber musket ball to the family jewels. He leaves behind quite a legacy, including nine offspring and a shitload of bills!"

He punched a stiff Shively in the arm lightly. "I'm playing, Shives! Continue. I need to catch up on some sleep." An involuntary smile flickered across Dr. Trumbull's face.

"Conserve your creative energy, gentlemen," he said. "You've got an audition tomorrow."

A collective double-take shot through the foursome at the word *audition*.

"Well, isn't this a fart in the soup bowl," said Myles. "I thought we were locked in for this gig."

Dr. Trumbull shook his head. "Nothing is *locked in*. Your continued employment at the Fort hinges on performance. Please the tourists, and you please me. Please me, and you keep your jobs. It's in the contract. Follow me."

We traded grumbles under our breath as Dr. Trumbull steered us to an unremarkable wooden building behind the soldier's barracks exhibit. *Audition?*

The guide shack was small and weathered, with peeling paint and a sagging roof. He shoved the creaking door open and beckoned us inside. Dust and the sharp scent of old pine hit us as we squeezed through the entrance.

Inside, the shack felt spartan and utilitarian. A single bare bulb dangled from the ceiling. A rickety wooden table occupied the center, encircled by mismatched chairs, while a filing cabinet leaned precariously in the corner. Along one wall, a row of lockers stood next to some cabinets and a small eating area with a refrigerator from the '50s humming irrhythmically. Dr. Trumbull shut the door behind him.

"The day after tomorrow at 10:30 sharp, I expect you all to be ready to reenact history before a living, breathing audience," he said. "No muskets or cannons for this performance. Just impress our visitors with your, how shall I say it? *Theatrical prowess.*"

He cast a glance at Myles. "Some of you already appear comfortable with that." For a moment, he froze, a montage of worst-case scenarios flickering across his face. He shook it off and pointed toward an off-white armoire.

"Inside that cabinet, you'll find your costumes, clean and sorted. Should you need adjustments, get them done in town. Greta Fortenberry, a seamstress who bartends at the Murray Hotel, offers us a discount. Keep your receipts."

Dr. Trumbull pulled a stack of papers from his shoulder bag, distributing them with the care of a professor handing out final exams. "Here are your scripts. This is a shortened version. It's light on historical depth, but it is easy to memorize. If you manage this successfully, we'll proceed to the next phase of your training."

He took one last scan of his new team and seemed to deflate visibly. He then spun on his heel and walked out. The shack door slammed shut, leaving us silent, except for Myles's anxious, unconscious finger snapping.

Rollie broke the silence. "This is bullshit, man! I didn't sign up for homework. I passed up a job writing wedding announcements and obituaries for the *Island Gazette* for this gig, and now I gotta study?"

With a smug grin, Myles leaned in and said, "Haven't you heard? Obituaries are a dead-end gig." Rollie chuckled, pulled out a pocket-sized notebook, and scribbled a few notes.

"Great line, Myles," he said, inspired. "I'm gonna use that."

Myles swung open the cabinet and reached in.

"Use it for what?" I asked.

Rollie kept scribbling. "I don't know yet."

"I want royalties," Myles muttered absently, holding up a blue colonial soldier's jacket and inspecting it skeptically.

And with that cryptic load of nothing, my job as a guide at Fort Mackinac officially began.

CHAPTER 12

"Privates" McGuinn

"Just a second. Almost ready," I called through the curtain, staring at my reflection.

I had imagined myself looking like a dashing Revolutionary War hero from the paintings in Dr. Trumbull's office. Instead, I looked more like the runner-up in a junior high Halloween party. I was drowning in the costume. What seemed so studly on Derek and his tall, irritating Yale pals looked ridiculous on me. The epaulets drooped over my shoulders, and the blue coat's sleeves swallowed my hands.

If Jenna saw me like this, she'd pat me on the head, toss a box of stale candy corn in my trick-or-treat bag, and send me off to the next house.

"It's not my usual style," I called through the curtain. I was standing in the dressing room of the Blue Butterfly, my mom's dress shop on Market Street. The walls were adorned with vintage travel posters and old black-and-white photos of the island. The scent of lavender filled the small but comfortable space. I was there for a fitting. Mom was a dress designer, so I didn't need some random bartender at the Murray Hotel to adjust my trousers.

Still, I didn't want to leave the dressing room.

Mom's voice drifted back. "Of course it's not your usual style, Jack. It's a uniform from 1780. Just get out here! Let's see what we're working with."

Another voice chimed in. "It can't be worse than the last uniform, with that poofy shirt and knickers. I'd call this a promotion. Front and center, soldier!"

The voice belonged to Smitty, who likely stopped by the Blue Butterfly to drop off a shipment of dresses for Mom. Smitty was as close to a brother as I'd ever have. Loyal. Street-smart. Born and bred on the island. I loved the kid.

Right now, a brother was the last thing I wanted.

My transition from real busboy to fake soldier needed some breathing room. It would take time to adapt, and Smitty was notoriously unfiltered. He taught me the meaning of "the truth hurts" at the tender age of six by pointing out a massive booger hanging from my nose in front of fifty tourists at Ryba's Fudge Shop.

Every single face turned to look at me. Smitty didn't mince words because he never learned how, and now he was about to behold his old pal Jack looking like Alexander Hamiton's scrawny nephew.

"Get out here, Jack!" Mom ordered again. "I have another fitting at noon, so if you want alterations, I need to see you. Now!"

I adjusted my tricorn hat to the perfect tilt, as I'd seen Derek do, and stepped out of the dressing room into the shop's warm light.

"Private McGuinn reporting for duty!" I announced, spreading my arms wide in a lame attempt to put a positive spin on my new look. I still wasn't convinced I'd made the right choice taking this job, so I sold the moment with exuberance. I didn't just have to delude my friends and family; I had to delude myself.

"Ten-*hut!*" Saluting with an exaggerated grimace, I clicked my way-too-tall leather boots together at the heels for good measure.

Smitty's jaw dropped. Mom took a few steps back, her hand flying to her mouth to stifle a gasp. An awkward silence fell over the Blue Butterfly. Then, like a dam bursting, laughter erupted, echoing off the coral-hued walls. Mom shrieked and doubled over, gasping, while Smitty mock-collapsed beside a mannequin draped in a frothy pink sundress, nearly knocking it down. Two freaked-out customers bolted for the exit, throwing scandalized glances over their shoulders before shoving the door open and fleeing to Market Street. For some odd reason, I noticed my mom had the same door chimes as Beth.

"What?" I inspected my uniform in a distant mirror. Yes, I was floating in it, but I had made peace with that. It needed alterations, but that could be handled. Hell, that's why I was there. I faced the mirror and stood up straight.

"Dude!" Smitty gasped from his position on the floor, arm in the air, pointing at me.

"Get back in the dressing room!" Mom yelled. I looked closer at my reflection, baffled.

My jaw dropped. The linen flap of my white soldier pants was unbuttoned and folded down. For reasons I could not explain—perhaps it was the flustered rush of changing into the costume for the first time—I was *sans* boxers.

Private McGuinn, indeed.

CHAPTER 13

Wingin' it

We cut sharp figures in our crisp blue coats, pristine white linen pants and hats perched. Our muskets, silent props today, gleamed. A crowd of tourist's faces waited for the newest team of bluecoats, ready to bring history to life. Dr. Trumbull hovered near the front, his nervous eyes flicking between us and his watch.

I had the first line. I opened my mouth.

Nothing came out.

I was as blank as the pages of the spiral notebooks I bought every fall for high school but rarely used for anything other than practicing drawing KISS and Van Halen logos. Beside me, Myles stood cool as a cucumber, grinning with his big white teeth. Shively fidgeted, his head crammed full of history yet unable to help. All the correct answers dripped down his face in rivulets of high-noon sweat. Rollie stifled giggles. Apparently, he found my panicked lockjaw hysterical.

Finally, I found the right words. "Ladies and gentlemen," I called out, the words tripping over my tongue.

"We welcome you to an extremely historical ... thing. A demonstration ... reenactment. It's, um, historical and, er, essential. Obviously."

Objectively, I was blowing it. A wave of indifference crested and rolled over the audience. Silence followed my introduction, a yawning chasm of nothingness you could fall into and never be heard from again. A ferry boat horn blasted in the distance. For a moment, I fantasized about being on that ferry, sailing away from the Fort forever, trading this nightmare for a job as a lighthouse keeper or a librarian.

"The battle of ... um ..."

I stole a sneaky peek at my left palm, where I'd scribbled a detailed script outline in red pen. It was a sweaty, illegible tomato soup of ink. I could only make out one thing: the number eighteen. So I said it.

"Eighteen ... *something*." I repeated the word, hoping it might somehow make more sense on the second attempt.

"Eighteen ..."

A sea of sunhats and squinting faces began to whisper. Their confusion swirled like dust devils across the parade ground. The collective verdict? *Ripoff.* Wristwatches were checked, gum was snapped, and restless eyes wandered, searching for anything more interesting than what was happening in front of them.

Myles stepped into the breach, voice as low and clear as a politician's. "Private McGuinn means to say that there was a lot more going on during the battle of Eighteen ... *Something* ... than anyone has ever been told."

A ripple of chuckles rolled through the crowd, a lifeline thrown my way. I received it gratefully with both hands. "Yes, indeed!" I blurted, a tiny spark of confidence igniting. "Our valiant Colonial Army stood shoulder to shoulder, fending off …" *Shit*! My mind blanked again. "The bad guys?"

Myles slapped me on the back. "The *bad guys*, Private McGuinn? These weren't just bad guys. They were *Redcoats!* The baddest of the bad. The Roman Centurions of their time! Picture it, folks!" called out Myles, his mustache framing a visage of pure passion. "The battlefield, a chessboard of Redcoats and Bluecoats, was practically …" He turned to Shively. "Private Shives, what do you get when you combine red and blue?"

He was taken totally off-guard. "Um. Purple?"

"*Purple!* Exactly!" Myles was winging it with gleeful abandon. "The air was *purple* with the sounds of battle and the scent of gunpowder. Aztec warriors moved like shadows among the chaos, their allegiance shifting like the tides."

Aztecs?

"Of course he means *Chippewa* warriors," interjected Shively.

"No! I don't! I mean what I said. *Aztecs!* Because that was a strange day. See, the Aztecs were in town, visiting the Chippewa tribe, all the way from Mexico City. It gets hot down there in the summer. Awful hay fever. Mosquitos. Sweat. Legend has it, they'd seen a brochure for Mackinac Island and thought, 'Hey. Looks nice!' So they came to the island for a little weekend getaway. Trade some trinkets. Buy some fudge. Do some … I dunno … Private Shartz, help me out here."

"*Networking!* Rollie called out.

"Yes!" Myles said, snapping his fingers with excitement. "Now let's not gloss over the local heroines from Madame Beatrix's Boarding House. And I think you all know what I mean by boarding house." He leered, tracing an imaginary set of curves with his right hand. There were random gasps from the crowd but mostly laughter and a few good-natured hoots. "These fine ladies armed themselves with nothing but their wits," continued Myles. "Wait, did I say wits? Sorry. Not wits. Let's just say it rhymes with wits. *KnowwhatImean?*"

He elbowed Rollie, who feigned like it hurt. A bigger laugh.

"That man knows!" Myles shot a finger at a chunky dad in a button-down. *"Grits!* Those fine ladies sashayed through the crossfire of the battle, offering their ... *grits* to the weary soldiers! Breakfast of champions, they say!"

We were all so fired.

Shively looked stricken. "That's not even remotely—"

Rollie stepped up, shutting Shively down with his left hand, and gestured to the hillside with his right. "The local children perched on the ramparts right over there, watching this madness go down like it was a movie, munching popcorn and sipping ... *chew-spit!"*

"Ew!" moaned the crowd, but they loved the grossness of it all. Rollie beamed, basking in the response, arms out.

I stepped forward. Suddenly it all was becoming easy. "Wait! It sounds disgusting, but remember, those were different times. Chew-spit was a delicacy back in Eighteen *Something*. It was like the Mountain Dew of the era. Kids loved it! In fact, it was hand-mixed on Market Street by a local island vendor ... " I was out of ideas and turned to Myles. "Private Fordham? What was his name again?"

"You talking about 'Spit-pot' Stauffer?" Myles offered.

"That's the guy!" I called back.

Myles took the baton. "'Spit-pot' Stauffer later got into the fudge biz. Made a lotta money." Myles pointed to the barracks. "And over there, French fur traders hawked their finest beaver pelts, claiming just one pelt could stop a musket ball dead in its tracks!"

Rollie jumped in. "Which greatly offended the fine ladies of Madame Beatrix's Boarding House, who were well-known for *their* beaver pelts and none too happy to be outdone." The kids didn't get it, but scandalized giggles and hoots rippled across the parade ground from the adults.

"A scuffle ensued," said Myles. "The ladies naturally won." Myles winked, magnetic, and shook his head in wonder. "As they usually do."

"*Whoo-hoo!*" yelled the fired-up women in the crowd.

"And let's not forget the cheerleaders," Rollie called out. "The unsung heroes of the day! Pom-poms crafted from the finest raccoon tails, leading the charge with their spirited chants: 'Gimme a K!'"

The crowd roared back in unison. "*K!*"

"Gimme an I!" A louder response. "*I!*"

"Gimme an L!" Even louder. "*L!*"

"Gimme another L!" They were going nuts now. "*L!*"

"What's it spell?" we all called out.

Everyone yelled together: "*KILL!*"

Admittedly, it was a twisted little chant, but what the hell, it was the '80s. At least in our version, nobody died, and everybody laughed. I stepped forward, addressing the crowd with arms wide. "And there you have it! The infamous but little-known Battle of Eighteen *Something.* Proof that war is not always hell."

Myles took over. "Sometimes, it's just …" With a grin, he finished, "*Heck!*"

Shively raised his arm for attention, and his scholarly eyes scanned the crowd. "Ladies and gentlemen, *none* of what you just heard is true!"

The crowd hesitated and then erupted in a rowdy roar of cheers. We took a synchronized bow, basking in the waves of laughter and applause that washed over us.

Out of the corner of my eye, I caught Dr. Trumbull's slow, bewildered clap. He was clearly blindsided by our mangling of Mackinac Island's storied past. His expression was a mix of confusion and horror. But his clapping continued. I had no idea what was buried in his expression, but at least I knew what *I* was thinking:

Please the tourists, and you please me. Please me and …

CHAPTER 14

Training Montage

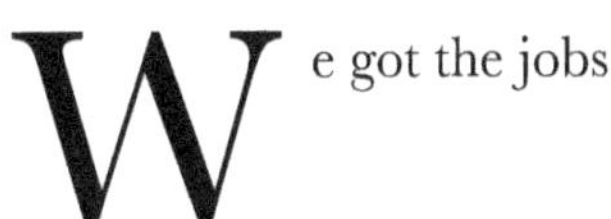

We got the jobs.

An hour and a half before the Fort opened, we found ourselves lazing about in our uniforms on the long wooden porch of the soldiers' barracks, killing time before our week of formal guide training was set to begin. Myles reclined on a creaking rocker with his soldier boots propped on the railing, reading the real estate section of the *St. Ignace News* aloud to us while Rollie taught Shively and me how to play a card game called Pig. With only three people, it was lame.

"This one looks promising," Myles murmured, "Riverside retreat with a rustic outhouse. It's not a bad spot for a business. Call it Fish and Crap."

Rollie called over without looking up from his cards. "Nah. Call it Fish and *Shits.*"

"Yup. Yours is better." Myles flipped to a new page.

"You have a gift, Rollie. A useless gift, but a gift just the same."

Rollie looked up from his cards and froze, squinting toward the far end of the parade grounds. "Am I seeing this right?" Then, with a neck-wrenching convulsion, he let loose a loud sneeze that echoed down the porch.

We swiveled. Seeing Dr. Trumbull's portly frame stuffed into a frayed Continental Army uniform caused the Bubble Yum to drop from my mouth and plop to the wooden porch floor. Although it was easy to laugh—the man was twenty-five years past his peak uniform-wearing days—it was still strangely admirable. None of us expected our scholarly bossman to play dress-up for training. Yet there he was, appearing out of the misty morning sunlight, tarnished medals jangling on his blue coat, his boots squeaking, and his white linen pants one karate kick away from splitting down the crotch. But there was a rigid pride from beneath his colonial hat that I hadn't seen before.

It shut me up. No smartassery.

Myles folded his newspaper and stood straight, saluting Dr. Trumbull with exaggerated flair. "Looking sharp, Doc!"

Somehow, Myles had already gotten away with calling Dr. Trumbull—the most respected historian north of Gaylord, Michigan—*Doc.* He scrutinized Dr. Trumbull's medals as he stood before us. "Wait, don't tell me. I know this one," he said, snapping his fingers in his now customary fashion. "You won Best Dressed, class of 1809!"

I expected Dr. Trumbull to shoot eye-daggers, but Myles's charm was disarming. Dr. Trumbull offered a pithy touch to his brim and replied, "Why thank you, Private Fordham. Looking sharp yourself."

"So," Myles continued, "you ditched your office to join us plebes for a little mission? Perfect timing. Tonight, we plan to strip ol' Rollie here naked and duct tape him to the flagpole at the South Sally Port. We could use an extra hand. Our boy may be witty, but he's definitely been shopping at the Big and Tall Store."

Rollie, who seemed to be impervious to insults, beamed like a rookie with the game ball, thrilled to be the butt of an original Myles Fordham dig.

Dr. Trumbull climbed the five steps to the porch. "We all have our struggles maintaining, Myles," he replied. I thought I saw the tiniest trace of a smile. "During my doctoral studies, I was a guide myself. It must've been the summers of '64 and '65." His eyes wandered to the parade ground. "So, I thought I'd suit up for today's first lesson." He looked down at his gone-to-hayseed physique and slumped a bit. "I was quite fit in the sixties."

"So was David Crosby," said Myles. "But time marches on."

Dr. Trumbull snapped back to his role as trainer. His spine bolted upright. He paced across the planks of the porch, hands clasped tightly behind his back. "Gentlemen, the upcoming visit from Governor Belkin is crucial. His impressions of the Fort Mackinac experience could be our lifeline, especially with his potential presidential campaign on the horizon."

A cloud crossed the parade ground, fading the blindingly white walls. "We need to present an impeccable— and let me make this very clear—*historically accurate* reenactment. Our funding, our very future, could depend on it. We may only have one chance to ..."

He looked away, straining for the right word. "What's the best way to say it ..."

"Dazzle?" Rollie suggested.

"Yes. *Dazzle*." He took a deep breath and used his palm

to wipe the sweat from his forehead. "Thank you, Mr. Shartz. That is the ideal word."

"Dazzle," I repeated under my breath. Dr. Trumbull was right. It was the ideal word.

"What unfolded the other day was, frankly, a travesty. You disregarded every last one of our State Park protocols. You decimated our proud Mackinac Island history. And you embarrassed me personally. He breathed deeply enough to pop the middle three brass buttons on his blue coat. "But, sadly, our visitors loved it."

"Sadly?" I asked.

"Yes. Sadly! In another era, crude hoots and cheap laughter wouldn't be enough to suppress my disgust for your performance. But in 1984, with the statewide economy being what it is, I'm finding myself more open-minded to whatever it was you did."

"It's called improv," said Rollie helpfully.

"Fine. *Improv,*" Dr. Trumbull repeated, his face twisting as if he had just inhaled the stench of a rotten carp. "Hopefully, with some serious training and a proper script, you can entertain our guests with historical accuracy. And maybe spare me a lawsuit in the process."

Shively lit up, nodding eagerly, entirely on board with Dr. Trumbull's approach. The rest of us just shuffled our feet like grouchy kids, knowing that "historical accuracy" meant only one thing: memorizing pesky, tedious facts.

"I make no apologies for adoring history," Dr. Trumbull said, the statement landing awkwardly in the silence. Nobody had suggested he should. "No apologies at all."

Dr. Trumbull turned and gestured toward the mainland of Michigan in the distance. "Out there," he said, waving his hand at the horizon and all its modern complexities, "the world gets more complicated every day. Technology. Speed. Does it make things better? More channels on TV to watch more crap performed by circus clowns? We're sixteen years away from the year 2000, gentlemen, and what have we done?"

We shared glances.

He continued. "Has anything come close to the power of a cannon fired from a bluff at an advancing enemy? Or the creativity of making candles out of bee's wax? Signal flags and drum beats to convey orders instead of screeching radios?"

Rollie glanced at me with a funny little grin and mouthed, *"Bee's wax?"*

Dr. Trumbull didn't notice. "Here at Fort Mackinac, it's as if time has frozen. The past breathes around us. It *breathes*, gentlemen! If only it could stay this way forever."

There was a long, weird pause, and we all waited to see if there was more to his impromptu sermon. He shook his head, shedding his utopian dream like a dog shaking off a Halloween costume. There was no room for nostalgia now. He had the mundane tasks of balancing budgets, securing funding, and ensuring the Fort's survival. No time for bee's wax.

"I trust I needn't spell out what a disappointment failing to impress the Governor at the Gala would be for all of us. There's not just pride on the line. There's money. And God knows, right now, we need it."

He stood for a moment too long, glaring at us as if willing the dire warning to stick. "Okay, then." He broke, turned, and walked toward the guide shack. "Follow me. The first order of the week: muskets."

Over the next four days, I guzzled down more historical knowledge than I could digest.

I learned that bayonets attached to muskets were not just for removing enemy bowels on the battlefield; soldiers used them to skewer food for cooking, which I found both fascinating and nauseating.

I learned to eat something called "hardtack," which tasted like particleboard and was essentially compressed, stale bread rolled in salt. Soldiers in the War of 1812 ate it because it lasted forever. We ate it because Dr. Trumbull made sure we ate it.

Because, well, *historical accuracy.*

I learned about flintlocks, haversacks, blockhouses, and mustering. I learned the intricacies of the Charleville musket model, a ten-pound rifle that felt like twenty after a few hours of drilling. I learned to use my teeth to tear open a cartridge filled with gunpowder and spit out the paper.

Bubble Yum was no longer on the menu.

I'd blown up enough model airplanes with my pyromaniac pals to know that gunpowder was stuffed inside those M-80s we used. And I'd seen enough Bugs Bunny cartoons to know what it could do to Wile E. Coyote when things went wrong. By the end of each training day, I reeked of the stuff. It was in my hair, on my skin, and probably even on my breath.

But I loved it.

Gunpowder didn't quite smell like victory, but it beat the hell out of the smell of ranch dressing, dirty dishrags, and leftover Redcoat sandwiches. It beat the smell of busboy.

CHAPTER 15

The Fight

We carved out the final training day to immerse ourselves in the pièce de résistance of our guiding repertoire: *The Fall of Fort Mackinac.*

Earlier in the week, we'd bluffed, joked, and lied our way through the audition show, barely snaking by due mainly to the cheers of a friendly crowd. But there was no way Dr. Trumbull would let that spectacle slide twice. "Improv," starring chew-spit, hookers, and Aztecs, might have been a hit with the masses, but in Dr. Trumbull's curated world, that brand of silliness was not going to cut it.

We assembled on a patch of grass beneath the snapping, fluttering flags just outside the North Sally Port, the spot where the carriage tours dumped their loads of wide-eyed tourists. That day, uniforms were optional—a rare gesture of leniency from Dr. Trumbull. Aside from our varied ages, we could have passed for a freshman orientation group on a campus tour.

Dr. Trumbull handed us each a battered, xeroxed script that looked like it had been passed down from the original apostles, its edges frayed, and the ink smudged with a thousand thumbprints. As Dr. Trumbull began reading through the script, I noticed Shively shifting from foot to foot, like a kid standing on hot asphalt. Each line sent electric shocks through his body, his reactions escalating from subtle twitches to outright flinching, scoffing, and dramatic eye rolls. Dr. Trumbull, oblivious, was piercing Shively's rawest nerve without anesthesia: the tale of Luther Shively, Bert Shively's great-great-great-great-grandfather.

Finally, Shively could no longer restrain himself. His voice trembled, then surged into a shout. "You're aware that none of what you're reading is true, right? I mean *none!*"

Dr. Trumbull lowered his script, pausing deliberately before responding. "Mr. Shively, I'm well aware of your family's contention with the historical record. I understand it has caused some consternation for you over the years."

Shively's lips quivered. *"Some consternation?* It's caused us complete humiliation!"

Dr. Trumbull nodded. "I understand that. But you can rest assured it doesn't reflect on you personally or your family. Lt. Luther Shively was under incredible stress that morning in 1812. He had no way of knowing that the British, along with a group of six hundred allies, had dragged a cannon up to the highest point on the island right behind us. For Pete's sake, the poor man didn't even know war had been declared."

Shively's face turned as red as raw sirloin. He quivered just like he had that day at Wild Style, but this time he seemed ready to erupt, Krakatoa-like. We all took a few instinctive steps back, sensing the imminent explosion. Dr. Trumbull eyed him warily, like a lion tamer sizing up a particularly temperamental beast, one wrong move away from a mauling.

Then it happened.

Shively spat on the ground like Sonny Corleone in *The Godfather.* He was not trained in the manly art of hocking a loogie, so only a little came out. But some stray saliva caught a gust and flew directly into Myles's eye.

Myles flinched, recoiling as if he'd just been slapped. "Jesus, Shively!" he barked, squinting from one eye like Long John Silver. "Learn to spit like a man!"

Shively threw up his hands, eyes wide. "I'm so sorry, Myles. That was an accident. I'm just really not okay with this story!"

Myles leaned in, his voice dropping low and threatening. "So practice your aim … *and spit on the Doc!*" He jabbed a finger toward Dr. Trumbull, who watched the exchange with detachment. "I didn't make up this crap. I'm hearing it for the first time right now!"

Shively's voice rose. "My great-great-great-great-grandfather did not surrender Fort Mackinac to the British without a fight. It's a damnable lie!"

Ah, here we go. *The damnable lie.*

Dr. Trumbull's expression was a study in patient indulgence, like a schoolmaster humoring an overzealous pupil. "And how can you prove it's a 'damnable lie,' as you so eloquently put it? I'm not trying to stir the pot here; I'm genuinely curious."

"I can't prove it!" Shively seized up. It was painful to watch. "I just know it's not true!" Shively spat again. It went better this time, hitting the grass without catching a breeze.

Dr. Trumbull's shook his head slightly as if speaking to a small child insisting on doing things the hard way.

"You know it's not true? As a PhD candidate in colonial studies, you should understand better than anyone here that simply *feeling* something is false does not dictate historical accuracy. There is no question that Lt. Luther Shively surrendered after a single warning shot was fired from the hill above us. Every historical record aligns with this account. He admitted it himself after he was imprisoned by the British. Resistance was futile, and surrendering was the only viable option to prevent the slaughter of all his soldiers."

"But—"

"—how about we leave it at that, Mr. Shively?" Dr. Trumbull looked at his watch. "*Facts*, Mr. Shively. *Facts.*"

Shively stewed, glowered, and kicked the ground.

Myles broke the tension. "Who the hell cares?"

All heads snapped around like we were at Wimbledon. "I'm dead serious. So, your great-great-great-great-grandfather got the jitters. Who wouldn't? Who needs a Brit musket ball through the nutsack and a hatchet haircut by some pissed-off Indian, all because you bought into a recruiting poster when you were seventeen. That's not surrender, that's brains." On the word brains, Myles tapped his temple, eyes alive.

"And what was he defending anyway? John Jacob Astor? Some pelt-slinging billionaire lounging in a Manhattan mansion? I say unless Astor was personally funneling a few thousand shekels into the Fort Mackinac Whiskey Fund, screw him! Wave the white flag and head home to the missus. Seriously. The only thing Luther should've felt bad about was being handed command of a fort that wasn't on the high ground! I'm no military genius, but even I know 'build on the high ground' is page one of the fort-building manual! Hell, man, he *shoulda* surrendered! God bless 'em, I say!"

A long pause as Myles's subversive history lesson landed. Shively froze in place, visibly processing. Rollie's eyes unconsciously tracked the hill rising above Fort Mackinac, where the British had, indeed, blasted their warning shot. The high ground.

"How do you know all that stuff?" I asked Myles.

He shrugged. "I taught junior high history for three years in Boca Raton."

I thought for a moment that Myles's take on Luther Shively may have broken the dark spell, that hearing a version of history in which Luther was actually a victim rather than a scapegoat might just work.

But Shively's face went pale, and his eyes went even darker. He turned to Myles and looked at him for a long moment.

His voice was low and menacing, a growl that sounded almost inhuman. "I told you, Luther Shively … did … not … *surrender!*"

And with wild eyes, he launched himself at Myles, knocking him to the dirt. After a few seconds of intense struggle, Shively straddled Myles, his right fist raised high. But before it could land, Myles twisted and flipped Shively into a pretzel-like hold, his limbs coiling around the wiry nerd like a tarantula. For a few seconds, I contemplated jumping in to pull them apart, but it was pretty obvious the skirmish would end soon. Myles was shockingly quick. Besides, I had always considered myself more of a lover than a fighter.

Once Myles neutralized Shively, he leaned in close and spoke in his ear, almost intimately. "You're in luck, Shives.

I'm not going to break your face. But the next time you jump me, you better bring an entire baseball team, all with Louisville Slugger bats. Otherwise, you won't have a jaw when it's over. I'm a lot older and a lot stronger. Clear?"

"Clear," gurgled Shively, his drooling lips mushed against Myles's right bicep. "I'm so sorry, Myles." It sounded like *I'm fo forry Mylef.*

"It's okay, pal. I understand. Family stuff can make ya nuts." Myles softened a few degrees. "No more silliness?"

"No. No more filly-neff. Promiff."

Myles let him go and lithely hopped to his feet. He extended his hand. Shively hesitated, and then took it. Myles pulled him up and looked him over. Shively was dirty, stunned, and embarrassed—but not broken. Myles smiled at him like a proud father, and then brushed the grass off his shirt. Good as new.

Now I had a new reason to ask an old question: *Who was this guy?*

"Yes. That'll be all for today," said an obviously frazzled Dr. Trumbull. He turned away and hastily fled to the safety of his office. "Learn your lines!" he shouted over his shoulder. He didn't look back.

Later that night, after the lights went out, we walked along the barracks porch as Rollie fumbled with his Walkman. Myles stopped and leaned on the railing, and we joined him.

I hadn't seen adults fight except in the movies, and it rattled me. It reminded me that I was sixteen, five years younger than the youngest team member, and probably seventeen years younger than Myles.

I was still a kid.

And today, I felt like it.

Myles looked up at the sky and shook his head. "Insane. It's really something up there." We followed his gaze. Above us, the stars formed a shimmering dome, arching from one stockade to the other, casting a protective glow over the Fort.

Mackinac Island stars weren't ordinary—something about the lack of cars made the night sky almost surreal in its clarity and brilliance. Without the usual city lights and pollution, the stars seemed closer, as if we could reach out and touch them. The Milky Way stretched like a ribbon across the sky.

"How would you describe it?" I asked Myles. "Dazzling?" I was hoping Myles would catch the reference from earlier in the day. He let out a chuckle, but he was transfixed by the stars.

Without looking away, he called over to Shively. "One-Shot. We good?"

My stomach tensed as I prepared myself not to break up another fight. I glanced at Shively, who was also looking up at the stars. It took a moment, but a reluctant smile crept across his face.

"Yeah, Myles," he replied, his voice tight. "We're good." He shot a sharp look in my direction, and then Rollie's. "But nobody else calls me that. *Ever.*"

We nodded solemnly. "Damnable lie," I muttered, almost to myself.

"Damnable lie," Shively echoed softly, his voice laced with lingering frustration. "Damn right."

Rollie reached down and clicked on his Walkman, and the tinny sounds of Phil Collins's *In the Air Tonight* seeped from the foam headphones hanging on his belt. A slow grinding guitar. Weird, haunting beats followed by the shocking, avalanching drum breaks like carpet bombs, even through headphone speakers. We listened to the entire song and stared at the stars and didn't say another word.

The day's history lesson was over.

CHAPTER 16

Seduction

The Blue Butterfly was closed for the afternoon.

The shop echoed with the sounds of *Monty Python's Flying Circus,* the British sketch comedy TV show Big Jack and I had embraced as our humor benchmark. Big Jack had worked out a casual arrangement with Mom to help restock and organize the shop on weekends when he came up from his Oldsmobile dealership downstate. The agreement was that we could continuously play Monty Python reruns on a small TV/VHS combo player Mom kept behind the counter, making stocking dresses slightly more tolerable.

At that moment, I was walking down the accessories aisle, small as it was, re-reading my *Fall of Fort Mackinac* script for the tenth time. Nothing was sticking. This week was the Governor's Gala, which was pretty much the only reason I got hired. Trina would be there, and everything had to be perfect. *Historically accurate.* Even Trenton Feagler was making an appearance, so there was, as Dr. Trumbull had said, potential funding on the line.

Meanwhile, Big Jack was practicing for the Ministry of

Silly Walks, a classic Monty Python sketch. With each exaggerated step and ludicrous lunge, he kept a precarious grip on an armful of flower-printed fabric.

Today, nobody felt my pain.

"Look, Ana," he called to Mom. "I've perfected it!" He was performing some three-step waltz with a dainty spin. It was all very, *very* silly. "They'll have to let me into the Ministry of Silly Walks with this sweet baby!"

"It's a TV show, honey. And it's been off the air for ten years."

"Don't be a killjoy, woman! I worked all week on this silly walk!"

"I'm sorry, dear. I know," she said, reaching up and patting him on his head as he sashayed past her. "I'm proud of you. It's ridiculously silly."

"Thanks, Ana. That means a lot to me," he said, never breaking his silly stride.

The door chimed, and a vision of understated elegance glided into the shop. There was something familiar about her. She was tall, in a sharp blue blazer and expensive running shoes—smart for Mackinac Island. Her hair was neatly pulled back, and her brown eyes were all business. As I moved closer, recognition dawned. She was the same woman I'd seen on the dock with Feagler. The oversized green handbag swinging from her shoulder by a strap was a dead giveaway.

She floated through the shop, inspecting Mom's designs with a smile.

"I'm sorry," Mom politely greeted her while pointing at the CLOSED sign in the glass front door. "We're not open right now. Doing a bit of restocking."

The woman's eyes shifted to Big Jack, who attempted to un-silly his walk, no doubt struck by her relaxed style, a stark contrast to the usual tourist drop-ins. She turned toward Mom. "Ana McGuinn?" Her voice cut through the Python laugh track on the TV. "I'm Helen Chandler. I represent Todd Feagler's non-pizza enterprises."

She extended a business card to Mom. "I'm not here to shop."

Big Jack lowered the volume on the TV and sidled up, scrutinizing the card over Ana's shoulder like a skeptical bouncer at the Pink Pony Bar.

"Actually," she said with a smooth, lineless smile. "Let me correct myself. I'm not here to shop … *for clothes.*"

"Wait? Is this one of those 'get it in 22 minutes, or it's free' deals?" Big Jack asked, his car dealer cornball charm kicking in like a nervous tick.

Helen responded with a patient smile and chuckled. "That's so hilarious." Her eyes said otherwise.

"Jack McGuinn." Big Jack extended a hand, and she shook it. "I happen to be Ana's loyal assistant and occasional husband. And that useless punk over there, trying to make sense of his script, is Jack Junior."

She smiled, and I raised my hand with a half-hearted salute.

Her eyes drifted back to Ana. "A true family business. How sweet." The word 'sweet' rolled off her tongue with the condescending tone of a preschool teacher admiring a child's macaroni art, and though her smile was warm, it felt as switched on as a sunlamp. Switch it off, and things would get as chilly as the windows of a corporate boardroom in winter. With her in the store, the boho walls of the Blue Butterfly felt too small, too exposed.

Or maybe it was all in my head.

"Mr. Feagler's been monitoring your progress, Ana," she continued, inspecting a blown-up black-and-white photo I had snapped of Mom posing with Christopher

Reeve and Jane Seymour on the set of *Somewhere in Time* during the summer of 1979.

"*Monitoring?* How flattering." Mom said. "And, frankly, a little creepy."

Helen smiled. "Yes, well, it's always best to be honest. Your work on *Somewhere in Time* didn't go unnoticed. What a wonderful story." Her eyes never left the photo. "Summer resident gets a job dressing Hollywood. Just, wow. Now, all this." She opened her arms to include the entire shop. "The Blue Butterfly. They say it's the best thing to happen to Market Street since Little Bob's famous cinnamon rolls."

"Little Bob's isn't on Market Street," I called over. "It's on Astor Street."

"Hush, Jack," Mom shot back, but Helen was calm and unflappable.

"Close enough," she said with a *nobody's perfect* shrug.

"You seem to know the island pretty well. It's funny we haven't seen you around," said Big Jack, whose eager-to-impress smile had dropped into neutral.

"I keep a low profile in matters of business. Mr. Feagler prefers it that way." Helen's eyes scanned the shop. "This place ... it's more than just a shop. It's art, pure and simple." Her face warmed, and, for a moment, she was a child again. *"God, I could just move in!"*

Mom blushed. "Thank you. We put our heart into it."

Helen nodded, shifting back to business. "Of course you do. That's why Mr. Feagler is interested. He's creating a new tourist destination on Beaver Island. And he wants the Blue Butterfly to be one of its cornerstones."

"Beaver Island?" said Ana, looking toward Big Jack. "Isn't that ... where is that, Jack?"

"Lake Michigan. Past the bridge, twenty or thirty

miles," answered Big Jack. He was gazing at Helen closely now. His smile was gone.

Helen nodded. "Fifty-five square miles. Thirty-five miles offshore from Charlevoix. It's an island that respects history, yet looks to the future." She continued, "Imagine, Ana, a place where colonial history and modern luxury come together. Your designs would be showcased alongside the biggest names in fashion."

Helen continued unveiling Feagler's grand vision. "Think of it as a destination for history lovers, merged with the allure of high-end shopping. A one-stop destination that redefines leisure and learning." She paused for effect, her brown eyes scanning for reactions. "Think Greenfield Village in Dearborn, the heart and soul of historical Michigan, but elevated. Transformed even. Now, picture the elegance and exclusivity of Rodeo Drive in Beverly Hills. Mr. Feagler calls it *upscale history*," she said. "A totally unique, new concept. We're not just building a resort. We're crafting an experience. And for it to work, we need the charm of boutique shops like the Blue Butterfly. It's *perfect* for this vision. Just … *perfect.*"

Mom looked drugged. It was all too much. "Are you talking about a franchise? Like Corleone's Pizza?" asked Big Jack.

She shook her head the way you do when talking to an unsophisticated rube. "I'm afraid not. Exclusivity is one of the major draws of this business model. You'd have to relocate." Helen let it land and then continued. "Of course, Mr. Feagler is prepared to support your move generously. And your expansion."

"Expansion?" asked Mom.

"Of course. He knows talent when he sees it and is never afraid to put his money where his mouth is." She looked around the tiny shop. "This is quaint, but it's cramped. You're an artist, Ana, and you'll need a big enough canvas to spread out and show the world what you have to offer."

Big Jack broke in with a groaner. "Hear that, Ana? Feagler wants a *Pizza the Action.*" Neither Mom nor Helen smiled.

Helen handed Mom a sealed envelope from her green handbag. "There are some initial term sheet ideas in this envelope." She checked her watch. "Oh boy! I should get going. I don't want to miss the last boat. I'm heading downstate tonight. We're also in talks with a boutique in Birmingham. Pirini's. Heard of it?"

"*Heard of it?* Danielle Pirini is the best designer in …"

But Helen was already half out the door. "Great to meet you, Ana McGuinn. Boys. We're all big fans of your work. Bye for now!" The door chimed shut, leaving us all as still as pine trees. Monty Python's *Lumberjack Song* skit flickered on the TV.

> *I cut down trees.*
> *I wear high heels*
> *Suspenders and a bra*
> *I wish I'd been a girlie*
> *Just like my dear Papa*

Nobody laughed.

CHAPTER 17

Showtime

We had draped ourselves around the guide shack like discarded sportcoats, struggling to remember our lines for the Governor's Gala to benefit the Allies of Mackinac organization. Shively was distracted, staring into space with a vapor of gloom hanging over him. His hair was particularly elevated that day, and I could only hope his hat would help solve the issue.

The clock was ticking, and our faltering attempts to memorize the script only added to an overall feeling of doom. The guide shack was filled with a low hum of both refrigeration and frustration as we repeated lines and gestured uselessly, trying to coax Dr. Trumbull's dialogue off the script and into our brains.

"I can't do this!" Shively finally shouted, hurling his script against a far wall. Myles stared at the discarded script as if expecting it to take wings and fly around the room.

"It's okay," I said, playing the wise acting mentor. "It's

tough to memorize. But if we get close enough, it'll be fine."

"It's not that," Shively shot back. "I can memorize anything. I have a photographic memory. I've been tested. It's this crap with Luther Shively. The surrender." He shook his head, too flustered to finish.

Myles looked over. "Shives, I mean this with much love. Why the hell did you sign up for this gig?"

Shively's reply was quiet. "I love history. I thought somehow I'd be able to …" He trailed off.

Myles nodded like an understanding therapist. "Have you considered the possibility that your 'love' of history is turning you into a lunatic?" He raised his hand. "Now, don't get me wrong. I have no problem with lunatics. Many of my best friends are lunatics." Myles glanced at Shively's crumpled script on the floor. "But we can't go through this again. You know exactly how this little tantrum ends."

Shively gave a resigned smile. "Me in a headlock, unable to breathe?"

"Bingo," said Myles.

"I agree," I said. "You gotta get it together. Governor Belkin's coming. Feagler's coming. Shit, my whole family will be out there." I almost slipped up and mentioned that Trina LaFromme could be there, monitoring my performance, but that was a different can of worms.

Shively kicked a folding chair, sending it skidding across the floor with a clattering crash, and then grimaced with pain from the impact. "I thought I could do it, but I can't. I can't go out in front of the entire island and repeat the same old damnable lie." His voice broke, a raw screech of desperation cutting through.

The same old damnable lie.

Myles flung his script to the ground, pages scattering.

"Dammit, Shives!" he growled, running a hand through his hair. "You just knocked all the lines out of my head!"

"Wait, guys," said Rollie, hands raised and eyes sparkling. "I have an idea. What if it's not the 'same old damnable lie.' But a *Super* Lie."

"A Super Lie?" said Myles.

"You mean like last time?" said Shively.

"Bigger. A Super Lie so outrageously untrue, that nobody'll be thinking about Luther Shively's *alleged* surrender because they'll be too busy pissing their pants laughing." We all appreciated that Rollie snuck in the word "alleged."

Rollie reached into his backpack and pulled out four scripts and a stack of neatly printed cue cards.

"Because I wrote something good." He spread the pages out on the table. We leaned in like a pack of hungry cats.

"Wait. We have to *memorize* this?" I asked, a nervous glance toward the clock on the wall. Showtime was in an hour.

"It's easy. A lot of improv. A lot of cue cards. I wrote it for guys just like you," Rollie said, growing more wicked by the second.

"… *Idiots.*"

We took our positions on the parade ground, facing a sprawling crowd that overflowed the field's edges and spread onto the sunlit grass. The sight was almost overwhelming: Governor Belkin, dressed in sharp tennis whites, stood with his fancy entourage, including Feagler, incongruous in his ever-present suit. My family hooted from the front row, obnoxious cheers cutting through the chatter of tourists. Looking like a nervous soccer coach, Dr. Trumbull paced at the edge of the lawn. It felt as if everyone I'd ever met in my entire life was there, craning their necks for a better view.

Under the branches of a cedar tree, off to the side, Trina LaFromme sat on a cheap foldable lawn chair. She cooled herself with an ivory-handled fan and wore a wide-brimmed hat with fake flowers that swayed with the fan's gusts. She appeared as a slightly odd relic from another era to the uninterested bystanders. But to me, she was judge, jury, and executioner.

Rollie started us off. He gestured expansively, and a hush rolled over the crowd. "When the War of 1812 broke out, the fort commander, Luther Shively, was not informed."

Shively chimed in, "But–"

I raised my hand, cutting him off, and said, "The U. S. secretary of war, a man named Useless—"

"—*Eustis,*" Shively corrected.

"*Eustis.* Sorry, that's right. *Eustice*—who also happened to be *useless,*" I continued, loving the groove of Rollie's easy-to-process sketch. Having cue cards conveniently hidden around the parade grounds didn't hurt either. "Eustis chose to inform Luther Shively, the commander here at the Fort, that America and England were at war … *by mail.* No Pony Express. No UPS. Not even FedEx. An ordinary letter!"

A groan of amazement rippled through the crowd. I continued, "True story. He walked to the Washington, D.C., post office and dropped a letter in the mailbox. It supposedly said—"

"—*duck, suckers!*" Myles interjected. "It's on!"

A bigger laugh.

Rollie continued. "You probably heard the expression,

'didn't get the memo.' Well, Luther Shively didn't get the memo. Or the letter." Rollie continued. "First of all, a little background on the War of 1812. It's a very, very weird war." Rollie was in his element, an ear-to-ear grin striping his puffy cheeks. "You don't hear much about it. America invaded Canada—technically England at the time." He paused and pretended to check his notes. "I think." It got a laugh. "And while America claims victory all these years later, it's untrue. If America won, why do nineteen-year-olds from Michigan need to sneak across the Detroit-Windsor tunnel into Canada every weekend, where the legal drinking age is nineteen, not twenty-one? We clearly *did … not … win."*

Myles jumped in. "And if we won, why don't we claim the rock band *Rush?* 'Tom Sawyer'? 'The Spirit of Radio'? Those would be classic *American* rock anthems! And more importantly, Wayne Gretzky would be playing hockey for the Detroit Red Wings, not the Edmonton Oilers! All together now! Let's hear it good and loud!"

"We did not win!" the crowd roared back.

We had them.

Shively picked it up. "On July 17, 1812, the British landed in the middle of the night on the island's far side, at a spot called British Landing."

"An incredible coincidence, if you ask me," interjected Myles.

"Indeed," Rollie continued. "The British were led by the great juggling genius, Captain 'Three Balls' Robinson. He got that nickname not for any anatomical anomalies but because he could juggle three cannonballs with one hand tied behind his back. Small ones, mind you—two-pound balls. Still, it was impressive."

Then I jumped back in, gripping an imaginary telescope and eyeing a perfectly placed cue card. "I can almost picture ol' Three Balls in his canoe full of soldiers scanning the darkened beach that fateful night. 'Where should we land? Well, there's French Landing. Nope. Greek Landing. Probably not. Italian Landing? Wait! I see the perfect spot! There's even one of those green historical marker signs: *British Landing!*'"

Shively joined in. "So, after feasting on peanut brittle and fudge and downing two sixers of Molson Canadian beer for some liquid courage, they dragged a cannon through the woods to a ridge above the fort. Once they reached the island's highest point, Three Balls eyeballed Fort Mackinac below and said ..." Shively raised a thin hand. "'Gentlemen. This is going to be very easy!'"

A laugh rippled. Buoyed by the reaction, Shively pressed on. "Now, here's the kicker. Fort Mackinac wasn't built on the high ground! Which, as we all know, is page one of the fort-building manual. Three Balls fired a single warning shot, which, according to the historical record, nobody heard. He then sent his best men down to the fort."

Myles jumped in. "Being a sporting Brit, Three Balls was sorely disappointed by the Americans' complete lack of readiness for the siege of Fort Mackinac."

"It was almost as if they hadn't gotten the memo," I said, stealing a look at another perfectly placed cue card. "So instead of deploying his entire 600-strong force— which included soldiers, fur traders, poop sweepers, fudge makers, chimney sweeps, cocktail waitresses, two members of the Jimi Hendrix Experience, Mary Poppins, and three local Native American tribes—he chose a much smaller, far more flamboyant group to storm the North Sally Port."

The audience hung on every word.

"They knocked for a while and were eventually let in

by the sleepy night watchman. See, Three Balls didn't want death. He didn't want destruction."

"No," Rollie cut in, "he wanted to dance! Outnumbered, having lost the high ground, and very sleepy, the American garrison agreed to the first and only historically documented … *dance-off.*"

Now, it was Myles. "This situation was made even more dire by the fact that the British had a 600-person field party going strong on the high ground, with a live band and three kegs of, you guessed it, Molson beer, which had just been shipped in from another part of the island, now called 'Molson's Landing' by the locals. They were *hammered* and ready to dance."

Back to Rollie. "The outnumbered Americans were in no position to refuse," he added. "It was then that the Americans made a request. To save face, they asked permission to discharge their muskets so the townspeople below would *think* there had been an actual battle. The British agreed, as long as the Americans promised to fire horse manure from their muskets as a symbolic admission of what a crappy job they did defending the fort. The Americans agreed."

The four of us lined up for the musket firing demonstration.

"Present arms!" Myles's command echoed across the parade ground, and we went through our musket-firing protocols with precision. Myles, standing tall, bellowed, *"ready … aim …"*

In perfect unison, we leveled our muskets. The tension built, the crowd leaned in.

Myles broke the moment, grinning. *"Poo!"* he shouted. BLAM! A cloud of gunsmoke mushroomed across the parade ground.

The crowd erupted. I caught Rollie's eye, and he gave me a slight nod. We were nailing it.

Rollie hit *play* on a hidden boom box as the haze settled. The unmistakable beat of *You Should Be Dancing* by The Bee Gees kicked in from the speakers. With the music weaving through the smoky air, we all launched into horrible disco dancing. Myles's arms flailed spastically like he was fighting off a wasp attack. Rollie gyrated weirdly, boots shuffling in exaggerated, awkward motions. Shively threw in some robotic pops and locks with stiff, mechanical moves. I gleefully butchered the Hustle, which Mom had taught me when I was little, and the disco craze was in full swing.

As we each floundered through our horrific dance moves, Rollie addressed the crowd. "There is no known historical record of what dances were performed on that fateful night, but we can only assume it wasn't pretty."

Now, it was my line. "And thus, the siege of Fort Mackinac ended not with a bang but with ... *disco!* The day was saved, timelines were all screwed up, and history was not made ... but *un*made!"

I glanced at Trina. She was on her feet, arms out, twirling to the music, her ancient dress and purple boa flowing in the breeze like a geriatric Stevie Nicks. The governor, who was surprisingly agile, did the Sprinkler dance, and he wasn't half bad. My entire family was doing the requisite Hustle, including Gramps.

Even Dr. Trumbull couldn't resist a tiny sway, although he looked incredibly uncomfortable, unsure if he was saving his beloved fort or ruining it.

I caught a glimpse of a cute college girl among the governor's crowd. She was all energy and enthusiasm, skillfully executing the wild, flailing arm moves that were the hallmark of the '80s, punctuating her routine with dramatic hair flips. She was decked out in an oversized Iowa sweatshirt and aviator Ray-Bans, throwing looks Rollie's way now and then. Rollie noticed, turned her way, and shot back with his best nightclub singer double-point.

Myles had the last word, his voice booming over the applause and laughter. "Let's hear it for the wild, ridiculous, and totally peaceful tale of the fall of Fort Mackinac!"

Rollie stepped forward, his face beaming with confidence. "And remember, folks," he announced, his voice carrying across the crowd, "*none* of what you just heard is true!"

"History!" we shouted in unison, throwing our fists into the air. We didn't know it then, but this would become our signature ending, the perfect punctuation to our historical nonsense.

Based on the response of the roaring crowd, big Rollie Shartz was one hell of a writer.

CHAPTER 18

Kurt the Busboy

I burst through the Tea Room's break room door with the force of a caffeine-fueled linebacker. My heart raced, though I couldn't pinpoint why. Something about the sound of laughter—the laughter of tourists, the governor and his family, my parents, and Trina LaFromme dancing—had me keyed up like a toddler on pixie sticks. The screen door swung open too fast and slammed against the stone wall as my eyes adjusted.

It was silent, except for the electric fan.

Squawbait, deeply absorbed in his *Motocross Action* magazine, glanced up. His eyes took a slow, deliberate tour of my new uniform, trying to decide if I was an apparition. He was no doubt mentally reconciling this new, dashing version of Jack to the last one he'd seen, a whining little peasant boy who smelled like ham.

He flipped to a new page.

"Ten-hut. Officer present," he said, dry as a bone. He was doing everything I would expect him to do. Dishwashers called 'Squawbait' were not put on earth to give compliments.

"Funny stuff," I said. "And I'm a private."

His eyes briefly met mine. "And a week ago, you were a busboy. What's with the new look."

"Movin' up in the world."

I struck a catalog pose, opened the blue coat, and froze. "So, seriously—what do you think, man?"

His eyes went back to the magazine. "I think Bob Hannah got robbed at the Anaheim Supercross," he said. "And the new Suzuki RM 250 looks fast."

He glanced up and squinted at me again. "Wait. Are you wearing friggin' *eyeliner?*"

"No!" I said, turning away, my cheeks heating up. I reflexively rubbed under my eyes and checked it. It was a smudge of gunpowder.

Another blank once-over. "You wear it well." His words hung like a wet sheet. I wore *what* well? Was it the uniform or the eyeliner? I let it go.

"Yeah, so I can't join you for lunch anymore. Guides run on a different schedule. And as for training the busboy, I can make time tomorrow morn—"

"—already handled."

"Handled? What does that even mean?"

"Maya brought in a new guy. Kurt. He started two days ago. Didn't need training."

"Wow. Great."

He looked up, eyes now bright. "Yeah, this kid's a real pro. The way he stacks those plates, my gawd, you'd think he was born to do it. Plus, he organizes all the dishes on the machine rack, which speeds things up a ton for me. I guess he's some sort of pro dish jock from Indian River. He's been doing it for years." He flipped to a new page. "So yeah. We're covered. No training necessary."

Pro dish jock? This was the first I'd heard of such a job

designation. "I did it for years," I pointed out, trying hard not to sound defensive and pathetic.

"That you did. That. You. Did." *Cryptic.* "Anyway, we're covered," he looked up. "Covered … *well.*"

His addition of the word "*well*" was a pointed little dig I didn't think was necessary. I indicated the kitchen. "Does Kurt know about the three-tiered wheeled dishcart? I usually store it behind the wait stand in case—"

"—no need," he interjected. "Kurt doesn't use 'em. Everything's cleared so fast he doesn't need the crutch."

Crutch? "Well, I mean, it's not really a crutch. It's just a backup in case things get too busy. You don't know what it's like out there during the lunch rush. It can get pretty hairy." What I wanted to say was, "While you're nestled in your little stainless steel dishwashing cacoon in the kitchen, wearing motocross boots and a doo-rag and listening to Foghat on your boombox, I was on the Main Stage, clearing plates to keep the tourist flow uninterrupted." I didn't say any of that, but I did find myself getting more irritated by the second.

He must've sensed it. "At ease, soldier. I'll say it differently: He doesn't need a *backup plan.*"

"So, uh, does Kurt know where we keep the extra soap for the dishwasher?"

"He makes his own."

"He makes his own what?"

"Soap."

"He makes his own soap?"

"Yeah, some organic, eco-friendly stuff. Smells like lavender or some shit. Dishes have never been cleaner … or more aromatic."

He looked up at me and smiled widely. "Anything else?"

"Wait? Aren't you the busboy?"

I looked across the breakroom. It was Jenna Bonnet. Seizing the chance to escape Squawbait's relentless mind games, I eagerly dove into Jenna's warm, blue-eyed gaze. Jenna, whose interest in me now seemed real. Maya was right. Just a week before, I wouldn't have dared take a step in her direction. Now, here I was, strolling over like some colonial stud, the heels of my boots echoing on the wood floor.

"I *was* the busboy; now I'm a bluecoat."

"Yeah, well, they couldn't do worse than the last crew. Weirdos." She squinted. "How old are you?"

"Almost seventeen," I replied, feeling a sudden urge to shift my gaze away from her probing eyes. "But I have a car downstate. It's an Oldsmobile Omega. It's red. I'm thinking about getting tinted windows." I stared at her with a lunatic smile.

What the hell was I talking about?

Squawbait coughed conspicuously from across the room. I ignored it. I was too busy fighting the urge to pass out.

She smiled, graciously allowing my ramblings to pass without comment. "Well, anyway, congratulations on the promotion." She adjusted her *Cider House Rules* paperback in front of her. "Rumor has it, the governor loved the show today. They say he was cracking up. Normally, he's in and out. Only sticks around for the photo op, but today, he's staying to see all the attractions. Could be the best Gala ever." Jenna shook her head, her eyes sparkling with curiosity. "You guys must've done something pretty wild."

"Can I get a Redcoat sandwich?" I suddenly blurted out, raising my voice aggressively toward the kitchen. No idea why.

The kitchen door creaked open, revealing the shiny-faced, bald chef. Sweat beaded on his forehead, glistening under the lights. His eyes locked onto my uniform, and his face settled into the same blank stare Squawbait had given me earlier.

"Wow. Maya wasn't lying. Trumbull really *is* desperate." A snort escaped him, dissolving into full-blown laughter. Squawbait joined in. I stood and took it, a Revolutionary punchline.

"Seriously. Can I just get a sandwich?" I cringed inwardly at my high-pitched, whiny tone.

"Calm down, Private Dishrag. I'll get to it." He disappeared back into the kitchen.

I spun to face Jenna, my ears blazing like signal flares. "Can I get you an ice cream puff or something?" The words gushed out. Jenna's eyes met mine, a hint of amusement dancing in them. She seemed to consider my offer.

"It's a sweet thought," she said, glancing at her watch with a slight furrow of her brow. "But I'm already running late for the ticket booth." She rose, smoothing her uniform. "Congratulations on your debut, Jack." With that, she turned away and left, the screen door clattering shut behind her.

It was just me, Squawbait, and the rattling sound of the old fan—just like old times. Outside, I heard the shuffling and clinking of an incredibly efficient busboy clearing a table.

Probably Kurt.

"I dunno, man. I think she really likes you," Squawbait said. He stood up, gathering his dirty plate and an empty can of Sprite with exaggerated care. Then, unable to contain himself, he exploded into laughter again.

Still chuckling, he carefully rolled up his magazine and stuffed it in his back pocket like it was a treasure map. With a final snort, he ambled back to his stainless steel dishwashing cocoon.

CHAPTER 19

The North Keep

In the following weeks, word spread that something new was sparking hot at Fort Mackinac, and it wasn't just the gunpowder flaring from the mouth of the cannon. It seemed like overnight, our nutty little production had become the talk of northern Michigan, with lines getting longer every day, soon stretching down the fort ramp.

Why did it hit home? It beats me. Maybe people sensed our love for the Fort, the island, and its history even as we gleefully tore it apart. It could've been our twisted take on the dusty tales they'd snoozed through in high school. Or maybe, in a time when Michigan was battling a rough economy, people simply wanted a good old-fashioned, stupid giggle. It was just fun.

Whatever the reason, attendance shot up. The gift shops couldn't keep fake muskets and colonial hats in stock. Beth made a few bucks selling T-shirts that simply said 'HISTORY!' Even the crustiest old-timer Islanders were spotted reluctantly trudging up the ramp to check our unmaking of history.

For a few glorious weeks during the summer of 1984, we were celebrities. Big fish in our small, fudge-and-horse-poo-scented pond, the hottest attraction that couldn't be bought by the slice. I, for one, loved it.

Bluecoats:
Come to my office for an important announcement.

Crossing the parade ground toward Dr. Trumbull's office, I mulled over the cryptic note we'd found tacked up on the guide shack door.

Scribbled with urgency in Dr. Trumbull's recognizable script, the message smelled of trouble. Fallout from our unlikely success? It wasn't beyond the pale.

The office door cracked open just enough to invite a peek.

I nudged it wider and looked around. The guys were already assembled. Rollie paced, engrossed in a copy of *Mad Magazine*, the buttons of his jacket undone, and his gut free to roam. Myles was sprawled on an old leather couch, snoring lightly, his boots propped up on the coffee table as if he owned the place. Shively was absorbed by a map spread out on a long table, his concentration was intense. Myles's eyes snapped open the moment I stepped in, instantly alert.

"Busboy! How'd it go?"

"How'd *what* go?"

He shook his head. "Are you really going to stand there and tell me you haven't rolled back to the Tea Room to impress the ladies with your newly acquired stardust? I'm not stupid. Spill it. I live for this stuff."

How did this guy know so much?

"No! I—okay, I've stopped by, but only to grab a few things," I stammered, feeling my face go hot.

"A few things? Like, maybe, phone numbers?" Myles chuckled, sliding forward in his seat. "Can't bullshit a bullshitter. What's her name?"

My ears were burning, and I couldn't think of a comeback. Just then, the door swung open, and Dr. Trumbull rushed in. "Big news," he announced, striding to the long table. "Gather around."

"Don't tell me. You saw your toes during weigh-in?" said Myles, getting up as slowly as a jungle cat. "That's great news, Doc. I thought you were looking svelte lately."

We formed a semi-circle around the map spread out on the table.

"Witty, Mr. Fordham, but no. It's better than my toes. Governor Belkin has greenlit the opening of the North Keep. It's happening, gentlemen!"

I leaned in, trying to make sense of the intricate web of lines on the map. "What does this mean for us?"

"Truthfully? Nothing. I just wanted to share the news."

Myles gave a sideways squint to Dr. Trumbull. "I think it's time to admit it, Doc. We're growing on you. Just take a deep, nourishing breath and let it all out. You'll feel better." Dr. Trumbull froze. His face dropped, and his gaze drifted away as if considering the implications of this horrifying possibility.

He shook it off and continued. "Last fall, the park commission ran into a major funding freeze right after we discovered a passage to an underground storage area north of the fort walls." He traced the line on the map gently as if pressing too hard might vaporize his dream. "We're calling it the *North Keep*. We think it may have been a sort of antechamber that was sealed off around 1860 and forgotten over time."

Rollie nodded. *"The North Keep.* Great name. Very cinematic."

"I'm glad you approve, Mr. Shartz. We had to stop everything last fall and secure it. The State couldn't release funds to send a proper team from Lansing to break the seal. It's under the State Park's jurisdiction, and as you know, the current economy isn't ideal for funding these types of projects."

Shively indicated the plot map, eyes guarded. "Dr. Trumbull, this North Keep. Is it the records room you mentioned during my initial interview?"

"Well, that's the theory. Records. General storage. Who knows what else? Of course, we haven't entered the space yet."

Shively tugged at his wild, untamed hair, his temperature visibly rising. "The site that might date back to the early eighteen hundreds?"

"That's the one. Attendance is spiking so Governor Belkin gave the nod for a team from Lansing to arrive next week to unlock the antechamber. Word is, Trenton Feagler is the one funding this new venture."

Dr. Trumbull sighed deeply and removed his glasses, his eyes drifting to the birch bark canoe suspended above his desk as if it were his patron saint.

"We're on the brink of opening up the most significant site in decades, a discovery so monumental that ..." Dr. Trumbull's excitement abruptly dimmed, and his smile vanished as if he'd just noticed us standing there. "Wait. Let me back up. None of this means I approve of the ridiculous farce you four have been foisting on the public. It's outrageous, what with the dance-off, Molson beer, and whatever else you throw in." He shook his head as if catching a whiff of a baby's diaper. "Truthfully, I've tried to forget the whole crude spectacle."

"You mean, like, 'Three Balls' Robinson?" I asked. We stifled laughs.

"Right," he responded, but a tiny crack of a smile flashed and then vanished. "'Three Balls' Robinson. *Unbelievable*. Donald R. Hickey would never forgive me."

"Who's Donald R. Hickey?" asked Myles.

Shively jumped in, eager to impress. "Hickey wrote *The War of 1812: A Forgotten Conflict*. It's probably the most comprehensive history of—"

"—I actually don't care," Myles interrupted. "I was just being polite. And I've learned my lesson. I have no plans to be polite again."

Dr. Trumbull sighed, his shoulders slumping. "I don't want to like what you're doing, but I can't deny it's working. As much as it pains me to admit, the funding might've come through because of your performances. We're on the verge of uncovering something significant here, and I have to overlook my distaste for what you do and focus on the big picture."

We stood in awkward silence.

"But seriously. *Ready, aim, poo?*" said Myles in a low voice, dripping with joy. "That bit absolutely kills."

Dr. Trumbull's face twisted like he'd chewed a lemon. "I'm sorry, but I refuse to acknowledge that travesty as a representation of history."

"The Governor liked it," I chimed in. "I saw him dancing."

"Yup. He was doing the Sprinkler," Rollie chimed in. "It looked something like this." He extended his right arm like a sprinkler nozzle, his left hand rhythmically slapping the back of his head, and began rotating his body as if dousing the office in water, a sight made even stranger by the fact that Rollie was wearing a Colonial Army uniform with his jacket unbuttoned and his gut hanging out.

Dr. Trumbull waved it off with a grunt and returned to tracing lines on the map. The room fell silent again, the only sound the scratching of Dr. Trumbull's pencil on a notepad.

A small, high-pitched chuckle—a squeak almost—escaped his lips, bird-like. At first, it was so soft we nearly missed it. The squeak grew into a full-on laugh, louder and squeakier by the second. Dr. Trumbull's shoulders began to shake. The laugh spread like a slow wave, picking up momentum.

He looked up, now in hysterics. "You people … are *nuts!*" said Dr. Trumbull as he yanked off his glasses and dried tears with his shirt sleeve. The office was roaring now, giggles ricocheting off old maps and book-loaded shelves.

But Shively stood apart. He was not laughing.

The plot map transfixed him. With his eyes narrowing, he mentally traced the lines and details like a hawk eyeing a mouse half a mile away.

An intercom buzzed on Dr. Trumbull's desk. A woman's voice. "Dr. Trumbull. Herb Craven from the A.J.A. is on line three."

"Wonderful!" said Dr. Trumbull, rubbing his hands together. "That's the writer from the American Journal of Archaeology. He wants to do an article on the North Keep dig." He trotted toward his desk and picked up the receiver. "I need to take this."

We exchanged uncertain glances, waiting for direction. "Should we … split?" Myles asked. Dr. Trumbull, his laughter fading, straightened his posture and adjusted his glasses.

"I need the room. So, yes. Kindly … *split.*" He took a breath and punched line three on the phone. His face had already shifted back into *respected historian* mode with jarring efficiency.

Later in the guide shack, Shively meticulously fastened the top button of his blue coat, his face pale and hair floating like strands of seaweed. Myles, inches away from him, whispered in his ear like Original Sin incarnate.

"You heard the good doctor. The funding dried up. That's why they never cracked the seal on the dig site. But now that the governor got his disco on? He got Feagler to open his wallet."

His words tumbled out. He then swiveled to Rollie and me.

"You guys get it?"

I was busily attaching my bayonet while Rollie was fiddling with the brass buttons of his white soldier pants. Both of us nodded along like curious disciples, more than happy to agree with Myles, but neither of us knew where he was going with it.

He continued. "You ask me? *We* deserve to go in there first. *We* made it happen. That antechamber would be on forever if it weren't for Rollie's crazy dance-off idea." His eyes locked onto me. "You, busboy. Aren't you curious what's in there?"

"Um. Kinda." Truthfully, I was more curious about why Myles was so interested.

"*Kinda?* Shit, when I met you, you wouldn't even take my order at the Tea Room, you were so beaten down. Now look at you! You're scoring phone numbers. Breakin' hearts! You're a goddamn *actor!*"

"I'm a *reenactor*," I corrected.

"Same thing! You're a soldier. You're a comedian!

You're a Renaissance man!" He opened his arms wide. "All of ya!"

Rollie, done buttoning his pants, looked up. "What's an antechamber?"

Myles shrugged. "The exact opposite of a chamber? Who cares? Let's find out. Because once the boys from Lansing show up, the window closes." He turned to Rollie. "You. Writer. You can get new material. I can almost see it." Myles hopped up on a creaky wooden chair and framed a scene with his hands like a director.

"I can see the movie. It's all about our boy Bert Shively and his immortal quest. Call it *Raiders of the Lost Dork.*" His voice dropped low, in full pitch-mode. "He and his idiot friends break into an antechamber called the North Keep to avenge his disgraced family history. Once there, he discovers a dusty old crate that contains … *hell, I don't know what it contains!* What remains of his pride? The busboy's nonexistent sex life? Then the Recoats break in." He looked us over, arms dropping. "This is living, boys!"

I couldn't bite my tongue any longer. "Myles, what's got you so worked up about seeing what's in there?"

He didn't reply immediately. "Excellent question. At the moment, the best I can come up with is, 'Why not?'"

Myles stroked his chin. "Two weeks ago, I was ordering 'battlechips' and lemonade at the Tea Room and sweating my balls off. Jack here was wearing knickers and stacking dirty dishes, too chickenshit to even take my order. Shively? He was ironing decals on T-shirts. A legitimate academic! A scholar! Working the steam iron!" He pointed at Rollie. "And who knows what Shartz was up to? Probably shoveling Little Debbie Swiss Rolls down his throat and writing haikus about his impressive pair of man-boobs."

Not the least offended, Rollie pulled out a notebook

and started scribbling. "Good stuff, Myles. I'm *definitely* stealing that."

Myles vaulted from the chair, sending it clattering behind him.

"Now look at us! We turned a reenactment into a disco brawl that got the governor of Michigan doing the goddamn *Sprinkler!* We got the Pizza King to cough up the funds to crack open the North Keep antechamber, whatever that means. It's all happening! We gotta smoke this summer right to the filter!"

His eyes had a fire I hadn't seen before. It was more than the standard Myles glint. Tonight he was a zealot. "I didn't know what to expect when I came to this island, but it sure wasn't this. It's way, way, *way* better. I want to see it through to the end."

He pivoted on the heel of his boot and pointed at Shively. "I don't know what's going on in our boy's oversized brain, but one look at his hair when he was checking out that map, and you know he's cooking up a theory. *So let's help him!* If we get busted, so what? We plead ignorance, which, in Jack's case, isn't even a lie."

I nodded. *Not untrue.*

"One-Shot stays One-Shot, and we all get a new story for the memoirs we'll never write. Enough *talking* about history." Myles's voice dropped low and quiet. Almost seductive.

"Let's *make* some."

CHAPTER 20

Breaking In

If I ever wrote the memoir Myles mentioned, there would be more than one chapter titled *Breaking In*. While I'm convinced most of these illegal entries were for the greater good, I'm also no choir boy. For a precise definition of "greater good," consult your spiritual advisor.

Results may vary.

Tucked into a hillside, a stone's throw from the North Sally Port, a dirty, decaying wooden door dug into the base of a hill shielding the North Keep's entrance. Discovered the previous fall, the site had yet to be inventoried. *Funding issues,* as Dr. Trumbull said. The door was chipped and faded, its once-white paint peeling to reveal the rotting wood beneath. It sat slightly askew in its frame, the kind of door that begged to be unlocked.

Greater good.

Shively's face was a mask of concentration as he pulled

a folded scrap of paper from his khakis. He'd jotted down the combination to the lock during his morning shift as an intern in the admin office. He unfolded the paper without making a sound. The slightest slip could bring Fort Security down on us, and we all knew it. Granted, I knew Fort Security. His name was Duke Maples, and he was likely passed out in his apartment after closing down the Mustang Lounge with his rowdy pals.

Myles was uncharacteristically quiet, his earlier bravado giving way to a restless, fidgety vibe. I couldn't help but think that he never expected us to follow through after his passionate, rousing, John Belushi-in-*Animal House*-style speech. Here he was, the oldest and, theoretically, most responsible accomplice to a break-in. Or maybe he was just tired. After all, it was 2:00 a.m., and he was getting too old for this shit.

Rollie's eyes scanned the periphery of the dig site for any signs of trouble. He was satisfied to play the part of the lookout, although he wore glasses and it was dark, so I'm not convinced he could've spotted a neon 18-wheeler if it rumbled down Huron Road. We all watched in somber silence. Shively spun through the numbers, and with a final turn, the lock clicked open.

"History's mysteries await, gentlemen," Myles murmured in relief. Shively removed the thick cable coil from the door handle and placed it around his neck like a scarf, and we shuffled in, flashlights scanning the passage ahead of us,

"Guys, you're not gonna believe this," Rollie whispered as we made our way in.

Myles looked over. "Wait. Don't tell me. First wet dream?"

"Close. After our last show, I met Governor Belkin's daughter. Turns out she also goes to Iowa. She came up after and wanted my autograph. *My autograph!* She said she loved our show and thought it was—and I quote—'brilliant.' I told her I wrote every damn word. She freaked. Thinks I'm some sorta creative genius."

"Even though half of it was improv?" I said, giving him a shove.

"Minor details," he laughed.

The idea that pudgy Rollie was getting hit on by political royalty while I couldn't maintain three unbroken seconds of eye contact with Jenna Bonnet made me quietly nauseous.

The governor of Michigan had an official residence on the Island maintained by the State. Rollie continued. "So I've been seeing a little of her for the last few weeks." He paused. The next part rushed out. "Okay, fine. I've been seeing a *lot* of her!"

"Hear that, busboy?" said Myles. "Ladies love creative types. Be like Shartz. Study the arts."

"Hey. You made a rhyme," I said.

"Yeah, but there's something else you guys should know," Rollie added, his voice dropping. "She's got the Secret Service with her almost all the time because her dad's making a run for President."

"Wait." Shively spun around, his light blinding Rollie. "Secret Service? Like with the black suits and earpieces?"

"I don't think they're on to me. But it's possible. I've snuck into the Governor's Mansion the last three nights."

Myles shook his head in wonder. "Shartz brought the heat, the horny little rockstar."

"I didn't bring the heat. *She* brought the heat."

"Shhh," Shively hissed without a flicker of a smile. We ducked through the last low stone entrance into the antechamber. The air was a thick mix of ancient wood and musty stone. Stealthy hook-ups with the Governor's daughter instantly felt like stupid gossip from a less serious era, as the conversation ceased.

We ducked under a low wood beam. The North Keep wasn't exactly King Tut's tomb. The space was smaller than I'd imagined, no bigger than the basement at Wildcliffe. Shelves groaned under the heft of books and manuscripts, and the floor was a patchwork of worn wood and dirt. Antiquated military supplies and weapons lined the stone walls.

Shively directed his flashlight toward a decaying wooden table piled with hand-scrawled journals and scanned the spines. Dust particles twirled in the beam. I moved toward a stack of tri-folded, faded American flags. The fabric was delicate, almost ghostly. Next to the stack, a corroded rack of Charleville muskets leaned in a rack. I reached out, my fingers grazing the rough, cool metal as I breathed heavily.

The dust invaded my lungs—pungent, moldy, and earthy. It was like inhaling a punch, disorienting and almost euphoric. I crouched, feeling like a drug-tripping baseball catcher, and tried to steady my breath. The room spun around me.

My brain rushed with strange thoughts, memories and realizations swirling like the dust in the air. The musty scent seemed to be unlocking parts of my mind.

I saw myself as I truly was: a selfish opportunist. The tour guide job? Just a cheap stepping stone, a way to catch Trina LaFromme's eye and land a dockporter position, haul luggage, earn cash, make friends, and meet girls. My interest in history was as shallow as a spray-on tan. The only historical facts that intrigued me were how George Lucas created the X-Wing fighters in *Star Wars* or the details of Dan Marino's first college pass.

Even the *word* history made me a little sleepy.

But now, crouched in swirling century-old dust, something was changing. I was awestruck. For the first time, I saw Dr. Trumbull—historian, fanatic, scholar—for what he truly was: a guardian. And though I'd shown no genuine interest and had no claim, at that moment, so was I.

"Holy shit, it's Armand Duval!" Shively's voice echoed off the walls. I shook off my surreal buzz, unsteadily got to my feet, and joined him as he traced his finger across a lineup of dusty journals with names scrawled on the spines. His hands shook slightly as he slid one from the shelf. He flipped open the journal with one hand, the other wielding his flashlight.

"Who?" I asked, leaning in close.

"Duval. He was French. My uncle is a professor at Albion College. He mentioned him to me once. He was Luther Shively's aide de camp," he whispered. "They'd become friends during their training, and Duval came with him to Fort Mackinac. After the siege of the Fort in 1812, he was never heard from again." His eyes scanned the pages. "Thing's written in French. It's gotta be his personal journal." With eyes fixed on the intricate penmanship, he moaned lightly. "This is going to take forever to decipher."

As Shively thumbed through the journal, a folded piece of parchment slipped out, fluttering to the floor. I stooped to grab it. The parchment was delicate, its edges frayed. It was a poem written in the same precise hand as the journal, but written in English. Da Vinci-style sketches of island landmarks framed the text, adding an artistic flair. Swirling patterns, arrows, and geometric shapes highlighted sections of the poem.

I focused on a name scrawled below a detailed sketch

of what looked like the Holy Grail. My heart rate spiked again.Even a low forehead like me recognized the name:

Pere Jacques Marquette.

It was a name woven into the fabric of Michigan. You'd find it on colleges, monuments, rivers, museums, and towns. There was a statue of him in the grassy park across from the Island marina. Like Henry Ford, Stevie Wonder, Iggy Pop, and Joe Louis, Father Maquette was a legend, known to every Michigander from Monroe to Whitefish Point, Oscoda to Muskegon.

Even if he *was* French.

I spread the paper on the ground and quickly pulled out my Instamatic, capturing a series of shots. Discovering what we'd soon call the Chalice Paper was enough to make my head spin, but another name suddenly crashed into my thoughts like a freight train:

Trenton Feagler.

The queasy sensation in my gut the day Helen Chandler breezed into the Blue Butterfly with her high-quality business cards and swinging green shoulder bag to discuss the Beaver Island vision was back, and I knew exactly why.

I announced it loudly to the room. "Feagler's is going after Marquette's chalice. That's why he funded the project."

Myles, in the far corner inspecting a rack of cannonballs, looked over. "What's Marquette's chalice?"

Shively's shoulders slumped in disappointment. "The French Jesuit explorer? I thought you taught history, Myles."

"In *Florida*. It's different." Myles walked over. "Listen,

Professor One-Shot, some of us missed the 'Legendary French Jesuits' lecture. Save the lecture and enlighten us heathens."

Shively paused, assessing the sarcasm level, found it acceptable, and launched into his lecture.

"First off, Father Jacques Marquette was no ordinary Jesuit. This guy was an explorer, a man of courage and ideas. Way ahead of his time." Shively's voice quivered as he paced the space, his hands slicing through the air. "Marquette's spiritual journeys took him everywhere. Get this: the man was 500 miles from the Gulf of Mexico and *still* made it to Mackinac Island. By canoe!"

Myles raised an eyebrow. "That *is* impressive. I drove to Mackinac on I-75 from Florida in my Ford pickup—which is pretty roomy—and still, I whined like a baby the whole way. Marquette paddled."

"Wearing one of those black ... whattaya call 'em ... *frocks,*" added Rollie. "Had to be hot."

"But the most amazing part," Shively continued, "was how he connected with the tribes along the way. He mastered six Native American languages. *Six!* They didn't just respect him—they revered him. They saw him as a bridge between worlds." He paused, his voice dropping to a near whisper. "Marquette died in 1675. After his death, the Ottawa and Huron tribes cleaned his bones and placed his remains in a wooden box—*with his chalice.* The chalice disappeared around 1690, somewhere in northern Michigan. From there, history blurs into legend."

Shively scanned the room. "Some people believe the chalice is still on the island."

We all stood over the poem laid out on the floor. "But nobody up here really buys into that," I said. "It's like all those ghost stories about Mackinac. Stop by the Island Bookstore, and you'll see a rack full of them. Marquette's chalice is no different." My words dripped with skepticism, yet I couldn't tear my eyes away from the poem.

Shively nodded. "Maybe. But legends usually start from the truth. What if Marquette's chalice *is* here on the island?"

"I guess it would be like the Holy Grail of ..." I trailed off. "You know ..."

"Holy Grails?" Rollie finished.

"Exactly. It'd be the Holy Grail of Holy Grails. Think about it. Feagler's constructing this historical shopping attraction on Beaver Island. What if he donated money just to get in first and see if there are any treasures to snatch?"

Now it was my turn to pace. "The guy's a businessman, always looking for an edge. He gets access to the North Keep under the guise of charity, but in reality, he's looking for artifacts."

Myles nodded. "If he had the chalice, people would probably flock to see it. His historical shopping mall would be on the map on day one."

Rollie shook his head. "He can't just haul stuff out of here, could he? Trumbull and his State Park Nerd Herd would have a shit-fit."

"How would they know?" Myles said. "If Feagler brings in a team of official-looking eggheads with the right badges, impressive tools, and plenty of cash, who'd question it? Easy to sneak out with some papers. Hell, if we can break in, imagine what *he* could do."

"In 22 minutes or less," I said.

Shively spoke. "Well, if that's the case, then I'm taking this journal." He stuffed Duval's journal into his shoulder bag. "Let's get outta here. Now."

"Never pegged ya for a criminal," said Myles as we

hustled back toward the entrance. "One-Shot, my boy, you remain an enigma."

"Bitterness and humiliation will do that to a man," Shively said as he slid the lock back on the door and clicked it into place.

It wasn't until the following day that the realization hit me like a bolt of lightning: we'd left the poem in the North Keep, spread out on the floor like a welcome mat.

With painstaking care, I eased the back porch door open inch by inch, to avoid the piercing creak of the rusty screen door. It took forever. I slipped inside, silent as a shadow, and moved through the kitchen in the dark, resisting a monstrous urge to finish the leftover tuna casserole I knew was waiting for me in the refrigerator.

Then Beth's voice. "Gramps? That you?"

Gramps? I thought.

Beth flicked on the kitchen light. Mom stood behind her in a robe, displaying her 'you got some explaining to do' arch of the eyebrow—trademark pending. Beth smirked with glee, always curious to hear what new jive I might spin.

"Jack, it's 3:00 a.m.," she said, her voice laced with a sigh that told me she knew damn well the old 'home by ten 'o'clock' era was long over. I was on the edge of seventeen now, and Mackinac Island had a new set of Teenage Master Rules. At the top of the list was *Don't do stupid shit, and we won't ask questions.*

Her eyes roamed my dusty black T-shirt and jeans. "Good God, Jack. You're filthy. What have you been up to?"

I was half-tempted to hit her with the truth. A little shock value for old time's sake. "Well, Mom, I just broke into a State Park antechamber called the North Keep and pilfered some papers that might lead to the century's most important historical discovery. See, Mom, Feagler isn't just poaching dress shops. He's on a quest for the Holy Grail of Holy Grails."

... Nah.

The chalice theory was too insane to drop at this hour, and I was dead tired. "I got roped into helping Dr. Trumbull at the dig site, lost track of time. Then I fell asleep." Over the years, I'd discovered that "then I fell asleep" was an insanely effective closer when lying to my parents. Add an *oopsie* shrug and a sheepish Jack Grin, and it was foolproof. There was just no way to poke holes in it.

"What's going on?" I asked. "Why are two you up so late?"

"It's your grandfather. He never came home."

Alarm bells clanged in my head for reasons unclear, but I played it cool. "Since when do we ask him to punch in?"

"He took his shaving kit," Beth added, biting her lower lip. "We think he left the island."

"I'm about to call your father," Mom said. "Gramps always checks in. What worries me is he's been moody lately."

I shook my head. "Please don't call Dad. He's probably just off being ... Gramps." Mom offered an uncertain nod, and the three of us reached an unspoken consensus: Let the night hold its breath. We'd exhale at dawn.

Under the covers, I mulled over the night's mission, the musty aroma of rotting journals and rusting musket steel still fresh. But something caught the periphery of my eye. A soft streak of light from the barn cascaded across my bedroom ceiling. Odd. It shouldn't be there. I padded across the floor and looked out my window. The barn door was closed, but a sliver of light cut across the overgrown lawn, where undoubtedly, in some previous century, horses had grazed.

I threw on my jeans, descended the stairs, and crossed the dew-drenched grass to the barn, the light from inside pulling me in like a tractor beam. I cracked open the door and peered in. Gramp's gold Sears Fleetwood, the bike I'd had serviced just two weeks ago at his request, was gone.

My grandfather, the blazing, growling alpha star of any front porch gathering, had been retreating into shadows for the last few weeks. His regular pool hall stool above Horn's Bar was left empty. His rowdy drinking buddies stopped by Wildcliffe, asking for him—and more than a few times, I'd found him asleep in his room, curtains drawn. In those moments, Gramps looked like a snoring cadaver. How old was he then? Just south of sixty-eight?

Too young to look that old.

But I'd turn away from his sleeping form and quietly shut the door. I had other things to do. His withdrawal from us was a passing cloud, a minor glitch in a busy summer. But now, no bike. No toothbrush. And Mom was right, it wasn't like him. He may have run on his own clock, but he always told us where he could be found. Big Jack had always joked it was in case his bookie called; but we all knew it was deeper than that. He cared. We were his responsibility, as he was ours. That was what families did. They kept track of each other.

And here I was, wasting my summer foraging for relics

like some ghoulish grave robber while the most precious relic in my life, a man who slept two doors down the hall, was fading in front of me.

NO!

He was on an adventure.

Right?

It was just a summer moment. That time Gramps vanished. McGuinns knew all about stories. Hell, someone could write novels about our summer moments. But guilt chewed on my toes like mice.

I crawled back into bed. In my dreams, Gramps pedaled his bike straight off the Mackinac Bridge. A bungee cord shackled him to the bike on one leg and the chalice on the other.

He plummeted into Lake Huron, the icy water shocking my dream-self awake. Now I was with him. We sank fast, the pressure building in my ears. The water darkened as we descended, a bone-chilling cold. Gramps' eyes met mine, wide with panic. I'd never seen him panic.

We drifted down, down, down to the cloudy, freezing bottom of Lake Huron. The murky depths swallowed us, stealing the air from my lungs. Just as the final bubbles escaped my lips, I jolted awake, gasping and tangled in sweat-soaked sheets.

Dockporters yelled out hotel names, voices competing with shrill seagulls overhead, beady eyes patrolling the Arnold Line dock for stray popcorn or fumbled hotdogs. Everyone was looking for something. Tourists meandered in a vacation daze, maps in hand, oblivious to the chaos around them.

Amid that chaos, I stood with Smitty, preparing for a

delivery of plywood to a cottage on the West Bluff. He leaned against a luggage cart, practicing a birdcall he'd been teaching himself.

He said it was a European Starling.

This summer, he'd traded his job wiping down tables at Louie's Horse and Buggy Drive-Inn for a job as a dray driver. Stocky and strong, Smitty fit right in with the rugged freight dray drivers. Like me, he was sixteen, but the green Teamsters' coveralls and dirty, calloused hands made him look older. My childhood friend was becoming a regular working stiff.

I waited.

After a few more failed attempts at the European Starling whistle, Smitty told me his deep, philosophical theory on Gramps's missing-in-action status. "The old guy's gettin' some," he declared.

I looked away. The image was not pleasant, but it beat the one of him riding his bike off the Mackinac Bridge to an icy death.

"Ya think?"

"Of course!" Smitty nodded, playing the working-man-sage. "The guy knows everyone on the island, so he can't get away with any dirty deeds here. Trust me. He'll stumble off this very boat with a big grin and an overnight bag like nothing happened. I'd bet the house on it."

The *Straits of Mackinac II* ferry thudded against the dock's pilings. The impact, cushioned by oversized tractor tires, sent a minor jolt through the crowd waiting on the dock. With a metallic roar, the ramp slid down.

I watched as the first few tourists tentatively navigated their way across the ramp. Gramps stepped onto the dock with an overnight bag slung over his shoulder and proudly wheeled his Fleetwood, which had a long cardboard box precariously balanced between the handlebars and the seat, held in place by a bungee cord.

Smitty turned to me, supremely self-satisfied. "Toldja."

I gave him a look of genuine admiration. "You're a psychic! How did you know he'd be on this boat?"

"Oh, that? He told me."

"What? When?"

"Yeah, I saw him leave yesterday," he chuckled. "He said he'd be back on the three o'clock from St. Iggie." I punched him hard on the arm as he grinned sheepishly. "Oh. Sorry. Did I not mention that part of the story?"

"You're a genuine asswipe, pal."

"And that's *exactly* why you love me."

Gramps looked sharp in a crisp sports coat, and his Michigan baseball hat tilted on his head as he rolled his bike up and stopped.

"Hello, boys! Didn't expect a welcome committee." Smitty shook Gramps' hand, his usual mischievous grin melting into a warm, genuine smile. Smitty loved my grandfather, and Gramps loved him back. Maybe it was because Gramps knew how rough Smitty had it on the island when winter rolled in, the tourists vanished, and he was left with a tiny house, a father who drank too much, and a mother who always seemed to want a different life. Smitty had it tough, but he never let it show. He hid his struggles behind non-stop movement, next-level fart jokes, and a beautiful naivety that I envied. Gramps saw it all, admired his spirit, and made sure Smitty always had a second family when he needed one.

"Wondering what the old man's been up to?" Gramps asked us with a twinkle.

I nodded, noticing a red smudge on his collar. "I've got a pretty good idea."

He twisted his neck and looked down. "Oh lord. I

better get that cleaned up. The last thing we need around Wildcliffe is a minor scandal." He paused, putting a finger to his lips, pretending to reconsider. "Scratch that. *I ain't cleanin' shit!*"

Smitty and Gramps high-fived, both grinning.

"You got the ladies on the homefront sending out a search party, Gramps. You should've let us know you were leaving the island." I spoke cautiously, aware I was trekking into dangerous territory. Gramps was a man, not a child.

He shook his head. "How many times have I told you about getting shot down in the Philippines? Just a guesstimate."

I rolled my eyes, a smile creeping in despite myself. "At least fifty. Maybe more."

He nudged and winked at Smitty as he asked, "And what's the grand finale of that epic tale of survival?"

"Your fighter plane was shot down. You ejected, swam to a deserted island, nearly drowned, survived with a busted arm, and lived off nothing but bark and seaweed for a week until you were rescued by a recon plane," I dutifully recited.

"Hear that, Smitty? Bark and seaweed! In more pain than you'll ever know!" He looked at us with mock indignation and held up his left arm. "My bone was visible! Stuck right out like a busted umbrella. It still hurts like a sonofabitch when it rains. You think after that, I can't survive a rowdy night in St. Ignace?"

He turned to Smitty. "This kid worries too much. Did I raise a neurotic?" Gramps asked, shaking his head.

Smitty shrugged, flashing a sly grin. "Not sure what that word means, sir. But I will say that lately, Jack here's turning into a real …" He glanced around and leaned in "… a real pussy."

Only Smitty could say something like that to Gramps and get away with it. It was one of his many gifts.

Gramps howled, his laughter echoing off the nearby buildings. He jerked his thumb toward the freight shack. "Follow me, Jacky. Got something to show you."

I trailed him as he wheeled his bike under the shelter, carefully leaning it against the wall of the freight shack and setting his overnight bag on an empty cart. He spun around, pointing to the awkwardly-shaped box. "Open it up."

I lifted the flap of the box. Inside, nestled in packing paper, was a weird, vintage-looking device with a long metal handle, a black grip, and an oval-shaped base adorned with faded blue markings. Wires coiled around the shaft, leading up to a blue control box with knobs and dials.

"What is it?"

"It's a goddamn metal detector!" He cackled again as if he'd heard the most hysterical joke since the Cold War,

I stared at him blankly as I slid it out of the box.

"You know! For hunting down those coins in the back-yard. Or whatever. Picked it up at a thrift store."

I hadn't searched for change in the backyard in about six years, but I was strangely moved that he remembered that phase in my life. Gramps stood back and marveled at the device. "By the way, I get a fifteen percent finder's fee on whatever you dig up with this little beauty."

"Fifteen percent?"

"You know damn well the old man wets his beak on every deal. Who knows? You might just find a chunk of gold in the backyard, and we can finally knock down the barn and build a helicopter landing strip!"

I rotated the dial to the on position, and the machine screeched, then pulsed a series of beeps and odd squawks, sounding like a constipated seagull. Tourists turned their heads, eyebrows raised in curiosity. I had a hard time imagining ever switching the antiquated banshee on again in public, but I felt hot emotion swelling just behind my eyes. I blinked it back.

"She's got her quirks but gets the job done," Gramps said. "Took her for a spin in St. Iggie last night. I picked up some souvenir charm bracelets from the Hope Chest on Ferry Lane. The jangly ones with *St. Ignace* etched in fancy letters? I had 'em buried in the park by the marina and let her rip. The damn thing really works!"

"And your date? Was she any help?" I said, thumbing his lipstick-smudged collar.

Gramps pushed away my hand. "*Date?* Who said anything about a date?" A sly grin crept across his face. "Alright, fine. I had a lady friend with me. And yes, she was a big help. She hid the bracelets in the ground. Buried 'em so I wouldn't know where to look. Afterward, I gave her one of the bracelets as a thank you."

"Who's the lucky lady?"

He gave me a conspiratorial look and mimed zipping his lips, locking them, and tossing the invisible key into Lake Huron. "Go find your nickels and mind your own damn business," he said, redirecting the talk with a wave of his hand.

I propped the metal detector against the wall and, without thinking, wrapped my arms around Gramps in a fierce hug. The move surprised even me. He pulled me in tight, his embrace solid and familiar as a Fort wall. He patted my back, his calloused hand rough against my Wild Style T-shirt.

"Thanks, Jacky," he murmured, his voice gruff.

I stepped back, not bothering to hide the tears in my eyes. His were misty too, glinting like Lake Huron.

"Thanks for what?" I asked, my voice catching.

Gramps' eyes swept the scene—the gold Fleetwood, the battered metal detector, the vast expanse of the lake, the rumbling ferry, the endless Michigan sky. Then his eyes, sharp as ever, met mine.

"For noticing I was gone."

CHAPTER 22

The Chalice Paper

I'd read the poem about six times since we'd found it, carefully analyzing the rhyme scheme and symbolism. I was no scholar, but I'd searched for hidden meanings or historical references. Each time, I reached the same conclusion. It kinda sucked.

The Dying Whisper
By Armand Duval

In faint whispers of a wailing wind,
Lies a secret, treasure unconfined.
On Mackinac, where beauty thrives,
Beneath its soil, a chalice hides.

In the year of grace, a year of strife,
An epic story breathes to life.
Where battle's roar on Mackinac did cease,
A soldier whispers prayers for peace.

In retreat, his comrades gone with tide,

He lies bloodied, side by side
With death's cold grasp and heaven's door ajar,
Beneath the silent evening star.

"Blessing," his faint plea fills the air,
For sacred rites, he does declare.
The British, ruling o'er the isle's domain,
Seek out a priest to ease his pain.

With haste and heart, the priest does come,
No chalice in his hand, struck dumb.
A soldier swift, from fort's old keep,
Brings forth a cup from Marquette's sleep.

In freedom's grasp, the soldier takes his stand,
And buries deep the chalice in the land.
A symbol pure of sacrifice and love,
Beneath the watchful skies above.

And when the moonlight bathes the land,
Stroll the streets, a lantern in hand,
In shadows deep, the past will stir,
The chalice calls, in night's soft blur.

Find the place the Chippewa know,
The Crooked Trail where spirits show,
With heart and will, the truth unveil,
Good fortune, seeker, on your trail.

Tonight, Wildcliffe's barn buzzed like it hadn't in years. Once again, I'd brought my larceny home like a stray rabbit. It wasn't the first time. It wouldn't be the last.

The wind outside was a wavering moan that wound around the eaves and slipped through the cracks. All four of us leaned over a foldable poker table from the '60s; its green felt, rotted and devoured by moths, revealed a crumbling particle board in the shape of Daffy Duck. The Chalice Paper, the handwritten poem by Armand Duval, was spread under the lightly swinging light.

Well, not exactly. They were *photographs* of the original Chalice Paper. Because in true Jack McGuinn fashion, I'd forgotten to grab the genuine article when I had the chance. Chalk it up to the adrenaline rush of breaking into the North Keep or maybe the trippy history dust in my lungs, which had caused a sort of residual head rush.

Luckily, I'd had the presence of mind to snap a few pictures. I'd taken the film to Benjamin's Photo Shop, where the clerk had squinted at me suspiciously before enlarging the shots. Now we had crisp, if slightly grainy, images to pore over.

We huddled around the photos like we were decoding the Dead Sea Scrolls. We all agreed there was a connection between the chalice drawing, Jacques Marquette, and the poem's verses, but what the connection was remained frustratingly out of our reach.

Shively broke away and began pacing the barn, his hair at its highest level in weeks. Class was in session.

"What I'm gathering from this is that it's some sort of true story. Maybe this guy, Armand Duval, was a poet. Why else would he have kept it tucked into his journal?"

"Why is the poem in English and the journal in French?" I asked.

"No idea," said Shively, twitching a little. His brain was smoking like a piston.

"Maybe it was for a different audience," said Rollie. "Like … Americans." He practiced a slow-motion tennis serve with an ancient wood racket, mimicking the cheers of a roaring Wimbledon crowd, enraptured with his incredible tennis skills but still half-listening.

"Speaking of the journal," Myles interjected. "Learned anything yet?"

Shively shook his head. "It's in French, and the handwriting is tiny. It's a slog. But let's focus on the poem."

"Yes sir, Private Shively," Myles saluted. "The floor is yours."

"So, here's my theory so far. Bored with soldiering, Armand Duval, Luther's aide-de-camp, decides to try his hand at writing one of those epic poems. You know the ones. They were all the rage in the nineteenth century. Like *Hiawatha* or *Gilgamesh*." He looked around at our blank stares. "You do know the ones, right?"

None of us knew the ones.

"Jack, you're an island kid. You should know something about this stuff. Longfellow worked closely with Schoolcraft, who lived at the Indian Dormitory as a consultant on *Hiawatha*. Does any of this ring a bell?"

No bells rang.

"I'm sorry, Shively, but I have no idea who those people are."

"Me either," Rollie chimed in, as he finally won match point in the Wimbledon Finals of his dreams and dropped to his beefy knees in joy as the crowd went wild.

"What the hell is *Hiawatha?*" Myles asked, leaning against the wall and popping open his second beer of the night with a crisp *tsss*.

"And *Gilga* … what was it?" I asked. "Wait! Isn't that the monster Godzilla fights in one of those … you know … *Godzilla* movies?"

"Nah, that's Gamera," Rollie called over.

"Oh, right," I said. "Gamera."

It got quiet again. Shively placed both hands on his face, a pose I'd recognize years later from the movie poster for *Home Alone*. Then, he slowly lowered them.

"It's *Gilgamesh*. And *Hiawatha* is a famous poem written by Longfellow. These are the classics. You guys never read ... how ..." He trailed off, then pointed at Myles accusingly.

"You said you were a teacher!"

Myles shook his head. *"In Florida,* buddy. I already told you. We taught *Florida* shit. Ponce de León. Fountain of Youth. And speaking of the Fountain of Youth ..." He held up his beer. "I seem to have located it!"

Rollie and I laughed. It was good old fashioned guy stuff, but Shively wasn't having any of it.

"Read the first part of the poem, Rollie," Shively said, shaking his head in disgust.

Rollie picked up the enlarged photo of the poem and began reading. For some reason, he read in a strange upper-crust English accent that made him sound completely idiotic.

> *"In faint whispers of a wailing wind,*
> *Lies a secret, treasure unconfined.*
> *On Mackinac, where beauty thrives,*
> *Beneath its soil, a chalice hides.*

"We appreciate the commitment, but feel free to read like a human, Rollie," said Myles. "This isn't Shakespeare in the Park."

Rollie lowered the photo. "My accent brings the poem to life. It makes it more interesting."

Myles pondered this and then nodded. "You've convinced me, Sir Shartz-alot. Plus without that stupid accent, the poem is just *terrible*. Read on."

"Hold on," Shively interrupted. "Here's what I've

pieced together so far. It's about a fictional battle on the Island between British and American forces. In the poem, the Americans are outnumbered and outmaneuvered by the British and forced to retreat. They get shot up and then scramble back to their boats. But one soldier is left behind, mortally wounded." He looked at Rollie. "Continue."

Rollie continued in his bizarre Shakespearian voice.

"In retreat, his comrades gone with tide,
He lies bloodied, side by side
With death's cold grasp and heaven's door ajar,
Beneath the silent evening star."

Shively, caught up in the tale, added, "Imagine him alone, the battle noise fading away. Musket smoke drifts across the field. He calls out for viaticum."

"What's that?" I asked.

"It's like last rights combined with communion. This poor guy thinks he's about to die. The British find him lying on the battlefield, bleeding out, and they call a priest to give him his final blessing."

"How civilized," said Myles.

Rollie read on.

"With haste and heart, the priest does come,
No chalice in his hand, struck dumb.
A soldier swift, from the fort's old keep,
Brings forth a cup from Marquette's sleep."

"Okay, stop!" Shively raised a hand. "So what I think this means is that a British soldier runs to the fort, rummages through the storage room, and grabs the first suitable cup he sees that might work for a communion." Shively's hands mimicked the soldier's hurried search. "He has no idea he's holding a piece of history: *Marquette's chalice.* Maybe it happened to be stored there. Besides, it doesn't matter. It's just a story. Back to the hero. He survives. Somehow he gets the chalice back from the Fort and buries it, symbolizing his own rebirth."

Myles pointed straight up. "Maybe a thank you note to the Big Guy upstairs."

"Buries it where?" I asked.

Shively nodded to Rollie as if he had been expecting the question all along. Rollie, back in character, read on.

> *"On the place the Chippewa know*
> *The Crooked Trail where spirits show*
> *With heart and will, the truth unveil*
> *Good fortune, seeker, on your trail."*

"Walks a crooked path," I broke in. "That's what *Wawashkamo* means. So this soldier in the poem buried Marquette's chalice, maybe on the exact spot where he almost cashed in his chips?"

Shively nodded, a look of pure PhD in colonial studies joy emerging like a sunrise. "Now you morons are getting it."

"That's where I'd bury it," Rollie shrugged. We all turned to look at him. "If I almost died in battle, received communion, survived, and then decided to track down the chalice and bury it as a thank you to God for saving me … that's where I'd bury it."

Rollie nodded with certainty and then headed off to find another toy.

Myles was no longer lounging. He leaned forward, eyes fixed on Shively. "So we think this poem is some sort of coded … I don't know… *map* … that points to the location of Marquette's chalice?"

"I think it's a distinct possibility."

The wind kicked up outside, causing a loose board to pound against the door.

"Do you think Feagler's team could figure this out?" Myles asked.

Shively nodded. "Of course."

"Why?" Rollie asked.

"First of all, we left the original poem in the North Keep, so they have the same information we have. And secondly, I think *we* figured it out, and let's face it, aside from me, we're not all that smart." He paused, looking around the room. Sensing no resistance, he continued, "I mean, Rollie? You're good for making a poo joke out of a musket firing demonstration. That's … something. Myles, you're charming but seem to be the world's most average teacher. And Jack here is still in high school and, from what I gather, isn't exactly headed for the honor roll." He glanced at me. "No offense, Jack."

I shrugged. "All good."

The barn was silent. Finally, Myles sighed. "You've raised at least three excellent points," he said, finishing off his beer. He followed with a reverberating sonic belch. He tossed his empty beer can, and we all watched it skitter across the floorboards with fascination. The can clattered to a stop next to a tattered golf bag, its fabric riddled with holes. A few ancient clubs stuck out at odd angles, along with a rusted weed whacker and the broken remnants of a fly-fishing rod.

Myles stared at the bag. The room quieted, all eyes on him, waiting for him to speak.

"You guys golf?"

CHAPTER 23

Going Golfing

I never liked golf. Still don't. My aversion to it was passed down from Gramps to Big Jack to me. Gramps was a board member of the Wawashkamo Golf Club, yet gleefully mocked golfers—a fraternity all his best friends belonged to—as "phony-baloneys." In hindsight, it was all a clever play to make him appear even more eccentric—a Michigan businessman who mocked golf.

Mocked golf! Sacrilege! Then they'd buy a car from him, which would, over the course of a decade, become ten cars. But all it meant for me was a genetic aversion to the one activity that might have helped my career.

"The Wawa Dig," as Myles deemed it, was on. Wawa was hosting a fundraiser for the Allies of Mackinac, so we'd all gotten the day off. Myles, Shively, and Rollie could easily pass for bona fide golfers, dressed to the nines in long, colorful pants, crisp short-sleeve polos, and golf shoes that gleamed in the morning sun. Myles had taken it up a notch: a snug leather glove adorned his left hand, and a clean Callaway brand visor was pulled low, shading his eyes but not entirely disguising his drooping blonde mustache.

The morning breeze had an unusual off-season bite that cut through my tucked-in, red plaid flannel, the only clean shirt I could find. I already felt spastic and twitchy, like the caffeine addict I'd eventually become, and we hadn't even teed off.

I'd secretly hefted the rotting golf bag out of the barn that morning, the odd weight of the vintage metal detector pressing against the small of my back, a guilty secret that clanked and rattled with each step.

"This is nuts," I muttered, but I felt the familiar rush of excitement coursing through me. *The thrill of the hunt,* as Gramps would say, had sunk its hooks in deep.

Myles was the first to tee off. He eyed the fairway and swung like an unrestrained beast. *Crack!* The ball sailed, a low drive that vanished until I saw it reemerge and bounce twice to continue its perfect little journey to the green.

"Jack, you're up," Myles called out. I could feel the eyes of the other golfers on us, curiosity piqued by our collective nervous energy, no doubt caused by the metal detector and four shovels concealed in our golf bags.

As I set up for my drive, I couldn't help but ponder the absurdity of our plan. Upon closer examination of the Chalice Paper, we noticed a sketch in the margins depicting a crack with double arrows pointing northeast. We decided it was the Crack-in-the-Island, a natural split in the limestone near the golf course that legend said was created when an angry Gitchi Manitou stamped his foot hard when the white man showed up. It was an understandable reaction. Once thought bottomless, it was now just a shallow rut. The arrows on the sketch aligned with at least six fairways on the Wawa golf course.

It was a long shot, a hunch pulled from the deepest recesses of our own cracks. But it was all we had.

The plan? Based on the sketch, hit each coordinate on the course, sweep the area with a metal detector, and dig fast at the first beep.

I took a deep breath and swung away, an embarrassing hook that had me cursing under my breath. "Great start, McGuinn," I muttered, staring after my wayward ball and swearing like a golfer who could've done better if he'd *just* held the club right. This was a load of crap. No grip, stance, or swing would ever make me better. My lack of golfing skill was carved in granite on the day of my conception.

"Captain Hook!" called Myles. Rollie started in on the requisite *Caddyshack* movie lines that all men born between 1960 and 1972 are required by law to memorize.

"Be the ball, Jack!" he quoted. The other three broke up. It was going to be a brutal afternoon. Rollie and Shively nailed perfectly adequate drives, and we were on our way to the first dig site. Myles popped a Stroh's beer when we were far from prying eyes. I had no idea where it came from. It was like some sort of magic trick.

"A little early for beer, don't you think?" I asked.

Myles squinted into the blue, cloudless morning sky and pointed. "What's that big bright thing up there?"

I followed his gaze. "The sun?"

"That's what I thought. Then no, sport, it's not too early." He took another deep pull on the beer and slapped me on the back. "Relax, busboy. We're not here for golf, remember? In fact, your pathetic hook shot took us right where we needed to be. Congrats. You're so bad, you're good."

As we reached the spot where my wayward swing had sent the ball, Shively pulled out a small notepad from his front pocket. His eyes flicked nervously behind us, where the steady advance of another foursome loomed.

"This is it. Fire it up."

I yanked the metal detector from my golf bag. Rusted clubs spilled out, along with a rotted Nerf ball and a bag of decade-old hotdog buns. Shively rechecked his notes and pointed at a large pine tree.

"Sweep ..." He looked back down, then up, down, up, down, up.

"*... there.*"

"Here goes nothing," I said, flipping the switch. The detector hummed to life, and the bizarre squawking sound returned, even more out of place against the sounds of seagulls and a gentle Island breeze rustling the pines.

"Do it fast, Jack," said Myles. "That contraption could wake the dead." I dutifully began sweeping the area.

For Marquette's chalice.

As if reading my mind, Rollie spoke up as he watched me lug the detector to a different patch of grass. "This is insane."

"Indeed," said Myles with bemused fascination, his club resting casually on his shoulder.

Shively, clearly in no mood for reflection, pointed to another grassy mound. "Now scan there."

I dutifully did as I was told. As I thought about the poem, the device emitted high-pitched, bird-like chirping noises. Was all this effort the result of a figment of Armand Duval's fevered French imagination? Admittedly, digging holes in a golf course was sheer madness, but deep down, I knew Shively was probably right: Feagler could be doing the same thing soon enough.

Find the place the Chippewa know,
The Crooked Trail, where spirits show

The metal detector squeaked.

"I got something!" I hissed.

We yanked the shovels from our golf bags and dug where we'd heard the signal like dogs after a bone. Myles, surprisingly spry for a guy who'd already downed a beer, attacked like a greedy prospector. Rollie was all grins while Shively scanned the horizon for the incoming foursome.

Clank. Myles's shovel hit something metallic. We froze, and then dove in with our hands, scooping away the wet, brown dirt.

"One precious chalice, comin' up!" said Rollie, pulling a square, dirt-clodded mass of something into the sunlight. We looked closer, pulling off chunks of mud.

"Antique beer!" said Myles.

It was a rusty six-pack of Meister Brau, still held together by its original six-pack ring. Myles shook his head, took it from Rollie, and plucked one from the ring.

"I'm not sure they make this stuff anymore," he said, popping the pull tab with a hiss. He took a long swig, then his face twisted in disgust. A violent cough followed, and beer erupted like a geyser from his mouth and nostrils. It was hard to tell if he was spitting or puking, but it seemed like a little of both.

"Damn! That's *putrid!* It tastes like it's been marinated in sheep piss." He dropped the five-pack back into its dirty grave, throwing the sixth offending can in after it. He stumbled to his feet, still coughing, and surveyed the course behind us with watering eyes. He took a few loud breaths, trying to recover.

Then, just like that, he was fine.

He clapped his hands and eyed the distant terrain.

"Time to beat feet, ladies. The foursome behind us looks like trouble." We all scrambled up, stuffing the shovels and metal detector back into our bags, and jogged toward the teeing ground of the second hole.

We barely had time to process how genuinely disgusting Myles's display was. For a moment, I wondered why a grown man would chug decades-old beer when he had perfectly good Stroh's on ice in his golf bag.

From the moment we met Myles, he had us wrapped around his pinky. He didn't need to douse his stomach with rotten beer to cement his legend status.

I let the thought go.

By the 7th hole, our treasure hunt felt increasingly futile. We scoured the rough and wooded areas flanking the fairways, our metal detector's beeps leading us through thickets and over uneven ground. But all we found was junk: an old *Six Million Dollar Man* lunch box, a rusted set of steak knives, a harmonica, seven brass buttons, a set of false teeth, and a bedpan. The odd assortment wasn't entirely surprising; the golf course had been the site of battles, parties, and impromptu dumping grounds for two centuries, leaving a bizarre archaeological record just beneath the grass.

With an impressive poker face, Shively convinced Rollie that the bedpan was a rare Victorian-era water pitcher. Rollie used it the rest of the summer, proudly mixing margaritas for guests, until his cousin, up for a wild weekend, inquired why he was being served cocktails from an old piss-can. After that, Rollie's relic went straight to the dump.

By the 8th hole, a hazy veil had descended, a blend of

the sun's relentless blaze and the seemingly endless supply of beers that Myles magically conjured from his bag like a golfing David Copperfield.

That afternoon, he gave me the first, second, and third beers of my life. By the time we reached the 9th hole, my interest in golf—and treasure hunting—had significantly diminished. Mainly, I wanted to share slurry stories about meeting Christopher Reeve and Jane Seymour in 1979 and regale the boys with how I'd broken into the wardrobe department of *Somewhere in Time* to save my parents' marriage. It was a fairly complicated tale, and I had to restart it at least four times. The more beer I drank, the less sense it made, a scenario that would continue for the rest of my adult life.

It got worse when I tried to weave in an element of an unsolved murder on the island and how I tried to "break" the case. But it spilled out like gibberish. And as the guys ramped up their merciless mocking, my tongue reacted by tying itself in slip knots. Eventually, I gave up on story-telling and moved on to more important things, namely walking.

The metal detector felt like an anchor, bulky and burdensome. I was hot and exhausted, and my hands were numb and filthy from digging.

As our enthusiasm for the quest waned, we came to an unspoken conclusion: The Wawa Dig was a bust. All we had managed was to turn the edges of the storied Wawashkamo Golf Course into a lunar landscape. Our efforts yielded nothing more than a lousy yard sale worth of junk. It was time to accept defeat and head back to the clubhouse.

We plopped our golf bags onto the rack with a collective sigh. Shively immediately set off to re-examine Duval's poem, muttering and grumbling under his breath, flipping through his notes to determine where exactly we went wrong. Rollie slipped away with a shit-eating grin, whispering about a planned clandestine hook-up with the governor's daughter at the Governor's Mansion and how he planned to give the Secret Service goons the slip.

That left Myles and me at the Wawashkamo bar.

CHAPTER 24

Drinks at the Wawa

"Come on, just one more," I pleaded with Myles as he signaled to the bartender. Apparently, I liked the taste of beer.

Myles shook his head. "Nope. I've got enough on my conscience, busboy. Just enjoy the rest of the ride." He shot me a sideways look. "And if you ever tell anyone about this little afternoon buzz, I'll deny it. Got it?"

I nodded solemnly.

Besides, it wasn't like I was drunk. Drunk people staggered and giggled. Yelled, barfed, and peed. I was pleasantly altered but saw no reason to debate semantics. Myles was probably right. I was known on the island. The sixteen-year-old son of Big Jack and Ana McGuinn, grandson of Jack the First and ceremonial mayor, couldn't be seen guzzling brewskis at the Wawa bar with some mysterious scoundrel with a handlebar mustache and a visor.

The bow-tie-wearing bartender, a lanky hillbilly-hippie with long, sandy-blonde hair and a name tag that read *Vance: Louisville, Kentucky*, glided over. Myles ordered a draft beer for himself and a tall iced water for me. We sat for a while, not saying much until Myles spoke. "I guess we should look on the bright side."

"What's that?"

"Your metal detector works."

I nodded. "It's strange. My grandfather gave me that thing out of the blue. He'd been missing for the night. We were worried about him. And then he gets off the ferry with a metal detector from some second-hand shop in St. Ignace." My voice rose. "Think about that! He comes back with a *metal* detector right when we're looking for–"

Myles raised a finger to his lips, cutting me off. I leaned in close, lowering my voice to a whisper, even though we were the only two at the bar.

"Right when we're searching for ..." I looked around the empty room.

"*Metal?*" he finished.

"Yeah! *Metal.*"

"Old men will shock you. Same with old women. They always know what we need."

"This whole thing is nuts, Myles. What were we doing on a golf course digging for a chalice? I mean ... right?"

"Nah. It's good, kid. The rest of the world sits around waiting for the clouds to part and a beam of light to shine down from heaven. But in my experience, it doesn't work that way. If you want treasure, you gotta dig some holes."

The bartender poured a beer from a bottle into a frosted mug and slid it to Myles. It looked like a work of art, and I watched as he took a deep pull from the sparkling glass of amber.

"Myles."

"Yeah?"

"What's your deal when you're not on this island?"

"What do you mean? I told you guys." He looked

straight ahead and stroked his mustache, removing a few stray suds. "I taught history. In Boca Raton. Remember?"

"Right. *Taught*. But what about the rest of the time? Like, what's your real job?"

It took a while, but he finally answered me. "Lately, I'm in real estate. Sarasota, Florida."

"Ah. In real estate," I repeated, nodding sagely as if I were acknowledging the vast opportunities in this exciting field. In reality, I was just trying to seem more adult. I had no real idea what "in real estate" even meant. Was he selling condos? Building malls? Managing skyscrapers?

"So why Mackinac Island?"

"The market softened. So I took the summer off. I heard this place was worth a look from a sailor pal in Florida. He worked here in the 70's hauling luggage on his bike."

I perked up. "They're called dockporters! And that's my plan—to be a dockporter. I only took the guide job to develop my "people skills," whatever that means. I was told I was lacking in that department by a few different people."

Myles snorted out a laugh. "Yeah. I'm pretty sure I was one of 'em." He looked at me. "And now check you out. Fort guide slash golfer slash treasure hunter."

I nodded along. I liked all those slashes. They made me sound fascinating.

"Those? Those are *people skills*." He raised his glass of beer, and I clinked him back with my water. Myles took another swig from his mug and set it down on the wood bar.

"What's up with those pictures? I saw your photo album lying around in the shack."

My pulse kicked up a notch. The idea of Myles poking

around in my secret little world was mortifying, although I had no idea why.

"They're not half bad," he said.

"Nah. It's nothing." An attempt at a manly shrug. "Just burning film."

He turned to me. "You're not hearing me. They're not half bad."

"Yeah, but I just—"

He raised a hand and shut me up. "I get it. You just want to be a normal skirt-chasing chimp, like all the other knuckleheads. If they think you have talent, they might think you're some sorta weirdo. Maybe even a little fruity. Am I right?"

Nailed it.

"I don't have talent, Myles. I told you, it's just something like—"

"—Listen!" Myles cut me off, his eyes suddenly intense. "One day, you'll hit a wall you can't just cruise around on your one-speed. When you've got *nothing* left. And in that moment, you'll wish you'd poured your heart into something you're good at."

He leaned in, his voice dropping. "Get good. The world's full of knuckleheads. Trust me, they're breeding like rabbits. What we need are people who actually give a damn about what they do."

The conversation was getting a bit too grown-up for me, especially with my brain floating on the clouds of my first beer buzz. The setting sun cast a warm glow that danced across the wooden surfaces and spilled over the counter. Across the clubhouse, golfers were rolling in, their voices mingling with Sinatra's crooning on the bar stereo. I liked it.

But I was certain I didn't want to talk about photography anymore.

"So, what about your folks?" I was momentarily confused. Myles had read my mind and shifted the conversation.

"My dad owns an Oldsmobile dealership downstate, and my mom is a dress designer."

"Ah. The evil spawn of a hustler and an artist. Could bode well for your future."

"Dad's not a hustler. My mom likes to joke he's the only honest car dealer in the Metro Detroit area."

"Sorry to hear that," he said. I couldn't tell if he meant it as a joke. "Honesty isn't always the best policy." He paused, and then added: "In certain trades."

"Where did you go to college again?" I have no idea why I asked him that.

For an instant, his face clouded over, and he blinked twice. Then he continued. "Flagler College. St. Augustine. Majored in history. But listen, Florida is a chapter best left closed," he said, sliding his mug back and forth between his open hands like it was a hockey puck on ice.

"Why?" I asked.

"Let's just say I dug a few holes myself." Myles paused, then chuckled humorlessly. He continued but seemed to be talking to himself. His mood had darkened. "Sometimes you strike gold. Sometimes, you strike … oh, I don't know … a power line?"

This time, his grin didn't quite reach his eyes.

I drew a breath to probe further but stopped when I saw Myles's shoulders tense and rise as if he were wearing a set of small but defined shoulder pads. He turned his head slowly and looked at me. He seemed ten years older, his face as hard as limestone. I barely recognized him.

"Any other questions, busboy?" he snarled.

What was happening?

A loud crash broke us out of our strange stare-down—a cacophony of coins hitting the floor behind the bar.

"Ah, day-um!" A strong Kentucky accent. "Not a-gin!" the bartender scowled. He wiped his hands on his apron before bending down to scoop up the mess. Something metallic rolled across the weathered floor of the bar, just out of my line of sight. Myles maneuvered around the stools and stopped the rolling object with a sharp, metal-on-metal clink from his golf spikes.

"I got it," Myles said, bending down behind the bar to help. He stood up slowly, holding what looked like a dented, tarnished trophy cup with a faded Wawashkamo Golf Course coat of arms plaque haphazardly bolted to one side. He set it on the bar and inspected it closely.

Then he picked it up, hefting it in his hands as if testing the weight. He slowly turned it in his hands. Thankfully, the thunderstorm of anger had passed, so I felt safe enough to move closer. He turned the cup upside down, slowly revealing the underside—floral, ornate, with undeniably old engravings.

"Not possible," Myles said, shaking his head in wonder. He whispered to me, "These designs …"

"French?" I whispered back.

"Peut-être," Myles responded.

I nodded, then leaned closer. *"What does that mean?"*

"It means … *maybe,"* he replied and then scratched his cheek. "I think."

The bartender scooped up pennies and old golf tees from the floor, the metallic clatter filling the bar as he dumped them back into the cup in front of us. We just stared at it, afraid to disturb a molecule, lest we be struck dead by the power of God for our drooling lust to steal the thing right off the shelf and run out of the bar with it.

"Apologies for the commotion, y'all," he twanged,

cheerfully resigned to his task. "I've knocked this stupid thing over three times just this summer alone. I can't figure out why it's always so close to the damn cash register. I set it up there on the shelf each mornin', and somehow, the sucker finds its way back to the cash register and I knock it over. It's like a bad penny. Well, I guess more like a bad penny *cup*."

"Got it," said Myles. He looked at the bartender's name tag and spoke slowly. "Tell me, Vance. Where did this … *penny cup* … come from?"

He shrugged. "Couldn't tell ya. It was a golf trophy in the 1950s. At least, that's what the plaque says. I never asked where they got it. Trophy store? Shit, there's all sorts of old crap around this clubhouse. I heard they dug up a lotta stuff way back when they first built the place. I think it was around the turn of the century. Arrowheads. Musket balls. All sorts of stuff. Who knows. Maybe they dug this up, too." He fixed Myles with a look. "Why you askin'?"

Myles's grin was back. "I'm just a curious sort."

"I got that problem too." Vance refilled the last of the change he'd scooped from the floor and returned the penny cup to the shelf.

"Now you stay," he said, pointing at the cup like it was a wayward French bulldog. Music echoed through the bar. "*Witchcraft*. Sinatra," he murmured. "Now there's a tasty selection." Myles and I shared a giddy look and then turned in unison to stare in awe at the penny cup behind the bar.

We had just located Marquette's chalice.

CHAPTER 25

Two Hunnerd Bucks

The bike ride back to the Wawashkamo Golf Course the following morning felt like a losing game of catch-up. I was the kid in the group, the speedster, the energetic rapscallion.

Right?

But rolling with two historians—one old, one young—both riding a crack-like rush of excitement made me feel positively sluggish. Dr. Trumbull and Shively stood up on their pedals, not the least bit winded. Dr. Trumbull was borderline chunky, yet he dropped me like he was wearing the yellow jersey at the Tour de France as we blasted through a canopied tree tunnel that led to Wawa.

"Just imagine, Dr. Trumbull," called Shively over the wind. "The chalice could provide new insights into the Jesuit missions and their interactions with indigenous communities. This could be a pivotal discovery in reconstructing the history of the Great Lakes region!"

"Yup!" Dr. Trumbull nodded, gasping for oxygen. "Plus, it will be a huge tourist draw!" Witnessing Dr. Trumbull's evolution from pure historian to raging capitalist was fascinating.

"Of course!" butt-kissed Shively. "Obviously, the more people we get through the turnstiles, the more research we can do!"

"Exactly," called back Dr. Trumbull. "I mean, that's the goal. More research!"

Right.

I found myself missing the comforting, corrupting presence of Myles or Rollie. If they were here, I'd be making sarcastic gagging gestures, finger to my throat, as these two eggheads rambled on. But they weren't joining us on this run to Wawa. They were, quite literally, holding down the Fort. Somebody had to entertain the tourists while we procured the chalice.

Myles and I had shared our discovery with Dr. Trumbull first thing in that morning, just as our day at the Fort kicked off. We caught him right as he walked under the arch for the South Sally Port, clutching his coffee thermos and a colossal cinnamon roll from Little Bob's.

When he heard the story, his face went a shade of beet red and contorted. He kept straightening up sharply, his movements jerky, almost like a marionette with tangled strings or someone having an epileptic fit. For a moment, we thought he was having a stroke.

But then he did something that left both Myles and I utterly bewildered. He leaned against the stone wall and calmly took off his left loafer. Then he peered into it as if he expected the shoe to offer him divine insight. Myles shot me a covert look, twirling his finger near his temple in the universal cuckoo gesture. I looked away.

Fast forward ten minutes, and, other than a mild stutter, Dr. Trumbull was now the original Man with the Plan.

"*G-G-G*-Get Shively. We're heading out now."

Thankfully, he never questioned how two knuckleheads like Myles and I recognized such an artifact, let alone knew where to find it. We were able to sidestep a massive lie by omission—that we'd broken into the North Keep, swiped a journal and a poem by some French aide-de-camp named Duval, and turned the Wawa links into a moonscape with four shovels and Gramps's prized metal detector.

The door creaked open, and we stepped in. The bar was quiet and empty. Old wood and the lingering vapor of last night's cocktails hung in the air. Now sporting a wild night's worth of stubble, Vance looked up from wiping down the counter.

"Hi, y'all! Back so soon?" he greeted, recognizing me from the afternoon before.

Did this guy sleep?

"We're here about the chalice," Dr. Trumbull began. For my taste, he sounded far too much like a government official, but it was too late to soften the approach.

Vance paused, his expression blank.

"Chalice?" He considered the request, and then brightened. "Oh! You mean the penny cup?"

"Yes, the penny cup," I said. "The one you knocked over yesterday. I was in here with my friend."

"Yup. The mustache dude. You tried to get him to buy you a beer, but he wouldn't budge. Said you had a 'nuff. For the record, I wasn't gonna serve you anyway. I *like* my job."

"That's ..." I looked back at Dr. Trumbull, my face reddening. *"Beer?* No. I mean, that's really ... anyway."

Vance was on a roll. "Mustache dude's from Sarasota, Florida. You kept nagging him about his past. You guys talked about a metal detector and diggin' holes."

"How did—"

"And there was something about your grandfather. How old people are, like, wise. You went on about photography and how yer, like, this reluctant artist-type. Yeah. I hear everything, and I remember everything. Comes in handy sometimes," he chirped. "Anyway. Yeah, I knocked over the penny cup for the third time this summer, and you boys picked it up."

"Yes, that's right."

"I have an amazing memory."

"Where's the damn chalice!" yelled Dr. Trumbull, his face expanding and his patience gone.

"You mean the penny cup?" Vance, unfazed, never stopped wiping the bar.

"Yes. The … *penny cup!*" It was like removing pints of his own blood for Dr. Trumbull to describe the sacred chalice as a "penny cup."

"Oh. It's gone."

"Gone?" asked Dr. Trumbull.

"Yup. Last night, the boss sold it." Vance produced a canister of Lemon Pledge and blasted the atmosphere with the sickly sweet-smelling carcinogenic. A cloud of chemical lemons wafted past us. Dr. Trumbull coughed but stayed still, processing the news in stunned silence.

"Yeah. Some super hot chick came in later last night. A real biscuit. Some sorta … *antiquer?*" He raised his voice on the last word as if it were a question. "Asked me if it was for sale. I asked the boss, and he said sure and … get this: she paid two hunnerd bucks for that scrap. Two hunnerd bucks! Ka-ching! *Boom!*" It came out like *bah-oom!*

Dr. Trumbull's face drained of color until he looked

made of wax. Shively seemed equally stunned and sat down slowly on a bar stool, repeatedly mouthing "two hundred bucks" like a mental patient.

"That chalice is a significant historical artifact!" Dr. Trumbull said, his voice back and booming.

Another blast of Lemon Pledge. *Sssssss.*

"Yeah, well, it was also a significant pain in my ass. I knocked it over three times already just this summer. Every time I'd put it up on the shelf—"

"It's priceless!"

"Obviously! I toldja. She paid *two hunnerd bucks* for it."

"That was Father Marquette's chalice! He gave communion to the local tribes from that chalice! Do you have any *idea* how significant it is?"

The bartender squinted at Dr. Trumbull.

"Wait. *Marquette?* You mean, like the statue in the park?"

"Yes!"

"That was a *real guy?*"

"Yes, that's a *real guy!* He's the most famous and revered—"

"—what did she look like?" I interrupted, hoping to change the subject before Dr. Trumbull leaped over the bar and beat Vance to death with his historian's shoulder bag.

The bartender knitted his brow. "Kinda New Yorky? Glamorous, but in a business-like way. She had a green sorta purse thing on her shoulder that swang when she walked in."

It was a spot-on description. It *did* swang. "Was her name Helen Chandler?"

He clicked his fingers and pointed at me. "Boom!" *Bah-oom.* "You got it! Ah never forget a name. Helen Chandler." He nodded, pleased with his memory, and turned back to his side work, hefting a case of Heineken off the floor and loading the bottles into a glass refrigerator.

Helen Chandler. Green handbag. The same woman who almost seduced my mom. Feagler had Marquette's chalice.

CHAPTER 26

A Bad Show

The ride from Wildcliffe to the fort was a treacherous, sludgy mix of mud and horse crap, thanks to the previous night's downpour. My mind felt the same.

Why was I losing sleep over a tarnished old cup I didn't even know existed until last Tuesday? Some Frenchie in a black cape and beard handed out free Merlot to the locals, and I was stressing over the cup he left behind? It made zero sense in the grand scheme of life. Besides, it was 300 years old, and if I had to be brutally honest, it wasn't the most impressive chalice I'd seen—not that I ever claimed to be some sort of chalice connoisseur.

Island history had always been Gramps' thing, not mine. He had books lying around Wildcliffe—many in the downstairs bathroom—with titles like *Lore of the Great Turtle* and *The Young Voyageur.* The intriguing drawings made bathroom breaks zoom by, but none of it really stayed with me.

So why had Marquette's chalice, of all things, suddenly put a hook through my cheek? I did love Mackinac Island. So there was that. Had my affection for the Island ignited a latent sense of civic pride? Had the Pizza King, Feagler, with his greasy, cheesy, 22-minutes-or-less schemes, roused a righteous fire of indignation I never knew I had? Or maybe there were traces of mercury in the dye of my blue soldier's waistcoat, and I was going nuts like the Mad Hatter. A teacher once told me that's why he lost his marbles: mercury poisoning.

Civic pride or mercury poisoning. As options, they were neck and neck.

But there was one other option.

The McGuinns weren't exactly gunning for Catholic sainthood. Our visits to St. Anne's were as unpredictable as Michigan weather, reserved for summer charity drives and whenever Mom felt we needed a spiritual tune-up. My most fervent prayers were usually reserved for emergencies that could be filed under the "please God, get me out of this mess and I'll never do it again" category.

But the chalice had stirred something deeper I couldn't name. For a smartass kid who cared more about himself than just about anything else, this was uncharted territory. Something was calling, a whisper just out of reach, and I couldn't stop straining to hear it.

I approached the North Sally Port and parked my bike in the rack. Myles slumped against the stark white of the fort's stone wall, his figure draped in a worn, pool-blue raincoat, the hood casting dark shadows over his eyes. In his hand, a cigarette smoldered.

I'd never seen him smoke.

The fort wall was bordered by a tall wooden stockade lined with red, white, and blue patriotic bunting. The contrast between the pageantry of the fort walls and

Myles's hangdog body language was striking, and I had to blink twice to convince myself it was even him.

He raised a hand, tossed the cigarette butt on the grass, and straightened, moving away from the wall to join me as I walked through the arched rear entrance.

"Everything okay?" I asked, eyeing him warily.

"Top notch." His response was too quick.

"I'm pissed about the chalice. We had it, Myles." I shook my head. "It was a quest, man, and we were so close."

"There'll be others," he said.

"Chalices?"

"Quests. There's always another quest." His laugh was dry, his gaze drifting off. "Let's suit up," Myles said as he looked over. "By the way, I'm playing Private Boone today." He didn't usually play Private Boone, but his tone left little room for discussion.

We were performers now, and performers needed to stretch occasionally. I'd read that in the downstairs bathroom too. I think it was in a *People Magazine* profile about the actor who played Remington Steele on TV.

The Court Martial of Private Boone reenactment staged on the Fort parade ground always drew a lively crowd, and today was no exception.

Done up in a colonial judge's outfit, complete with a gray curly wig, round eyeglasses, and a black robe, Rollie gestured to the passing tourists.

"Hear ye, hear ye! Welcome to the most ridiculous show trial this side of Cheboygan, Michigan! Hell, Sheboygan, Wisconsin, truth be told! Let's get this kangaroo court of a farce underway!" He did a little drum roll on a big red drum. The crowd moved in closer, buzzing already.

Playing the prosecutor, I stepped up. "Esteemed fudgies, jurists, tourists, truth-seekers, road-apple dodgers, cyclists, and psychos! Welcome to the Court-Martial of Private Boone. Private Boone is a *very naughty boy.*" The crowd chuckled.

Looking uncharacteristically dour, Myles as Private Boon, wearing handcuffs, sat at a table next to Shively, who played his attorney. Myle's hair was unkempt. His shirt was grimy and wrinkled, tucked loosely into his worn woolen breeches. The cuffs of his shirt were frayed.

Normally, the beat-up wardrobe was borderline silly, but today, Myles wore it like he was indeed on trial. His body language—slouched and glowering—was a touch too dark, and we all noticed it immediately.

The skit, as written, had the wacky, over-the-top vibe of a *Saturday Night Live* sketch. But today, Myles brought an intensity, even before he uttered his first line.

I shot him a wary look and continued. "Private Boone here has been accused of stealing fifteen muskets from the Fort Mackinac supply depot. He then sold them to a group of fur traders, who, in turn, sold them to the Chippewa tribe. What they did with them is anyone's guess, but since the Chippewa tribe has allied with the British—our sworn enemies—for the last decade, we can assume it wasn't to make lacrosse sticks."

"Or curtain rods," piped in Rollie. He held a finger to his lips. "Although I must say, it would add a certain vintage flair to any teepee."

"They also probably didn't want the muskets as backscratchers," I added. "One flinch could blow a hole through your buttocks."

"Although, it would effectively scratch the itch," added Rollie.

"You make an excellent point, your honor."

"I'm honored."

"The honor's all mine."

The crowd chuckled. So far, so good. We were grooving. "Rise and shine, Boone," said Rollie, gesturing to Myles.

Myles stood. He wasn't grinning. He usually held a gleam like he'd had a wild night with your sister, regardless of the character he played.

"How do you plead?" called Rollie.

"Not guilty," said Myles. "A moral compass guided my actions. I wanted justice for those history has forgotten."

His tone was severe, contrasting sharply with our loose, goofy banter. He was also making shit up.

Shively, as the defense attorney, jumped in. "Your Honor, this soldier, with his years of service to his country and fantastic facial hair, has a spotless record! You heard him. His reason for borrowing the muskets was honorable."

"Borrowing?" I leaned in, pointing at Myles. "Private Boone, isn't it true that you filched our precious muskets to sell to fur traders for a ridiculous profit?" A little blonde girl holding her dad's hand waved at me. I waved back. She blushed.

Myles shrugged, "I knew they'd eventually aid the Chippewa who faced threats from settlers. My intentions were just, even if my methods weren't. I knew the guns would get to the people who needed them."

We all paused, baffled by Myles's diversion. This was way, *way* off-script. Rollie and I passed quick glances, but Shively spun around, trying to save the moment. "See? A man of honor! Boone saw an imbalance and acted not for greed but equity!"

Okay, *maybe* I could work with this.

"Absurd!" I shouted. "So now Boone's some kind of blue-coated Robin Hood? Stealing muskets for the greater good?" I flailed my arms wildly. "What a hero! We should erect a colossal statue of him in the park, right next to Father Marquette! We'll have him holding a bag of cash over his shoulder and crying out VICTIM OF THE SYSTEM!'"

I'll just say it: it was some solid improv, considering the screwball Myles had just thrown my way.

Myles shot to his feet. "This is no joking matter. We talk about law and order yet ignore the plight of those we've displaced and wronged. I stand by my decision to help the Chippewa."

The crowd had been eating it up. But now they were shifting side to side. Confused faces. Was this all just part of the show?

In the corner of my eye, I saw Dr. Trumbull standing on the hillside, frantically drawing the shape of a giant smile with his finger, pleading for us to rediscover our crowd-pleasing goofiness. So crowd-pleasing that we'd recently had a glowing front-page review in the *Island Gazette* with the headline:

"Hilarious Fort Guides Make (Up) History"

But here we were, delivering a half-assed college lecture on the plight of the oppressed in front of an audience expecting the *Bugs Bunny/Road Runner Hour*. It was a colossal, mood-killing bummer.

Edging closer to Myles, I fished out an old, tattered

notebook from my leather shoulder bag and struck my best pre-*gotcha* stance.

"Private Boone. Is this your journal?"

"Yup," answered Myles.

I handed it to him. "Is this your handwriting?"

"Yup," answered Myles.

"Please read the highlighted section."

He read in a dead voice. "Today, I stole ten muskets from the supply depot and sold them to some stinky fur traders camping in the park. I couldn't believe how easy it was."

Shively jumped up. "Objection! How is Private Boone expected to recognize his own handwriting?"

"That's my handwriting," said Myles, deviating yet again and killing the joke. He was supposed to act shocked, argue, and throw his hands in the air. Wail. Flail. Maybe even cry. Rollie was fantastic with the crying. It always went over huge with the kids.

What he was *not* supposed to do was agree.

"Shut up, Boone," said Shively. "Nobody asked you."

"*I* asked him," I said.

It wasn't genius-level comedy, but we got some of the crowd back laughing.

"Alright, let's cut through the *bullshit!*" Myles said.

Mortified moms earmuffed their children, and rising whispers passed through the crowd.

Did he just say "bullshit"?

"I did it," he said in a dead voice. "I stole the damn muskets, okay? Plain and simple. And I lied earlier. It wasn't to help the Chippewa tribe defend itself. It wasn't because I care about humanity. I did it because I needed the money, and it was an easy scam." He turned to Rollie and pointed. "You idiots don't even have your guns labeled."

None of this was part of the script. We were in uncharted territory. Trying desperately to nudge the skit back to something funny-adjacent, I blurted out, "So, Private Boone, was it a buy-one-get-one-free deal on those muskets?"

The lame joke landed flat on its back, souring the atmosphere like curdled milk on a beach. I heard someone sneeze. My wide, terrified eyes scanned the crowd. The little girl, now bored and grumpy, was impatiently tugging her dad's hand, desperate to escape our monotonous, shambling disaster of a performance.

"Wait, that's not right. What I meant to say was, umm ... why bother denying it? Your journals are the proof!" My voice suddenly cracked like a thirteen-year-old under a full-blown puberty attack.

Myles replied coolly. "I'm *not* denying it. I took the guns, and I sold them for cash."

"Right, but if you say that—wait, what are you saying?"

The show was unraveling, and Myles was the loose thread. My eyes flicked left and right, looking for a lifeline, an idea, anything. They landed on Governor Belkin, wearing Kelly green pants and a salmon button-down.

Is he here today? *Wonderful.*

The Governor yawned so loud you could hear it downtown. There'd be hell to pay when this shitshow was over, but for now, all I could do was flounder like a whitefish on a dock.

Myles said, "I'm not here to preach about righteousness. I was a terrible soldier who saw a chance to make a quick buck and grabbed it. It's that simple. Jesus, man. There's no need to dig for deeper meaning."

"Sure, Boone, you say that now—*but we have your journal!*" I shook my finger at him like the world's hammiest actor. It made no sense. Apparently, I was terrible at improv because I hadn't heard a word he'd just said. "Acting is reacting," Rollie once told me.

Myles pounced, suddenly raging. "You're not listening, busboy! I did it!" The sudden intensity caught everyone off guard, most of all me.

Busboy?

His eyes were now wild and challenging. "You want the truth? Fine. I'm a thief. There, I said it." He paused, letting the words settle. "Lock me up, throw away the key. It won't change a *goddamn* thing."

Ooph.

Another bad word bounced off the walls. Half the crowd was gone. More were leaving. We were cooked.

We were frozen in place. Rollie's face cycled through confusion, frustration, and resignation before settling on determination. With a *show must go on* flourish, he banged the red drum, the sound cutting through the awkward silence.

"Well, folks," he called out, his voice strained, "I think it's time for the audience's verdict!" His eyes darted around, silently pleading with us to play along. It was beyond time to put this disaster to bed. "What say the jury?"

The response was tepid. A couple of hippies in the back cheered enthusiastically, shouting, "Preach, brother!" and "Yeah, man!" But mostly, it was crickets from what was left of the peanut gallery.

"Come on, folks! Let's hear it!" called Rollie. "Private Boone's life rests on your verdict."

"Guilty," echoed several bored voices in the audience. I also thought I heard someone mutter, "Who cares?"

Up on the hillside, I saw a slumping Dr. Trumbull. He looked as though he was having a chili pepper surgically removed from his butt. Rollie brought the gavel down with a thud that could wake the dead.

But it didn't.

"The jury has spoken. Guilty as charged!" he declared, his enthusiasm oddly out of place in the nearly empty parade ground.

Shively stepped up. "And remember, ladies and gentlemen, none of what you just heard is true."

With our last shred of energy, Shively, Rollie, and I shot our fists up and chanted, "History!" in our traditional closing line. Myles remained seated, head down, disconnected from the gesture.

The Court-Martial of Private Boone show was over. We'd bombed.

In the guide shack, remnants of colonial brick-a-brack mingled with modern-day clutter. George Washington's painted gaze, slightly askew from his frame on the wall, watched over a jumble of coffee mugs and styrofoam remnants from yesterday's lunch. An elderly maintenance worker finished a meal and flipped through *Popular Mechanics*. Rollie's Private Boone script, now a wrinkled casualty, lay amidst the chaos under a powdered wig. I shot a baleful look at Myles, who was calmly shedding his blue coat.

"What was *that?*" My voice, louder than I intended, bounced off the walls. "You made us look like complete amateurs."

Myles replied with a cold smile. "We *are* complete amateurs."

Struggling to remove the tall boot from his left foot,

Rollie was even more irked. "Why didn't you just stick to the script?!"

Myles shook his head as if we were all hopelessly out of touch. He turned to Rollie. "We made the show ridiculous because the previous script was predictable. Remember? Now, *ridiculous* is predictable, and predictable is, yet again, boring." He shrugged. "So I found a *new* ridiculous: boring."

Shively spoke up, his tone hesitant but genuinely curious. "Myles, what does that mean?"

Rollie didn't wait for an answer and jumped up, one boot off. "Ridiculous isn't boring, Myles! Not by a long shot. Our act was hitting its stride. It was funny, and even Dr. Trumbull was finally on board. You saw the article!" He threw his arms in the air. "And then you decide to go all dark method actor on us? Talk about boring!" Rollie's voice edged into a whine. "You didn't even do the Houdini handcuff bit! That one's gold!"

Myles slipped on a worn black T-shirt. He turned to face us and crossed his wrists as though shackled in invisible cuffs. "Guilty as charged," he said tonelessly.

When Dr. Trumbull burst in, a gloomy silence had settled over the room, broken only by the sound of the maintenance guy annihilating his bag of Fritos, a staccato series of crackling mini-explosions.

Dr. Trumbull kicked a chair theatrically. It didn't fall over. "You guys really shat the bed with that show!"

Myles, stone-faced and detached, combed his hair and checked his look in a mirror mounted inside his locker. "I thought you hated the comedy stuff, Doc," he said. "If I recall correctly, you once described our act as 'puerile antics fit for a schoolyard.'"

"It is *puerile antics fit for a schoolyard!* I despised it. Initially," Dr. Trumbull continued. "But I can't argue with the results. The crowds love it. The buzz around our reenactments has grown. Our attendance numbers lately have skyrocketed. And Trenton Feagler's donations to Allies of Mackinac? I wouldn't deny your shows played a part. In short, I was wrong."

Myles snorted.

Dr. Trumbull took a few steps closer to him. "Something you'd like to say?"

"Yeah. Feagler's a snake."

"Well, that *snake* just funded the opening of the most important discovery we've had here in twenty years." He turned to Shively. "Listen, I'd be *thrilled* if you returned to historical accuracy, just as long as it's still …" He trailed off.

"… dazzling?" piped in Rollie.

"I was going to say *entertaining*." He spun back to Myles, not done with him. "*And you!* Do you really think Private Boone would spout some confession like a sniveling little coward?"

Myles continued to work his mustache into shape. "Never met Private Boone, Doc. He's been dead, what's it been, a hundred and twelve years? So I have no idea what he'd … *spout.*"

"You know what, Myles, don't call me 'Doc'! I can't remember why I tolerated that in the first place."

Myles clicked his heels and saluted, but his eyes never left the mirror. "Yes, *sir.*"

Was he *trying* to get fired?

Dr. Trumbull paced, his fingers massaging his temples as if trying to knead away a migraine. "You want to know what Governor Belkin said after that train wreck of a performance?" He stopped abruptly, fixing me with a glare.

"I know because I was right there, soaking in every syllable. He said, and I'm quoting verbatim here, 'Well, that show sure sucked eggs.' And just like that, poof! He vanished. Sucked eggs!"

Dr. Trumbull's arms shot up, nearly taking out a coat rack. "He'd brought a writer from the *Detroit Free Press*. I'd just finished gushing to her about our 'hilarious' new guides. 'A fresh take on history!' I said. 'Innovative! Cutting edge!' And what do you lot do? Lay the biggest, fattest egg since the extinction of the dodo. Which you then proceeded to suck! You laid an egg, then sucked it! Amazing feat! You must be double-jointed to pull that maneuver off!"

Dr. Trumbull collapsed into a chair, the fight visibly draining out of him. He cradled his head in his hands, took a few deep breaths, then looked up with eyes that had aged a decade in minutes.

"You lot don't grasp the tightrope I'm walking these days," he said, his voice softening. "I'm a historian, for crying out loud, not some ... carnival barker. But here I am, forced to play salesman just to keep this place afloat." He gestured vaguely at the Fort around him.

"Our guests could easily ditch us for Harbor Springs to window shop for—" he waved his hand, searching for words. "Oh, I don't know."

"Cable knit sweaters?" Rollie chimed in.

"Sure. I don't know what people do in Harbor Springs. Or they can kayak at Pictured Rocks. Imagine they're ..."

"Lewis and Clark?" said Shively.

"Yes, I suppose. Although we all know Lewis and Clark never explored that region, as they were based—" He caught himself getting distracted. "It doesn't matter! My point is there are other places! Sea Shell City! 'Home of the Man-Eating clam'! God knows it's cheaper. Or they could spend their day watching an ore ship getting raised twenty-one feet at the Soo Locks. Wee! Or visit the Mystery Spot in St. Ignace, where they say 'gravity works backward.'"

He stood up. "You guys came up with something unique. Insane, stupid, and wrong—but unique. And it brings in the guests. It's a hit. I'm begging you: Don't ruin it."

He looked us over. We all stood at attention except Myles, who continued to groom indifferently. "Now get your act together. Quite literally."

With that, he turned on his heel and left the room. It was a long time before anyone spoke.

"Ya know, I like the Mystery Spot," Rollie said, finally pulling off his boot. He'd calmed now that Dr. Trumbull had taken the anger baton and was running with it. "All that anti-gravity stuff. It's trippy."

Myles snorted at Rollie's odd observation and shook his head. He slammed his locker shut, slung his backpack over his shoulder, and walked out of the guide shack without a word. The three of us finished changing out of our uniforms without saying much more.

CHAPTER 27

Out of Shirts

I had a day off. Big Jack was downstate at the dealership, Gramps was cruising around on his gold bike for the umpteenth time, Mom was peddling flowery frocks at the Blue Butterfly, and Beth was busy at Wild Style. Myles had vanished without a trace, and Smitty was stuck at work.

After decimating three dresser drawers, I accepted that I was out of wearable T-shirts. That summer, my day-off uniform was a rotation of *The Police*, *The Clash*, and *Black Sabbath*, relics of my musical awakening during the summer of '79. That's also when I got swept up in crime by a metalhead named Blaze and gave away a tiny chunk of my heart to a Hollywood New Wave angel named Jill. Both left their musical tastes ingrained in my memory like scratches in vinyl. I never saw either of them again, but my T-shirt collection kept their memories close to my heart, as well as other torso-centric organs. Unfortunately, these precious memories were currently stuffed in the hamper, smelly, crumpled, and unwearable even for me.

I needed Beth.

Wild Style.

Beth would slide free T-shirts my way, maybe two or three times a summer. She wasn't one to hand out freebies; she was in the shirt game to make a profit. But every so often, she'd pass me something cool. I'd like to think it was out of kindness and love, but that was just part of it. I was a visible island kid, the former paperboy, a current Fort guide, and, God-willing, a future dockporter.

I got around.

Having her little brother ride through town sporting her latest designs was not the worst marketing idea. The business gurus called it a *win-win*.

I pulled on a purple Minnesota Vikings hoodie I found in the back of my closet—probably left behind by one of Big Jack's auto dealer friends. As a Detroit Lions fan, I normally wouldn't be caught dead in Vikings Purple, but it would do for now. I set off to pay Beth a social call and hopefully hustle up some new threads.

"Can I try that one?" I had zeroed in on an exceptionally stylish T-shirt displayed on a freakish mannequin in a day-glow gas mask. At this point, the hood of the Vikings sweatshirt was pulled tight so only my eyes were visible, ensuring I couldn't be recognized outside Wildcliffe.

"*Try it on?* That implies you might give it back," Beth called over as she sliced through a stack of packages with a box cutter.

She looked over. "How about being straight with me? 'Beth. Confidant. Sister. Occasional therapist. I need a new T-shirt. I haven't done laundry in two weeks because I'm a lazy-assed teen, and I'd rather be given a brand-new shirt than learn the complex engineering of today's modern washing machine, what with all its knobs, buttons, and settings."

"Yup. That."

She smiled. "See? The direct approach. Much easier." She gestured. "Pick something off that rack. It's the new stuff."

A familiar voice boomed behind me. "Yeah, Jack! The direct approach is always best. How do you think I landed this killer gig hauling stuff?"

I turned to find Smitty grinning, setting down a box he'd just lugged in from the horse-drawn dray outside. He was clad in his faded green State-issued uniform, drenched in sweat after a grueling morning of hauling boxes.

"Let me guess: *the direct approach?*" I ventured.

"Bingo! I walked right up to Mr. Chambers and told him, 'Mr. Chambers, I want to haul stuff on a dray this summer. I'm strong, I'm a great worker, and I don't charge very much.'"

Beth was barely listening but unable to resist. "Shrewd bit of negotiating, Smitty," she called. "You really ground him down with that pitch."

"Thanks, Beth!" Utterly irony-proof, Smitty stretched his arm across his chest like a shot putter warming up for his next toss. "Be right back. Gotta few more boxes for you." He headed back outside to the dray. Beth smiled, her eyes following him as he hustled out the door.

"I love that boy," she said. "Of all the loser buddies you've had over the years, he's by far the least irritating." She snapped her fingers. "Speaking of losers, too bad about Gordon."

"What about him?"

"Rumor is, he's turning into a Grade-A jackass. My friend Janine saw him at the Grand pool with some sultry blonde, ordering waiters around like he was Louis the

14th. She said he was dressed in tennis whites and wearing hundred-dollar Porsche sunglasses.”

“His parents finally got divorced. Now they fight to see who can buy him the most expensive stuff,” I said, knowing it was a weak defense.

I could almost hear her eyes rolling. “Aw. Poor baby,” said Beth. “My heart just bleeds.”

I’d managed to ditch the Vikings sweatshirt, slip into the new T-shirt, and was admiring myself in the mirror. The shirt was electric blue, featuring a crisp white outline of the island. There were no frills, no clutter. Below it, in small letters, it read: “IF YOU KNOW, YOU KNOW.” It perfectly reflected Beth’s quirky style to a T.

Get it? To a tee?

To Beth, Mackinac Island was more of an idea than a place—a shape, a feel. And if you don’t know that, no problem. Keep shopping. Get something else. Only buy the shirt if you understand the island. But if you *do* understand, prove it. Buy the shirt. Wear it.

But what really mattered to me was not the complex psychological underpinnings of my big sister’s artistic inspirations. It was something far more important: the shirt fit perfectly.

“I’ll take it,” I called over.

“Looks like you already did,” she called back distractedly while folding. “Just don’t forget to tell anyone who asks where they can get one.”

“What do I get out of it?”

“The shirt, dumbass.”

The door chimed again as Smitty lumbered back in, hauling two more boxes and plopping them on the counter. He glanced at my new blue shirt. “Hey, Beth, that one’s pretty sweet. I like the design. It’s super, like ...” Smitty trailed off, his brow furrowing. He scratched his head as his mouth opened and closed a couple of times like a fish out of water. "It's, like, sort of …"

Beth observed Smitty's syntactical struggles with fascination, then threw him a lifeline. "Minimalist?"

"Sure," he nodded. *"That.* I was gonna say 'simple,' but your word sounds, you know, classier."

Beth chuckled. "No, I like 'simple.'" She indicated the rack of shirts. "Take one. You and my clueless brother can be twins. But you've got to promise to wear it at least twice a week in public. Deal?"

"Hell yeah. Shit, Beth. I'll wear it *seven* days a week if you want!"

"Ew. No. That's gross. Don't do that. It might have the opposite effect."

"It's my second free shirt this week." Smitty's grin widened as he shrugged off his green, dray service-issued jacket, revealing a white shirt underneath. Emblazoned in garish bold letters, it read "FBI," with "FEMALE BODY INSPECTOR" printed underneath. Beth's expression soured as she stared at his shirt with disgust.

"Really, Smitty?"

Smitty beamed, oblivious. "What? It says 'Female Body Inspector.' It's, you know … funny. I mean, right?"

Beth shook her head. "No, it's not funny. It's *creepy.* Where did you get that infantile rag?"

He glanced down at his shirt and then pointed across the street. "I got it from ParTees. Must have a thousand different shirts. Boobies. Fake tux shirts. 'I'M WITH STUPID' in about ten different colors. They have one that says 'I'M NOT AS THINK AS YOU DRUNK I AM.' They all say Mackinac Island on 'em. That place is awesome!"

I positioned myself behind Beth, frantically gesturing for Smitty to stop talking before she pounded his head into

Hamburger Helper with a hand iron. He finally caught my eye and quickly changed his tune about ParTees.

"I mean—*awful!* Did I say awe-*some?* I meant aw-*ful.* This place is way, way better."

Beth looked down and resumed slicing open boxes, the blade biting into the cardboard with quick, sharp motions.

"Not only do they sell the cheapest quality shirts with the worst designs, but people actually buy them!"

Smitty looked down at the floor sheepishly. "Sorry, Beth. They gave it to me for free."

Beth shook her head. "No, it's fine. It's not your fault you have bad taste. Most people do."

Smitty exhaled, shoulders relaxing in relief. She continued. "I just hate that ParTees took over the biggest storefront, and—day by day—they're going to lower the IQ of the average island tourist with their tacky shirts." She paused mid-slash, her box cutter poised in the air. "Wait. Smitty, I think this isn't our box."

Smitty leaned down to inspect the printing on the lid. "Speak of the devil. This is a ParTees box. It must've gotten mixed up with your stuff. Here, I'll take this back to the dray and—"

The box cutter slashed through the cardboard as Smitty pulled his hand away to avoid getting sliced. Beth ripped open the lid, looked up at us with an innocent little smile, and covered her mouth with her hand.

"Oopsie."

She reached inside the box, pushed aside some packing paper, and visibly recoiled when she saw the folded China-made T-shirts with neon print that read "BEER GOGGLES ACTIVATED."

"*Beer goggles.* Of course," she grumbled as she dug deeper, pulling out a pink shipping bill with a dot-matrix font. "What have we here?" She held it close. "Tradewinds Products, LLC. Livonia, Michigan. Interesting."

She glanced through the window at the ParTees sign across the street, her face grim. "Something stinks, and it's not just these horrible shirts." She pulled the beer goggles shirt out of the box, unfolded it, and held it in front of her, staring at it in silence.

CHAPTER 28

The Talk

Myles was MIA, leaving us a man short, and storm clouds were gathering, both literally and figuratively. The air crackled with tension, and not just from the approaching weather. After the train wreck that was the Private Boone fiasco, we were on thin ice. The show needed to be dazzling.

A herd of wide-eyed kids surged towards the platform overlooking the harbor, trailed by their parents who looked like they'd just survived a forced march through the island's trails. Shively, Rollie, and I exchanged grins as the crowd pressed closer. We were locked and loaded for the cannon-firing demo, ready to serve up a fresh helping of historical fiction, courtesy of Rollie's imagination.

He'd written another whopper.

One hundred fifty feet below, the view unfolded into steely blue-gray layers, the wind sketching whitecaps even in the shallowest pockets. Sailboat halyards clanked against masts in the marina as choppy waves snuck past the break walls. The Mackinac Bridge, seven miles away, looked like a mechanical beast from an H.G. Wells story as sheets of rain swallowed it.

Dr. Trumbull stood off to the side, plaid necktie flapping in the wind, sending a ripple of unease through the team. Yet, on closer inspection, he seemed oddly calm. The bad weather was closing in, but it appeared Trumbull's personal storm had finally passed.

A smattering of fort staffers huddled nearby. Among them was Jenna Bonnet, and suddenly, my colonial uniform felt two sizes too big. I straightened up, gripping the cannon's ramrod like a microphone. My eyes swept the crowd with lead singer swagger, then locked with Shively and Rollie. A quick nod. Myles might be AWOL, but the show must go on.

I stepped up. "Ladies and gents! Ever heard about the time Napoleon tried to invade Mackinac Island?" I began, watching the crowd lean in, instantly intrigued. "It's true!"

"No. Actually, it's not true," responded Shively, shaking his head, playing the disapproving father.

"Don't get hung up on details," I snapped back. "So. The story goes that Napoleon heard about our island's fudge through a French fur trader who'd been here and couldn't stop raving about the stuff when he returned to Paris. Napoleon, a man of great appetites, wanted himself some fudge."

A few tourists tittered, while the humorless waved the story away like an annoying black fly. But so far, nobody looked bored.

Rollie was up next. "Yep, the guy had a sweet tooth. Here's a little-known nugget: He kept a stash of Skittles tucked away in a secret pocket inside his general's uniform."

In unison, all three of us struck our most Napoleonic

poses, hands tucked inside our jackets, freezing like statues. Then, we each removed a bag of Skittles, ripped them open with the ferocity of children, and began chowing them down with disgusting gusto. We gnashed our teeth, rainbow-colored candy visible as we chewed with open mouths, occasionally letting out grunts of exaggerated pleasure.

"Hmm. Delicious," said Rollie, his mouth stuffed.

A kid in a black *Ghostbusters* T-shirt piped up, "But Skittles didn't even exist in those days!" I pointed a finger at him, my mouth still full. "Ah, but they did! Back then, they were known as *Les Skittelles!* Which is French for—"

Shively finished for me. "Skittles!"

We gulped down the candy as Rollie continued. "After the bitter cold of the Russian invasion and dying for a change of pace, Napoleon decided he needed some Mackinac Island fudge. It soon became an obsession."

"Fine," Shively sighed, as if reluctantly playing along with the ridiculous story, and gestured grandly toward Lake Huron. "He sent not one, not two, but *twenty-three* ships across the Atlantic, heading straight for the Island. Somewhere along the line, his craving for Mackinac Island fudge had overwhelmed him. The Americans, however, were ready. With this very cannon," he said, patting the nine-pounder, "they stood determined to protect our island's treasured confectionary industry."

"Nope." Rollie shook his head, looking out at the harbor. "Not on our watch, shorty."

I jumped in. "It was time to turn Napoleon Bonaparte into Napoleon … *Blown-apart!*"

Credit—or blame—for this gem goes to John Bakkila, who'd whispered it to me during a mind-numbing fourth-grade history lesson. The groaner got a surprisingly big laugh from the crowd.

"Ready," Rollie called out. "Aim," he continued, holding the smoldering fuse steady.

"Au revoir, Frenchies!" I yelled.

"FIRE!" The command reverberated off the fort's walls. I sparked the cannon's touch hole. A thundering boom and the cannon recoiled. A cloud of white smoke enveloped everything.

Rollie's voice cut through the haze. "When the smoke cleared, the soldiers of Fort Mackinac were treated to a wondrous sight. Look!" He pointed dramatically, and the crowd turned to gaze at the harbor.

"No French! The fleet was gone! They'd hightailed it."

"Split town!" I chimed in.

"Skedaddled!" added Shively.

We all joined in, unleashing a chaotic mix of clumsy similes: "Beat feet! Bolted! Booked! Made like bananas and split."

I finished. "Napoleon had decided that a land invasion, even for the world's best fudge, wasn't worth it."

Laughter and applause echoed across the firing platform.

Rollie raised his hand. "Little known fact: Shortly after his failed invasion of Mackinac Island, Napoleon attacked Switzerland. Why, you ask? Dark chocolate! And while he was there, he picked up a bunch of Swiss Army Knives, went skiing in the Alps, and opened a few numbered Swiss bank accounts. But that's a story for another time."

"It's also not true," said Shively.

"Shut up, Shively," said Rollie.

"Make me," said Shively.

They fake scowled at each other and then hugged. All part of the act.

I stepped up, raising my hands for attention. "On that note, let's be clear: nothing you heard today is remotely true." I paused for effect. "Thank you for coming." We launched into our now-familiar battle cry, fists pumping the air: *"History!"*

The crowd's applause swelled and then tapered off. A stiff gust swept across the platform as they began their trek toward the long exit ramp. Most were likely headed to Main Street for a cold beer and a whitefish sandwich, maybe to catch the Tiger game as the rain rolled into the harbor.

Dr. Trumbull's applause was distinct—a slow, deliberate golf clap cutting through the air. Moving against the tide of spectators, he made his way toward us, his eyes scanning the dark sky.

"Gather around for a couple of quick announcements," Trumbull called out, his voice slicing through the gusting wind. Ticket-takers, the office staff, a solitary security guard, a few maintenance men in work clothes, and several cashiers—it wasn't the entire Fort staff, but it was a notable turnout. A murmur of unease rippled through the assemblage. They edged closer, eyes darting around, exchanging glances.

Dr. Trumbull squinted at the darkening sky. "Looks like rain, so I'll make this quick. I know this is an odd spot for a staff meeting, but it's fitting. For a century, soldiers stood right here, scanning that same horizon for trouble." He paused, a smile tugging at his lips. "Though I doubt they were watching for rogue French fudge invaders."

He placed his hand on the cannon, seeming almost transformed by the storm clouds rolling in, ominous but holding back. "Now, thankfully, we live in more peaceful times. Today, in 1984, our sentries guard tourists and freighters, fudge and ferries. But the battle for funding never ends. And, as we all know, the economy is bad."

His eyes darted skyward as a gust whipped his hair and

tie. "I'll cut to the chase. The grant promised to the State Park via the Feagler Endowment fell through last night. I wasn't told why. This means a few things: The North Keep dig is on hold, and…"

Dr. Trumbull removed his glasses, pinching the bridge of his nose. Whether it was dust or emotion clouding his vision, we couldn't tell. "The Tea Room will be temporarily closed," he announced, his words met with a collective groan.

His eyes darted upward as the wind picked up, tugging at his necktie. "I also regret to inform you that Myles Fordham, one of our most popular guides, has resigned." The words hung in the air. "He will be … missed."

Stepping down from the cannon platform, his voice took on a determined edge. "Fort Mackinac has weathered many storms." As if on cue, the wind howled, nearly drowning him out. He raised his voice, almost shouting now. "We'll weather this one too! My office is open for questions!"

The first fat raindrops splattered around us as he turned to leave. In seconds, it was a downpour. Dr. Trumbull pulled his corduroy jacket over his head like a makeshift umbrella and made a dash for his office. We watched as he disappeared into the gray veil of rain, then, in a mad dash to stay dry, dispersed ourselves.

CHAPTER 29

Lifers

Mackinac Island's businesses were staffed by a humming, tourist-pleasing, fudge-producing hive of worker bees, each fitting not-so-neatly into their own categories: Year-Round Islanders, College Types, Neo-Hippies with their patchouli stink, Resort Rats, Fort Nerds, Backpackers Who Never Left (and probably never would), Jamaican Waiters, Enigmatic Characters, Lost Eastern Europeans, Cottager Kids, Hustlers on the Run, and Lifers. They mixed, intermingled, hopped categories, and often collided like bulls, creating a chaotic summer jam session that grew louder and wilder as the days got shorter and autumn's chill crept in.

The College Types, arguably, were the lowest on the Totem Pole of Respect but had the largest card-carrying membership. They flocked to the island when classes let out, seeking a wild summer of no-strings-attached antics and a brief respite from the looming specter of plugging into the matrix that is white-collar America. Arriving in Spring with funded bank accounts, they set out to work hard and play much, much harder. Their days were spent waiting tables, selling trinkets, renting bikes, cooking fudge, hauling luggage, and slinging drinks.

And their nights? Lit by the glow of beer lights and bar bands, they diligently went about blowing their meager savings on rounds of gin and tonics, cases of beer, Chippewa Hotel club sandwiches, and overpriced skunkweed, living each day as if it were their last.

And as September rolled around, they'd pack up their memories and head back to campus, leaving a trail of unpaid bar tabs, torrid love affairs, rugburns, and promises to return.

Some did. Some didn't.

Although most came from other categories, Lifers, arguably the opposite end of the Worker Spectrum, were a different breed altogether. They were the gears of the machine. Some were year-round residents, others were former college kids who had escaped the corporate grind, and a few were just Northern Michigan folks who kept coming back for the seasonal work. Although not exactly teetotalers, they didn't come for the party but for the grind. They worked not for fun but for necessity: school supplies for their kids, medication for their aging parents, and debts that never seemed to shrink. Everyone had their reasons that drew them back each season. But without them, the island simply couldn't function.

They knew how to work the decrepit fifty-year-old cash register and where the spare keys were hidden. They knew how to train—and sometimes fire—ingrate college students. They could reconcile payroll while simultaneously unjamming a stubborn coffee machine. They knew the secret trick behind mass-producing whitefish dip for the Knights of Columbus conference in May. They could dock a ferry and organize a delivery of fifty bags of concrete to the Grand Hotel pool.

In short, they were *Responsible Adults*. Their evenings weren't spent elbow-to-elbow with the rowdy crowd at Horn's Bar, shouting over the band's final set. No, they were tucked away in their rented rooms, balancing checkbooks. Every dime was sacred, carefully stashed away like acorns before winter. They kept their eyes fixed on that distant lighthouse of financial security, as if blinking might make it disappear.

Maya was a Lifer.

Squawbait too.

And they both just got canned.

Madonna's *Like a Virgin* blared from a radio on the floor. Maya sat at an empty table, meticulously counting her tips —ones and fives neatly stacked. Squawbait was wrestling with a tape gun that hissed stubbornly across a cardboard box of cleaning supplies, grumbling about the music. "You like this crap, Maya?"

Maya didn't bother looking up. "I *loooove* this crap. *Like a Virgin.*" She smiled seductively. "Emphasis on *like.*"

Squawbait grinned and reddened. "Wait, woman. Are you telling me you're not a virgin?"

"Ha!" She still didn't look up. "Ask my eight-year-old son about that one. And his deadbeat dad." She stopped her count. "Dammit, Squaw, you made me lose count. Again!"

She glanced up and saw me in the doorway, drenched from the rain. She brightened and hopped up to bear hug me, wet uniform and all. "Jacky! How's my favorite soldier boy?"

"I heard about the layoffs," I said, feeling a sick twist in my gut.

"Yup. It's a damn shame," She said and then deftly changed the subject. "I heard you guys are quite the hit with those crazy stories you cook up. Someone said it's not *historical* fiction—it's *hysterical* fiction." She cackled, eyes gleaming. "Hell, Jack. The whole town's buzzing about it. What'd I tell ya, huh?"

I looked at her closely. "How'd you know?"

"How'd I know what?" Maya asked.

"I dunno." I shrugged. "That I'd be good at it."

She motioned for me to sit and did the same, swiftly securing a stack of bills with a rubber band like a seasoned casino banker. I watched, fascinated. Waiting tables was her job, but those folded bills—destined for her tiny apartment in St. Ignace, where she lived with her kid—were her real life's work. You could see it in her eyes as she tucked the wad away: This was survival, pure and simple.

"Jack, honey, I didn't know. But sometimes you gotta be shoved out of the nest."

Squawbait, silently listening as he tacked shut another box, chimed in, "You dodged a bullet, Private Nutsack. You owe this lady big."

Another stab of guilt hit me. "What are you guys gonna do now?"

"Well, let's see. The first thing on the list is to panic," Maya said with a wry smile. "That's scheduled for tomorrow at ten. After that? Not too sure. They're opening some fancy-pants restaurants on Beaver Island. Kurt, the new busboy, knows some people. They're looking for staff with Mackinac Island experience, so a few of us are taking a little field trip to Beaver to sniff it out."

Try as I might to squelch it, a snort escaped. "*Feagler.*"

Maya's eyes hardened. "Jack, I know nobody up here likes him much. But I've got a little boy waiting for me at home. And Squawbait? He's looking after his old man, who's got the dementia real bad."

She leaned in close, whispering to ensure Squawbait couldn't overhear. "The poor man needs help with everything. And I mean everything. Last week, he started using Squawbait's clean T-shirts to wipe himself. He thinks warm cotton is the only thing that kills the demons ... *hiding in his ass!*

She threw back her head and laughed loudly, tears springing to her eyes. She covered her mouth to stifle the sound. She wiped away tears with the back of her hand and shook her head. "Good God, what a crazy world."

She paused, her eyes searching my face, no doubt reading the guilt etched like a gravestone. "We always kept our personal lives out of it for you, but this is what we're up against. We need work." The break room suddenly felt like a broom closet, the air thick. Outside, rain tap-danced on the patio floor.

"There's gotta be another way," I muttered, more to the universe than to them.

Squawbait's bitter laugh cut through the air. "Strap it on, musketeer. I've got no interest in moving to Beaver. I like my life here on the rock, weird as it is. But I'm a migrant dish-dog, like those Okies in *The Grapes of Wrath*. I follow the work. Just been lucky it's always been here."

Maya fixed me with a smile. What hurt most was seeing her more concerned about my feelings than her own truly screwed-up predicament.

"Listen, we gotta finish the side work, Jack." Maya stowed the last stack of bills in her purse and stood up, all business now. "This place needs to be locked up tight in two days."

There wasn't much more to say. I left, stepping back into the drizzle, the door slamming behind me.

The drizzle was doing its best to make me feel worse, patting against my skin like an terrible tap dancer. And there was a tightness in my chest. I'd heard people throw the word "privilege" around like a sharp rock, usually to hit someone square in the ego. But wasn't the whole point of life to ensure our kids and grandkids get to swim in heated pools or ride bikes on islands with no cars? Yes. I was lucky. I'd dodged a bullet. So why did I feel like I'd just swallowed a gallon of sour milk?

Why did I feel guilty?

Strap it on, musketeer.

But standing alone on the drenched Tea Room patio, staring at the misty harbor, rain running off the eaves, one question drowned out all the noise in my head. It wasn't the one I expected:

What the hell was "a dust bowl Okie"?

CHAPTER 30

The Pink Pony

The sailor from Mobile, Alabama, talked like he had all the time in the world. Each word dripped out slower than the last. I met him the same night Feagler broke ground on Fort Beaver.

First, though, a bit about the Pink Pony Bar.

"The Pony" was a fixture on the island as far back as what Gramps called his *salad days*, a term I never really understood because Gramps was not exactly a health nut. I eventually learned that *salad days* actually meant *wild days*, and then it made a lot more sense.

When I was a kid, my folks hauled me to the Pony with their rowdy Wildcliffe crowd, most of them buddies since their college days. For some twisted, magical reason, they'd decided that dragging their seven-year-old kid to the local watering hole at night and propping him up with lemonades was perfectly acceptable. It made me feel grown-up yet still a kid. Human with a dab of mascot. It's the kind of thing you'd catch hell for today, and I get it. Kids around booze is bad. *Bad, bad, bad.* But I saw a ton and learned even more, and I swear most of it was good. *Good, good, good.*

Mom often stole the show on those McGuinn Pony nights, claiming the pink upholstered piano bench as her throne. Her voice cut through the chatter, drawing everyone in. Her party trick was impressive: performing the 1960s song *To Sir With Love* blindfolded. It always brought the house down. Big Jack would sink into the pink booth couch, arms behind his head, beaming like the world's most laid-back king, quietly admiring the impressive talents of his queen.

In the 1980s, the Pink Pony was still the beating heart of island life, but there were other spots—Horn's Bar, the Village Inn, the French Outpost, and the Mustang Lounge. Locals drifted between these haunts as summer days stretched on. The nightly rotation through these watering holes kept the stories flowing, the deals brewing, and the arguments settling over clinking glasses. Despite thriving on tourism, the Island was still just a small town after the last ferry left.

That night, the Pony buzzed. The occasion was a good old-fashioned baseball game. In 1984, the Detroit Tigers were on fire. They won thirty-five of their first forty games and finished the season with 104 wins and a World Series victory, crowned by Kirk Gibson's magnificent mauling of Padres pitcher Goose Gossage, a legendary event in the Great Lake State.

The image of "Gibby," arms raised in pure joy as he crossed home plate, was immortalized on posters plastered across pubs, mancaves, rec rooms, and auto parts shops all over Michigan. But that madness wouldn't happen until October. These were still the dog days of summer. Our beloved Tigers had let us down before, and they would do so again.

Michigan sports had its own magnetic force that drew us together in ways beyond logic. Boston was at Tiger Stadium for a three-game stand, and Tiger ace Jack Morris was pitching. The great Manitou of Baseball had magically beckoned us to the bar that night, and nobody dared refuse. Some nights, it was simply understood that you might miss something special if you didn't watch the game.

Little did we know.

I sat at the bar next to Big Jack, who sat beside Mom. Beth didn't care much for baseball; she was off with her friends, taking a needed break from the worries of market-flooding, low-grade Chinese T-shirts by grilling hot dogs on the beach, listening to Grateful Dead songs, and maybe, just maybe, sneaking a kiss from a cute college boy in the orange glow of a bonfire.

Gramps glad-handed and grinned, rejuvenated since his secret trip to St. Ignace to meet his mystery squeeze. In another gaggle, the three competing fudge shop owners, all wearing different-colored V-neck sweaters and gripping bottles of beer, chatted away like old pals, as if they weren't locked in pitched confectionary combat during daylight hours.

The news earlier that week from the Fort kept my head spinning. My Tea Room friends were out of work, and Myles had vanished—although there had been sightings of him. I clung to the puppy-dog hope he wouldn't leave the rock without at least saying goodbye to me. Marquette's chalice was history, both literally and figuratively. Trying to unravel how all these events intertwined—or if they did— was beyond my mental bandwidth.

Desperate for a break from the chaos, I turned to something I understood: baseball.

I took another long pull of Pepsi, muffled a belch, and surveyed the bar like a gruff, old-school regular. Big Jack and Mom were engaged in an excruciatingly dull conversation that ping-ponged between the upholstery on the new model Cutlass and the silk fabric variations on her latest line of evening wear.

Behind me, clusters of conversation hummed with local gossip and adult banter. The air smelled of beer and fried food, punctuated by laughter and stories about property taxes and boat repairs. I was starting to feel like a kid at the grown-ups' table, trying not to spill my drink. Not a crusty local but an out-of-place teenage dope.

Alone.

I turned to my left. A stubbled stranger in a worn yellow T-shirt nursing a margarita stared intensely at the appliance commercial playing on the TV screen behind the bar as if seriously considering a new washer-dryer combo. He looked about thirty-five or so and had telltale raccoon sunburn lines.

Sailors were expected at the Pink Pony, especially during the Chicago- or Port Huron-to-Mackinac sailboat races, when they took over the place. The unspoken challenge of who would steal the porcelain pink pony hanging over the bar's entrance was legendary, proof the "grown men" designation was a myth, but "drunken sailor" wasn't. But this wasn't race week.

Lost as sea, at least socially, I joined the sailor in watching the appliance commercial on TV as if a student of washer-dryer combos.

When George Kell, the Tigers' play-by-play announcer, flashed on screen and read the opening lineup, and as the Tigers took the field, the place vibrated, glasses clinked, and chairs scraped against the wooden floor. Everyone knew this season was different.

"Here we go, boys!" rasped Gramps, voice cutting through the din.

"This is our year!" barked the normally reclusive Rick the shit-sweeper at the end of the bar. Thankfully, he wasn't wearing his usual stinking, green government-issue coveralls, instead sporting a threadbare Tigers jersey. He was considerate like that. At least on game days.

Then something strange happened.

A graphic slid over the screen just as Jack Morris was winding up to throw his first pitch. It said SPECIAL REPORT. The screen cut to a smiling female reporter with huge blonde, teased hair, holding a microphone in front of what looked like Fort Mackinac's blockhouse, only made of rich dark wood instead of whitewashed rock.

"This is Edie Canfield from Channel 4 Action News coming to you from Beaver Island, Michigan, for the event the state has been waiting for—the groundbreaking of Michigan's newest tourist destination," she breathlessly announced.

"What the hell! Switch back to the game!" a voice shouted.

The bartender held up the remote. "This *is* the game!"

The boos from the bar were sudden and deafening. Beaver Island? During a Tigers game? Why in God's name were we stuck watching some dimwitted reporter holding a ridiculous microphone, yammering about Beaver Island?

But Yammer on, she did. "Fort Beaver is the crown jewel of Michigan's most well-known entrepreneur, Trenton Feagler," the reporter continued.

Feagler?

"Feagler, the founder of Corleone's Pizza, is a massive donor to Michigan charities and projects. But his real vision has always been a project he calls Fort Beaver. And tonight, he's breaking ground. We have him right here."

"Fort Beaver?" someone hollered from the back. "Hey, Archie!" called out another voice. "Wasn't that what you called your room at St. Cloud your first summer?" Laughter rippled through the crowd.

"Not funny, Roger!" yelled a guy I could only assume was Archie. "I got my wife Janine with me, ya jagoff!"

Suddenly, Trenton Feagler's face appeared on the screen, exactly where a grim-faced Jack Morris was supposed to be mowing down Red Sox batters.

Feagler spoke. "Fort Beaver has been a vision of mine since I first visited Greenfield Village and Henry Ford Museum as a child. As many of you know, I love history. This is my attempt to create the ultimate historical destination."

"What makes Fort Beaver different?" asked the blonde, her manner manufactured in a lab to be as inoffensive as possible while still appearing human.

"Well, other places in Michigan might be similar. But let's be honest, most are just glorified T-shirt shops," he said. "Just last week, I visited one of the more well-known islands in the area. I won't name names, but let's just say they're more famous for fudge than class."

He paused for effect, then continued. "I saw the most tasteless T-shirt shop imaginable. Really, it was just ... gross. Fake tuxedo prints, shirts with cartoonish female breasts, and slogans about drinking. One even said, 'I'm not as think as you drunk I am.' I thought to myself, what the hell is happening to Mack—" He caught himself, but it was obvious the slip was intentional. "Oops. I'm sorry, I meant to say, what is happening—*in the world these days?*" A big salesy smile.

Across the bar, Large Sarge, the dray driver and former Marine, slumped lower on his barstool and tried to shrink his bulk. His right hand crept up, fingers splayed in a clumsy attempt to mask the neon letters blazing across his

ParTees T-shirt that read, "I'm not as think as you drunk I am."

The realization staggered me like a brick to the skull, and I immediately wished Beth were beside me to share the shock. Feagler was financing ParTees. He was deliberately flooding the island with tacky crap to make his own high-fashion vision gleam by comparison.

Why else would he be so specific about the shirt designs? He was setting Mackinac up to look like a lower-rent Coney Island, dragging our reputation through the muck to elevate his new destination.

The man is a genius.

I reminded myself to tell Beth the next day that her instincts were, as usual, spot on. I'd bet my two-speed kickback hub and toss in my left nut that Trenton Feagler had a financial stake in an obscure company named Tradewinds Products that shipped in T-shirts from China.

He continued. "I guess people know where to go if they're into that sort of … sorry for the language … but *crap*." He continued. "But Fort Beaver is different. We're building state-of-the-art AV experiences, a reconstruction of an authentic Revolutionary era fort, which you can see the bones of behind me, and top-of-the-line restaurants and retail shops."

As Feagler spoke, the screen flashed a slick montage of high-quality renderings: an impossibly glamorous street resembling Rodeo Drive, an expansive fort, and rows of soldiers in pristine colonial uniforms—only in Redcoats instead of the Colonial Army blue we wore at Fort Mackinac.

On my left, the sailor finally spoke up, his Southern drawl thick like molasses.

"Wow. That is immmm-*pressive*."

"Turn this off," called Gramps to the bartender, who

frantically flipped through the channels. But all the major networks were covering the press event. The bartender yelled to the heavens. "He bought out all three networks. *How's that even legal?"*

Big Jack muttered, "22 minutes or less buys a lot of airtime."

The reporter leaned forward. "There are voices out there questioning the authenticity of Fort Beaver. They argue that there's no real colonial history here, no original fort."

"Damn straight!" yelled Rick the shitsweeper at the screen.

"How do you respond to claims that you're merely fabricating a past that never existed?"

Feagler didn't flinch. "Perspective, folks," he began, eyes locking onto the camera like a pro. "Is Main Street USA at Disneyland authentic? How about Greenfield Village? Or Rodeo Drive in Beverly Hills? Technically, no. But that's missing the point."

His expression shifted, an enthusiastic spark igniting as he leaned closer to the camera, in his element. "You see, Fort Beaver isn't just about authenticity. It's not about recreating history. It's about crafting an experience, a feeling. It's about being ... *better than authentic!"*

His last words landed with infectious enthusiasm, a bold statement from a man who had spun pizza into a billion-dollar empire. His usual officious, overzealous suit-wearing vibe had vanished, replaced by the radiant glow of Walt Disney.

He repeated it. "That's it. *It's Better Than Authentic!"*

The sailor's eyes never left the screen. "Good God. That sumbitch can talk."

Even after everything, I wasn't ready for what came next. The camera slowly dissolved, revealing Marquette's chalice. It gleamed under studio lights. Perched on an ornate, rotating stand, the chalice was ridiculously impressive, turning slowly and gracefully on a silver platform. The intricate designs on its surface caught the light, casting mesmerizing patterns that danced across the screen.

I couldn't help but lean forward. The sailor let out a low whistle, and for a moment, the room was silent, all eyes drawn to the hypnotic rotation.

Over the shot, the reporter gushed, "Fort Beaver's crown jewel is Father Marquette's legendary chalice, a rare artifact believed only to be a myth. But myth no more! From 10 to 5 daily, visitors can see the famous cup Father Marquette used for communion. And the best part? Until Fort Beaver officially opens next spring, it's free to visit!"

Across the bar, Gramps stared at the TV and pointed at the chalice. "I swear that thing looks *exactly* like that penny cup at the Wawa bar. Used to be a trophy way back when."

"I was thinking the same thing, dad," said Big Jack.

I bit my tongue so hard it hurt.

"Turn this shit off!" yelled a voice.

The panicked bartender flipped through channels until he landed on MTV. A music video by the band Culture Club was now playing. Boy George pranced through the frame, dressed in a kimono. The crusty, Tigerless crowd sat frozen. They watched Boy George preen and prance, their expressions a mix of confusion and reluctant fascination. Fort Beaver's implications likely loomed, yet they couldn't tear their collective eyes away from the surreal spectacle on the screen.

Finally, Gramps spoke up. "I knew we should've let that rich phony into Wawa." It got a few chuckles but not many.

"Put the Beaver Island thing back on," someone called. "This video is freaking me out."

The TV switched back. Now Feagler was standing with a distinguished-looking group of dignitaries, including Governor Belkin, holding gold shovels. The camera widened, and four soldiers dressed in Redcoat costumes finished a twenty-one-gun salute. I squinted and leaned closer.

It was Derek and the Yale mushroom guides.

Feagler was poaching everything.

"Fire!" The muskets went off.

The fancy people with the shovels broke ground as still cameras flashed away.

"So much for the Sox," the sailor mumbled to himself.

I looked over. "You mean so much for the *Tigers?*"

"More of a Sox man, myself. No idea why. I was born in Mobile, Alabama." I looked closer at his faded yellow T-shirt, which read *Spooky Pete says Marco Island is for Lovers.*

"Hey! I know a guy from Marco Island. Actually, he's not from Marco Island. He's from some other place. Maybe Sarasota? Anyway, he's got a T-shirt just like that. He was wearing it the day I met him."

"No way." The sailor shook his head. "There ain't *no way* he got T-shirt like this. This one is from Spooky Pete's Pub on Marco Island. And let me tell you, it's a *hole … in … the … wall.* I know the owner Spooky Pete Priebe personally, and he sells about four of these goddamn T-shirts a decade."

"I'm telling you. My friend has that exact same shirt."

What's your friend's name?"

"Myles," I said. The sailor froze, then slowly set his drink down on the pink cardboard coaster.

"You tellin' me that Myles Christian Fordham is on Mackinac Island?" His scuffed, pricey sunglasses swung on his neck like a pendulum as he pointed down at the bar. "On this here island?"

"Yeah," I replied, shifting in my seat. "I work with him at the Fort. He's a tour guide."

He seemed to mull this over. After a long pause, he nodded as if he'd come to a conclusion. "I'm gonna pretend I never heard you tell me that," he said.

"How do you know Myles?" I asked.

He took a long sip of his drink, as if buying time. "Not sure it matters, but we sailed together a few times," he finally said, avoiding my gaze.

"Wait! You must be the guy he told me about!" I said. His eyes darkened. "What exactly did he say about me?" he asked, guarded.

"Nothing, really. He said he knew a sailor who told him about Mackinac Island. He mentioned you were a dock-porter a long time ago."

He leaned in, all business. "Here's the deal." He pronounced the word *deal* more like *dill*. "I like Myles. But if I knew he was up here, I might feel obliged to let certain folks down in Sarasota know he was up here. And, see, that might not go so well for our mutual pal Myles." He studied my face. "You gettin' me?"

I wasn't. "He said he was in real estate," I said.

He shook his head slowly, as if he was speaking with a hopeless idiot. "Real estate? That's funny. More like *fake* estate because that shit Myles sells *ain't real.*" He paused, then shook his head, softening. "Listen. Not a man more charming or quicker to lend a hand than Myles when the chips are down. But he's got a tendency to get in over his head, business-wise. Know what I mean?"

"Not really." But deep down, maybe I did. The breezy way he skated past details when pushed, his effortless charm. It was all too—*wait a minute! This was my friend!*

I took a sip of Pepsi, sucking in a few ice cubes and crushing them with my molars. The cold, rumbling crackle was comforting.

"Now, let me be real clear,"he said. "I know absolutely nothin' about the Sarasota dill."

"What's the Sarasota dill?" I asked.

"Deal! And I just told ya, I don't know nothin' about it. No details, anyway. But from what I hear, there are enough old coots—sorry, *retirees*—to field a damn football team that wouldn't mind seeing Myles Fordham hogtied and dipped in a big ol' vat of piss. He owes people a lot of money down there."

He scrutinized me. "What are you, sixteen?"

"Almost seventeen," I said. He looked me over.

"Don't worry, kid. You're probably safe. You ain't got nothing he wants. But remember, things ain't never what they seem with Myles." He signaled to the bartender and tossed twenty bucks his way. "Keep the change," he mouthed, sliding his battered Velcro wallet back into the rear pocket of his sun-faded khaki shorts with a sideways lean.

"Wait," I said, putting my hand on his shoulder. to stop him. "Did Myles ever get his PhD in history? Or teach history? Or I don't know. Anything about … you know … *history?"*

"History?" He broke out in a loud laugh.

"Buddy, that's freakin' precious. I doubt that dude could pick George Washington out of a lineup if he were the only one in it." He paused, reconsidering. "Although he'd definitely recognize Ben Franklin, and I think you know what I mean by *that.*" He rubbed his finger and thumb together in the universal money-money-money motion. "As far as education goes, I know for a fact Myles Fordham is a high school dropout. He let that slip on a wild night in Fort Walton Beach. Can't even remember why we were there, but it sure as shit wasn't to sell Boy Scout cookies."

He stood and put his sunglasses on, even though it was dark out. "Listen, I came here to watch a ballgame, not talk about the good old days." He moved toward the door and called over his shoulder. "Remember, keep one hand on the tiller and the other on your wallet." He patted his left butt cheek where his wallet lived and walked out the door of the Pink Pony.

CHAPTER 31

Searching for Myles

I propped James the bike against an ivy-wrapped fence and cautiously approached Casa Verde, a sprawling Victorian cottage. True to its name, the place was overwhelmingly green. Tonight, the front porch—usually alive with lights and well-heeled revelers—sat empty and quiet.

An hour earlier, the Pink Pony prematurely expelled grumpy patrons onto Main Street, their collective mood soured by the baseball game's interruption. Feagler had bought at least a full hour of programming, stuffing every second with ribbon-cutting ceremonies, gold shovel ground-breaking, and slick interviews in which he gushed about his new attraction.

For Tigers' fans, it was an egregious act.

The enthusiasm for Tiger baseball had evaporated, leaving everyone too sober—and worried—to keep the Pink Pony party going. Not only had our dreams of watching Jack Morris mow down Wade Boggs gone up in flames but we were forced to endure the Pizza King prancing around his maypole, crowing about his Mackinac-crushing attraction on Beaver Island.

As for me, I needed to find Myles.

I was pretty sure I didn't believe a word of what the man from Mobile had said. Too many sailor types who washed up on the island were dubious characters, ashore just long enough to escape the wife and kids for a week or so, drink rum, and hit on college girls.

Myles may have gone rogue during the Private Boone show, vanished for a few days, and then resigned without telling us why, but he was still a solid leader and undeniably the most interesting person I'd ever met. He'd given me my first through third beers and always seemed amused at my odd observations, a worldview that landed somewhere on the spectrum between Kerouac and *Caddyshack. If* I'd inched any closer to the level of confidence it would take to get Trina to hire me, Myles was the reason.

He was a philosopher, a businessman, a history teacher, a real estate seller, and arguably an American Renaissance man. He'd also let it slip that he owned a Viking 44 fishing boat moored on the coal dock. I almost felt foolish considering such half-baked gossip from a half-drunk sailor.

So why was my heart pounding?

I pressed the bell, and after a brief pause, the door creaked open. A graceful woman in her mid-fifties greeted me, her face creased by sleep lines and a hint of annoyance.

"May I help you?" she asked.

"Is Myles here?"

A trace of confusion. "There's never been anyone named Myles staying here. Are you sure you're at the right place?"

"Is this Casa Verde?"

Of course it was Casa Verde. I'd delivered newspapers

to this house a hundred times. The woman glanced at the sign swinging on the porch entrance as if checking for herself. The very same sign I'd just walked under. A sign lit by a small spotlight hidden in the bushes. A sign that read *Casa Verde* in bold, black, old English letters. Recognition dawned as she looked at me more closely.

"Wait. You're little Jack McGuinn, aren't you? Our paperboy from years back."

"Yes, ma'am, that's me, only not so little anymore, *haha*, but yes."

She squinted, baffled. "And you're asking me if this is Casa Verde? I must say, I find that, well, rather odd."

"I'm sorry."

Fantastic. Wait until this nugget got around. I could see the *Island Gazette* headline: "Teenager Harasses West Bluffer in the Middle of the Night (Asking Idiotic Questions)".

"I was looking for a friend. He told me he was renting your guest house this summer, and he … I swear he said Casa Verde."

"Oh no. We stopped renting that apartment five summers ago. Too many college kids making too much racket. It wasn't worth it." Her gaze drifted past me, taking in the line of large houses along the bluff. "Why don't you try some other cottages down the road?" She rubbed the sleep from her eyes, and her graying hair, held together by a barrette, came loose. She pulled it back quickly, not thrilled to be seen in this disheveled state.

"But do remember it's late. Tomorrow may make more sense. Unless there's some sort of trouble. Is there?"

She looked at me and waited for an answer I didn't have.

The Coal Dock was a different universe compared to the island's pristine Yacht Docks, which hosted vessels with names like *Edna's Windfall* or *Eclipse*. Over there, workers in crisp, quasi-military uniforms buzzed around, ensuring everything was immaculate. The restrooms gleamed, the harbormaster's office windows sparkled, and the mooring lines were coiled with precision.

In contrast, the Coal Dock, a place that hadn't seen a lump of coal in ten years, served as a long-term parking lot for the boats of Islanders. It was a place of practical necessity rather than aesthetics. Rusty cleats jutted from weather-beaten planks, and grumpy seagulls fought. I was genuinely surprised Myles had wrangled a spot for his 44-foot fishing boat, *Fishful Thinking,* at the Coal Dock. But then again, this was Myles we were talking about. In one summer, he'd already mastered the island's unspoken rules and hidden pathways. If anyone could make the Coal Dock feel like the Yacht Docks, it was Myles.

Now I just needed to find him.

The dock stood about six feet above the waterline, forcing me to peer down to inspect the small fleet moored to the rotting pilings, shielded by old tires or worn-out boat bumpers. It was dark, but so far, nothing resembled the kind of boat Myles had described. I didn't know much, but I was pretty sure a Viking 44 was forty-four feet long.

Most of these boats were shabby aluminum Lunds or Starcrafts, their decks littered with empty cans and half-hidden beneath decaying tarps. These were the speedboats Islanders used for mainland beer runs, impromptu fishing trips, or quick snorkels in the clear waters off Arch Rock. Junkers. Beaters. As Big Jack would say, "Rode hard and put away wet."

A small Boston Whaler knocked against the last piling, its bow shrouded by a blue tarp. Propped up by a pole, the cover gave the boat an almost pup-tent appearance. Patches of worn gel coat revealed the underlying fiberglass, frayed and mended in spots. The hull's distinctive slap-slap-slap echoed in the growing wind.

From where I stood, the island lights reflected across the harbor like a shimmering Christmas tree. It was the weekend, and the Yacht Dock's slips were packed—a beautiful mess punctuated by random laughs, the creak of hulls, and the clinks of riggings. This was my next target.

Finding *Fishful Thinking* would take time, but sleep wasn't an option tonight. I needed to talk to Myles.

As I walked back to the head of the dock, a sound sliced through the night like a rogue kite on a windy day. I'll never be sure why, but something made me glance back at the Boston Whaler. An unsecured section of the blue tarp thrashed, flapping and dancing like a distress signal. It caught the light from the halogen lamp mounted on a pole.

What happened next was even stranger. I returned to the Whaler and eased myself down onto the dock's edge, legs dangling. I lowered myself onto the deck. The boat rocked but then steadied. I lifted a section of the tarp and peered underneath. Two battered North Face backpacks were propped against the wooden steering console, and a sleeping bag was rolled out on a faded purple yoga mat.

Somehow, I already knew what I was looking at.

It was outrageously illegal, but I leaned down, unsnapped one of the backpacks, and dug inside like a marauding black bear. I spotted a snippet of yellow and knew exactly what it was. Myles's T-shirt. The same *Spooky Pete's says Marco Island is for Lovers* shirt he'd been wearing the day I met him at the Tea Room.

Spooky Pete's.

"He sells about four of these T-shirts a decade," said the sailor from Mobile.

Digging deeper into the pack, I felt rubber. Myles's bright blue rain slicker. I'd seen him wearing it just this week, leaning against the wall of the South Sally Port, smoking, lost in dark thought. A pair of white golf gloves. More clothes I recognized.

I scanned the deck. There was a battery-operated alarm clock, a small propane stove, and maps. Orderly and organized.

There was no Casa Verde apartment or Viking 44 yacht named *Fishful Thinking*. Myles was not the Renaissance man who chose to summer as a Fort guide for a lark to put his history degree from Flagler University to good use. Myles Fordham's home was a worn-out Boston Whaler, moored on the Coal Dock.

Myles slept under a tarp.

"Looking for something special, busboy?" I spun around to see him standing statue-still on the edge of the dock. He'd aged since I last saw him, and that was only a few days ago. I was holding his pack, struck momentarily dumb.

"You better say something fast," he said.

Finally, I found my voice, hoisting the backpack like evidence, assuming my prosecutor role from the *Private Boone* show. "You're a goddamn liar!" The words came out loud but shaky.

"Maybe I am. Maybe I'm not. But you? You're breaking and entering. And that's a fact." With a cat-like leap, Myles landed on the boat, sending it rocking. I staggered to maintain my balance as he snatched the backpack from my hands. His tough-guy persona had been on full display when he effortlessly twisted Shively into a pain pretzel on our first day of guide training. Knowing what he was capable of, I stumbled back a few steps. His jaw was set, eyes blazing, and fists clenched.

One thought screamed: *Who is this guy?*

"I'm not getting off the boat until you answer me!" I yelled.

He softened, shaking his head, and unfastened the ropes securing the tarp to the console one by one. Then he rolled up the tarp and stuffed it into an oversized bait box. He moved around the small craft quickly.

"I met a guy tonight who said he knew you from Florida."

He looked up, eyes narrowing.

"A sailor," I said.

Myles shook his head. "Don't tell me. From Mobile, Alabama?" He adopted a slow Southern drawl. "Talks *reeeaaaal* slow?"

"That's the guy," I said. "He told me there's a bunch of retirees looking to drown you in … wait, what was it? Oh yeah, *a vat of piss.* Ring any bells?"

He slammed the box shut, latched it, and straightened up. "You've got about ten seconds." He dangled a key with a faded rubber Mickey Mouse keychain, Mickey's hands on his hips, winking at me. "You're about to take a one-way trip to Swingin' Iggie."

"Swingin' Iggie" was our shorthand for St. Ignace, the mainland town at the north end of the Mackinac Bridge. He slid the key into the ignition and turned it. The outboard roared to life, sputtering before settling into a steady, throaty hum.

He uncoiled the bowline, then moved to the stern and did the same. "When we pull into the dock on the mainland, this boat slides right onto a trailer." He slapped the console a few times, like patting a favorite horse. "And me? I slide right into the bucket seat of my F-250 with Florida plates. Then the Myles Fordham Show leaves town." The Whaler was now unmoored, bobbing side to side on the increasingly choppy water. He took the helm and stared at me.

"Last chance."

I didn't budge. His old grin made an encore, but it was flushed with irritation.

"Have it your way. Hold on tight." He shoved the throttle. The bow kicked up, throwing me off balance, and I slipped across the deck. Myles powered out of the harbor with the reckless energy of a teenage thief stealing his first car. A wave smacked the boat, and I lost my footing, crashing onto the deck. A spray of cold lake water soaked me. I had to hand it to Myles: He knew how to call a bluff.

"What are you going to do to me?" I yelled over the roar as I struggled back to my feet.

Myles yelled back. "Do to you? I'm a professional bull-shitter, not Jack the Ripper. I'm gonna dump you in Iggy, like I said. Let you sleep on a bench. Freeze your scrawny ass off. Learn how the other half lives."

The Whaler roared around the break wall, banking sharply past the Round Island Passage Lighthouse and straight for St. Ignace. I grabbed onto the seat of the Whaler.

"Did you even go to college?"

"Strange timing for that question! Who the hell cares?"

He was right. But if I could understand one lie, other lies might make sense. His narrow eyes focused on the dark horizon split by the twinkling the Mackinac Bridge.

"I'm a third-generation janitor from St. Augustine. The closest I got to higher education was mopping the men's room at Flagler College. Or at least I was until I escaped to Marco Island to—as they say—reinvent myself. So no, I didn't go to college." He looked at me and smiled, the wind whipping his hair across his face. "Is any of this sinking in?"

"Why did you pick Mackinac Island?"

"Jesus! The questions! I came here because …" He trailed off, lost in thought, then regained his momentum. "Because I heard about it. I needed to hide. It's about that complicated. I was able to land a gig bullshitting people, which I think we can agree is something I excel at. Met an ambitious busboy. A fat comedy writer. A tortured PhD. Busted into an antechamber. Learned some history. Found a chalice. Did some golfing. Truth is, it's been the best summer of my life." He smiled through clenched teeth. "Until right about now."

Slap! Another stab of water washed over the deck.

The island blurred past on our right, a streak of dark land against the shimmering water. From this distance, Casa Verde on the West Bluff was just visible, a distant speck of light. An hour ago, I was standing on its porch, but it felt like another lifetime.

"You whine like a newborn when you get mustard on your pirate shirt. But it wasn't like that for me," he snapped. "Yes, there are people after me, so let's cut the bullshit."

I looked toward the expanse of the Mackinac Bridge. I was amazed by its beauty for the thousandth time in my life, but no answer blinked back in Morse code from its twinkling lights.

Myles called over, eyes fixed on distant St. Ignace. "There's something else you might as well know." The Whaler banked hard, and the engine revved. It was too loud to hear him, so I scrambled closer. "That chalice!" Water streamed down his face.

"What?"

"The chalice!"

"What about it?"

"I sold it to Feagler!" he yelled, his voice piercing

through the engine's roar as the boat crashed over another sharp wave.

Myles shot me a grim smile.

"What do you know! Finally got you speechless."

He continued, "After you stumbled out of the Wawa bar, I called a sharp, attractive woman I'd met at the Pony a few weeks back. She worked for Pizza King in business development, or so she said. Slipped me her card—and a few other things." Myles's eyes glazed over momentarily. "Let's just say she revealed some island hiding spots that aren't exactly in the guidebook." He chuckled softly and shook his head in amazement. I was certain I didn't want to know whatever salacious rerun was playing behind his blue eyes.

He snapped back to the grim, wet present moment. "Fifty grand later, Feagler had his magic penny cup, and I was one step closer to cleaning up the Sarasota Shitshow."

My brain short-circuited as I tried to process this information. Finally, I blurted out, "How do you sell something you don't even own?"

"They paid for the knowledge, not the hardware," he shouted over the boat's roar. "I knew where it was. I knew the fine folks at Wawa didn't know what they had. And I knew he'd pay."

"That chalice belongs on Mackinac Island!"

"I agree!" he snapped back, surprising me. "And two months ago, I wouldn't have given three squirts of piss about *Mackinac Island.* I couldn't even pronounce it. It was just another small town, ripe for the picking. But now? I'm not ashamed to say I'm ashamed."

He turned to me, lake spray dripping down his face, eyes intense. "But I did it. It's done. And now I'm leaving."

My knees buckled, but I steadied myself. A flashback of

his brooding performance at the Private Boone reenactment.

Call me a thief because that's exactly what I am.

A confession.

He inched the throttle forward. The motor screamed and we were skipping across the chop, racing faster toward the shore of St. Ignace. Myles stayed silent, eyes fixed on the approaching coast.

"I thought we were friends!" My words were lost in the roar of the engine and the crashing waves, but I saw a flicker of something—regret, maybe—in his eyes. Or was it just the glint of lake water?

He was easing the throttle forward. Faster.

Looking back, I'm about 95% certain that he wasn't planning on ramming the Whaler full-speed into the St. Ignace shoreline like some suicidal maniac, but at the time, I'd put the odds closer to fifty-fifty.

As the shore approached, the spray stung my face, and the wind cut through my clothes, but all I could think about was making it all stop. So I did something monumentally stupid. I reached out and wrenched the steering wheel hard to the left. Why? I dunno. Snap him out of his trance? Something along those lines.

It didn't quite work out that way.

"What the hell are you—"

The boat reeled violently, and a cresting wave knocked it sideways. Myles flopped like a stringless puppet, stumbling back a few steps. He tripped over the tackle box, his arms flailing.

And then he was gone.

The Whaler continued its wild, unmanned spiral, dipping down in a trough and accelerating on its own. I lunged toward the console, grappling for the throttle, my fingers slipping off repeatedly.

Finally, I got my feet underneath me and found the throttle. Pulling it back, I hit the kill switch, shutting down the engine. Rhythmic waves pounded against the boat's fiberglass hull.

Slap-slap-slap.

"Myles!" I screamed, racing to the Whaler's stern. Over the roar of the waves, I could barely hear his desperate thrashing and gasps for air in the choppy water. I scrambled for the flashlight I had seen in his backpack and flicked it on. The beam sliced through the darkness, and I could see him. Myles was drowning.

I snatched the wooden paddle from the gunnel. Each stroke was a battle against the current, the water seeming to thicken with every passing second. I inched toward Myles, but the lake tugged the boat sideways. My arms burned, muscles screaming as I fought the relentless current. It felt like trying to paddle through molasses.

Finally, I reached him, grabbed his jean jacket, and yanked. My muscles burned, but inch by inch, I managed to drag his limp form up and over the side. He flopped onto the deck, his chest hitching unevenly and his face alarmingly pale, even in the dim light.

"Come on, Myles!" I pounded on his chest and screamed, my voice raw with panic. "Come on, you stupid lying fucking snake!" My voice cracked with desperation. "You can die in Sarasota in a vat of old man piss, *but not here!*"

I pinched his nose, my mind racing to recall the least favorite lesson from my lifeguard class at the Chippewa Hotel pool two summers earlier. As I bent down, inches away from his lips, Myles convulsed. A torrent of lake water spewed from his half-open mouth and straight into my face.

I swear I tasted a hint of beer mingled with Lake Huron.

Disgusting.

Yet somehow, in that moment, it tasted sweet.

He twitched and gasped for air, clawing at his neck, and then sat up straight like a man shot in the heart with a needle of pure adrenaline. Choking out a few more breaths, he spat the remaining water onto the deck and fixed me with a baleful stare. I stared at him warily. We were in uncharted territory now.

Was he going to attack me or hug me?

His voice was a husky choke. "I can die in SARASO-TA!?" Then: "In a VAT OF PISS!?"

I stared at him hard. The only response I could muster was this: "*Fishful THINKING!?*"

That was it. We stared at each other, two exhausted, gasping rats, fresh out of interesting insults.

It started with him.

The chuckle grew louder and soon turned hysterical. It was insanity. Our situation, floating in the Straits. The fact that Myles was a con man. That I almost killed him. That I saved him. That he stole Marquette's chalice. We sat together in the slap-slap-slapping Whaler, drenched, and just coughed and laughed, laughed and coughed.

Myles finally released a final, heavy sigh, shook his head, and pulled himself up. He restarted the engine. I watched him navigate, still sitting in the stern of the boat, cross-legged, too worn out to stand. The Whaler spun around and accelerated.

"What are we doing now?" I shouted over the roar of the engine.

"We're going back," Myles yelled back. "You're gonna be a *great* dockporter."

I couldn't suppress a smile. I liked the way it sounded, and I wanted to hear more.

"Why did you say that?"

"Because you're very persuasive when you want to be. It'll serve you well on the docks." He leaned into a wave.

"Seriously, Myles, why are we going back?" I scrambled to my feet and joined him at the wheel. "I thought you were leaving!"

His champion's grin reappeared beneath a wet mop of hair that whipped in the gale like a bullet-ridden battle flag.

Slap-slap-slap!

"Why?" I yelled.

He willed the boat to jump a swelling wave by jamming the throttle forward and leaning back, putting all his body language into the maneuver. The boat leaped, the outboard screamed, and so did he.

Finally, he responded: "I CHANGED MY MIND!"

CHAPTER 32

The Plan

Beth let us use Wild Style before she opened in the morning. It was perfect for meeting privately, away from prying Island eyes. The night before, Myles and I, still drenched and battered from our near-death boat trip to St. Ignace, had agreed to meet up with Shively and Rollie to hatch a plan to recover the chalice. Despite discovering how shady, cunning, and immoral my former mentor was, I liked him even more. It says a lot about me, none of it good.

All I knew for sure was that Myles had turned the boat around and returned us to the Island. For some naive reason, I believed he was here to stay.

As I nudged the Wild Style door open, the door chimes jingled, and then the sharp hiss of a steam iron swallowed up the sound.

I halted. Myles stood behind the iron, working through a stack of T-shirts. Steam billowed around him, catching the orange morning light and giving him the mysterious aura of a '70s Rock God, live in concert.

He'd decided to play early bird for our meeting and

was chatting away with Beth, who sat smiling, legs crossed, atop the counter. Myles was deep into a rousing story about rappelling down El Capitan—which I assumed was some mountain cliff—when he discovered his shorts had fallen off, leaving him in only a jockstrap. Beth's customary skeptical gaze melted like butter on a skillet, and she threw her head back and laughed uproariously while he grabbed a fresh shirt from the pile.

Knowing Myles, I doubted the El Capitan yarn was true. I waited for him to finish. Finally, I cleared my throat with a theatrical "Ahem! Beth's smile vanished, replaced with big-sister annoyance at being interrupted.

"Oh. Hi. I met your friend Myles."

Myles stood up straight and saluted. "Officer present!" He slammed the press down again, the steam bathing him in another rock and roll cloud. Beth shot me a look of casual lust and mouthed: *your friend is hot!*

Perfect.

Beth, seasoned by twenty-one wild summers on the island, was as close to bullshit-proof as anyone on Earth. Yet, here she was, drinking in tales from this mustache-sporting stranger who'd wandered in off the street and commandeered her steam press.

Clearly, we were related by blood.

"Heads up," I said, pointing at Myles. "He's a border-line criminal. I won't bore you with the details, but he's on the run from a rabid pack of old coots—sorry, I mean *retirees* … from … where is it again, Myles? Naples?"

Myles glanced up, smiling through the steam. "Sarasota."

"Sarasota," I echoed. "Right."

Beth retreated a few steps, her eyes narrowing as she scanned Myles with renewed intrigue. "Really?"

"True story," I said. I was secretly thrilled to have

Myles back in my life but damned if I'd cover for his sins, least of all with my own sister.

The news of his questionable backstory didn't faze Beth. It had the opposite effect. She was positively glowing.

"Wait. You're an actual *outlaw?*"

Myles shrugged and held up his wrists like he was handcuffed. It was the identical gesture he'd used in the guide shack after he sabotaged the Private Boone reenactment. "Guilty as charged."

Beth's gaze flicked between Myles and me. "Now I *really* like him!"

She opened her mouth to continue, but the door jingle cut her off. Shively charged in, head down, loaded with two bulging backpacks and a stack of notebooks. His hair floated in disheveled tufts. Without ceremony, he heaved his cargo onto the Wild Style counter, causing a cloud of dust to rise and a few of Beth's Bic Banana ballpoint pens to roll to the floor.

Shively scanned the room, his eyes widening slightly as they landed on Myles. He pointed, words starting and stopping, before finally completing a coherent sentence. "Hi, Myles. Where have you been? I thought you—wait, are you working here now?"

Myles laughed. "Nope, just here for the clandestine meeting. Figured I'd contribute some labor to the McGuinn family business empire while I'm at it," he replied, gesturing toward the pile of T-shirts. "You know, I owned a T-shirt shop in Fort Lauderdale for about twelve minutes in the old days, so working the big press is like a trip down memory lane."

"Bullshit. He's hitting on Beth," I said.

"Now, now," said Myles. "Mind your language around the lady."

"She's not a lady. She's my sister."

Beth studied Shively. "You look like you've been up all night," she said, gesturing to his stained, wrinkled Oxford and wild Doc Brown hair.

"Not night. *Nights*," Shively answered, fishing a weathered journal from his bag. "I finally finished Armand Duval's journal. It's in French, so it took forever. It's mind-blowing! I was right!"

Myles flicked off the steam press switch and walked around the counter.

Shively's face shone like a convert at a revival. "Luther Shively was innocent." He carefully cracked open the journal and spoke first to Beth, getting her up to speed. "So, the backstory is, Armand Duval, the journal's author, met Luther Shively—my great-great-great-great-grandfather—when they were both teenagers."

Beth leaned in. "Wait. First. How did you even get this journal?" Shively glanced at me for approval. I nodded. *Family*.

"We stole it," he said.

"Thought so," said Beth. "Jack attracts crime. He's been that way since he was eleven. Go on."

He began pacing like a caged animal. "Armand Duval was French, but his father was an advisor to John Paul Jones during the Revolutionary War, and he was keen on having his son serve with the U.S. Army. Duval and Luther struck up a friendship at Fort Detroit while training. It's all in the journal."

"Slow down, One-Shot. You're giving us whiplash," Myles said as he watched Shively pace.

Shively stopped, took a deep breath, and resumed pacing, now slightly more self-conscious. "But as Luther climbed the ranks, Duval was sidelined. He loved Luther and saw him as a brother but lived in his shadow. Resentment was building. What he really wanted was to be a poet."

"Oh, God," Beth said, rolling her eyes. "Frustrated artist syndrome. They. Are. The. Worst."

"A frustrated French artist," Myles added. "What could possibly go wrong?"

Shively nodded. "It's 1809, and Luther Shively is assigned command of Fort Mackinac. He insists that Duval be his right-hand man, his aide-de-camp. During an inspection of the storage cellar under the soldiers' barracks, Luther discovers an old, neglected locker. Any guesses what's in it?" Shively paused, eyes twinkling with excitement as he looked at me and Myles.

"A penny cup?" I said.

"Correct."

Beth shook her head, baffled. "A penny cup?"

"Marquette's chalice!" I whispered, as if the walls might have ears.

"No shit!" Beth said, eyes wide. She scooted forward on the counter to get closer. "Okay, boys, you got me. I'm totally hooked."

Shively continued. "Even then, the chalice was only whispered about as a myth. Nobody really believed it was on the island. But Luther did some research and confirmed it was the real thing." His eyes danced. "But when he told his pal, trouble started. Duval felt the chalice belonged in France."

Myles nodded. "Makes sense. Marquette was French."

"Exactly. But Luther disagreed. In France, he said, Marquette was just another vessel of the King, using his black robe and crucifix to grab land. But he did his best work here in America. And specifically in northern Michigan. Much of it right here on the Island—spreading the word of

God. He was a bridge between worlds, blending cultures with humility and intelligence." Shively paused. "Luther knew his history and felt the chalice belonged on the island."

"Plus, there's another little-known bylaw," Myles said. His eyes twinkled. "It's called 'finders keepers.'"

Shively nodded. "There's also that." He continued, "They fought about it for months, even coming to blows at one point. But Luther never wrote him up for insubordination." Shively picked up the journal, his fingers tracing the worn edges. "Duval writes that even *he* was amazed at his friend's loyalty."

"Brothers," I murmured, my mind flashing to Gordon. In the good old days, he would have been right here with us, attending precisely this type of clandestine meeting. Old bonds fade.

"Flash forward again. In 1812, as the British landed and took the high ground, aiming a cannon down on Fort Mackinac, Luther ordered Duval to prepare for battle. He knew that day was coming and was ready with a rock-solid plan." Shively held up the journal. "It's all written right here!" he almost shouted, his voice croaking. "Luther was ready!"

I sensed where it was heading. "Let me take a wild guess: Duval dragged his poetic little heels? Didn't give the order."

"Worse. Duval attacked Luther, beat him unconscious, tied him up, and dragged him to the Fort's brig. Then he surrendered the Fort to the British without fighting, claiming it was on Luther's orders!"

"So it should've been more like One-Shot Duval," I said.

Shively nodded. "Luther broke out of the brig, but it was too late. The Union Jack was flying, and the Brits arrested him as a prisoner of war."

"Rough day at the office," Myles said.

"Rough day?" Shively exploded. "It was a tragic miscarriage of justice!"

"That's what I meant to say," said Myles.

Beth interjected, "Wait. Why didn't Luther speak up?"

"He was in jail," Shively said, shaking his head. "They hauled him off as a POW to Fort Detroit, also in British hands. He died later that year during an American attack on the prison."

Myles winced. "They should've called him 'Shit-Luck Shively.'"

Shively's arms flailed. "Enough with the stupid nicknames! That ends today!"

Myles raised his hands in surrender. "Easy, Shives. I got it."

"So what happened to the chalice?" Beth asked, steering the conversation back on track.

"That's where it gets really interesting." Shively continued. "In the craziness of the attack, Duval tossed it in a box, thinking he might be captured, and buried the box just north of the Fort. He planned to return for it when the fighting calmed down," Shively replied. "But he was taken prisoner. So during three months as a POW at the Fort, he wrote the coordinates in his journal. In code."

"Let me guess." Myles touched the side of his nose like a wise Santa. "Disguised in the lines of a poem. With a few helpful sketches."

Shively pulled out my photos of the poem. "Both the journal and the poem were eventually confiscated by the British, never read, and tossed in storage." He paused. "In the North Keep."

"Until we came along," I said.

Shively flipped through the journal. "After that, Duval vanished. No record where they sent him. But his last written entry is filled with remorse, praying for forgiveness for betraying the only friend he ever had."

"Your   great-great-great-great-grandpop,"   finished Myles.

"This," Shively held up the journal, "is Duval's confession."

We fell silent, a minor miracle considering the sheer mass of smart-asses and know-it-alls jammed into Wild Style.

A carriage clip-clopped past the window like a moving still-life. A few bikes crisscrossed the frame—morning workers with tool belts. Shively slowly closed the journal like a priest after a particularly moving sermon and slipped it back into his pack. We watched him curiously. I don't know if anyone else noticed, but to me he looked transformed. Maybe it was how the morning light streaming through the window lit the side of his face, contouring it. He was no longer an agitated, tortured, scholarly apparition. He was exhausted but oddly calm. In this light, he was almost handsome.

Relief.

Was it the lighting?

When I later became a professional photographer, I learned terms like *relief*—the perception of depth, and dimension. I didn't know all that art school jargon then, but it was the perfect word at that moment in time.

Different interpretations. Same word.

Relief.

Shively looked ...

... *relieved.*

Five minutes later, the door to Wild Style burst open with a resounding jangle. This time it was Rollie barreling in, wearing a BEER GOGGLES T-shirt from ParTees and leading a human shape swaddled from head to toe in a red Hudson Bay blanket.

"Everyone hit the deck!" Rollie's eyes darted around like a cornered fox. Nobody did. Instead we exchanged glances as he nervously peeked out the window, scanning Main Street through the glass. After a minute of hitched breathing and frantic glances, he exhaled.

"Alright, we did it. The coast is clear," Rollie said. "Those Secret Service goons tailed us for almost an hour!" He relaxed, shaking his head. "Had to use three carriages and a dray." Rollie looked at me. "Your boy Smitty hid us under a stack of mattresses heading to Stonecliffe. What a great guy."

A voice emerged from the blanketed figure. "Excuse me, Roland, but those 'goons' protect my father from harm, and they're perfectly nice people!" The voice was unmistakably female.

Rollie unwrapped the blanket, unveiling a breathless, long-haired brunette. Her tousled, static-infused hair framed a face that mixed confidence with a hint of blinking bewilderment. She took in the surroundings as she pushed librarian glasses up her sunburned nose.

"Oh, I love this place!"

Beth instantly beamed. I recognized the girl but couldn't place her. She continued her wide-eyed inspection of Wild Style with an open smile. "Roland, you need to swap that horrible shirt out for one of these."

Rollie looked down at his shirt. "I toldja baby. I'm wearing this ironically. That makes it okay."

"No. Actually, it doesn't." Then she turned to us as if

she'd just noticed she had company. "Oh, hi," she said with a cute little wave. I'm Cassie Belkin."

Rollie put a protective arm around her shoulder. "She's the First Daughter of the Great Lake State. And if her old man wins next November, she'll be a lot more than that."

"To which I say, gag me with a spoon," she said with a smile.

"Yuck," said Rollie. "Anyway, we've been seeing a bit of each other."

"Aw, Roland." Cassie patted his ample gut affectionately. "Don't undersell it. We've been seeing a lot of each other."

Rollie flushed red and turned to us. "Cassie's been keeping tabs on her dad for us. I told her everything. She knows all about the Feagler situation." He gave her the floor with a sweeping gesture. "Tell 'em, babe."

Cassie hesitated for just a moment, her eyes scanning us. Then in a flash, her expression shifted from a sweet smile to that of a steely-eyed football coach on the eve of the Rose Bowl. I blinked, caught off guard by the sudden change.

"I'll cut to the chase. Dear old Dad is caught in Feagler's web. Politics is all about money. Feagler is rolling in dough."

Rollie nodded along. "Get it? Dough? She isn't just smart; she's funny."

She waved off Rollie's joke. "Not now, Roland. I've got the floor." Cassie paced, her gaze locking onto each of us in turn. Then she softened, and a trace of the sweet smile returned. "I love my dad." She picked up a T-shirt off the rack with a funny design and chuckled. "This one's great." Then she was back to business. "Anyway, he bought me a pony when I was six. I had a Buick Regal at sixteen, and I'm pretty sure he pulled some strings at Iowa to get me into the MBA program. The man loves me. He also loves my dumbass brother and my mom. He's a very decent man. But let's not kid ourselves. He's neck-deep in the political swamp. He's running for President. He has no idea what he's got himself into."

Cassie's expression hardened. "Feagler pumped a ton of cash into Dad's campaign. But we all know nothing's free. So, when Feagler decided Marquette's chalice should be the centerpiece of his dopey new Disneyland, Dad jumped right on board." She paused mid-sentence, her attention snagged by another shirt on display. "Oh, look at this one! YOU'RE ALL NUTS. Love that!" She grabbed it, and then refocused. "Dad shut off the money to Fort Mackinac and funneled it to Fort Beaver."

She found another shirt on a rack and held it up to us by the hanger, gesturing to the saying: IT'S ALL PRETTY STRAIGHTFORWARD.

"So," she continued, "I did some digging. I talked with my dad's State Historic Preservation Officer. They're on a softball team together. I know. Softball. Lame."

"I love softball," said Rollie.

"You shouldn't. It's lame." She touched his cheek sweetly. "And please don't interrupt me again, Roland. But the good news? There's a loophole."

"There usually is," added Myles.

"You would know," I said, grinning at Myles. He feigned being shot with an arrow in the heart.

Cassie continued. "The chalice was dug up on State Park land."

"Dug up … at a bar," I added.

"Details. Right now, what matters is they've got it," Cassie said, her voice growing sharper. "It's all about possession—nine-tenths of the law and all that. By the time anyone could legally untangle this mess, Fort Beaver could be too popular to challenge. Feagler's smart. He's playing the long game. But here's the thing—if you can get the chalice back to Mackinac Island now, you change the game."

"Wow," said Beth, leaning on the counter, watching Cassie with a mix of intrigue and respect. "Like father, like daughter."

Cassie's boss-lady act dropped momentarily, and she grinned like a little girl before pivoting back to take-charge mode. "Now, here's the play. You can't just sit around. You need to act fast," she said. "You're 'reclaiming Mackinac's history.' It's a *legacy*. It's *history*. It needs to be in its rightful place, blah, blah, blah. You know, all that stuff newscasters love. Anyway. And trust me, my dad is no fool. He's got his finger on the pulse of public opinion. He likes money, but what he *needs* is votes. If that chalice somehow makes its way back to Fort Mackinac, he'll support it." She mimicked turning a tap on a faucet. "He'll turn the funding back on so fast it'll make your head spin. All will be well. Flowers will bloom, the lame will walk, and the blind will see."

"Is there a legal option?" asked Shively.

"There's always a legal option," she said. "But it could take years."

"What do you think we should do?" I asked. It was really the only question that mattered.

"Well, if I wasn't the Governor's daughter, I'd steal it." We all stared at her, trying to figure out if there was a punchline. She gave an adorable shrug. "You asked."

The room fell silent. Myles finally stretched his arms to the sky, groaning like a bear, and then stood up. "Time to gas up the Whaler, boys. Looks like we're going to Beaver Island. Wear your costumes and leave the muskets. It's not worth getting shot over."

He walked toward the door. "By the way, I'm the one who sold the chalice to Feagler." He pushed the door open with a jangle. "We leave in thirty minutes from the Coal Dock."

And with that, he was gone. After a beat of silence, Cassie held up the two shirts to Beth.

"Do these come in bulk?"

"For you they do."

"Aw, thanks doll. I'll take a case of each."

CHAPTER 33

Armada of One

Aside from the occasional slap of sea spray, Shively, Rollie, and I sat motionless, engulfed in the din of the motor and waves, holding our tricorn hats in our hands to keep them from blowing away. Myles had just wrapped up the story of how he brokered the shady chalice deal and netted a cool $50,000. The ride had gotten awkwardly silent.

Myles, clad in his colonial soldier get-up, cut a weirdly heroic figure against Lake Huron's deep blues and grays, especially considering he was piloting a beat-up Boston Whaler, its hull marred with Rocky Balboa-caliber scars from years of overuse. His unbuttoned blue coat fluttering in the wind made him look more like the captain of a wooden warship heading into battle against the British than a ragged reprobate pushing a floating flophouse to the screaming outer limits of its motor's capabilities.

We passed under the massive concrete-and-steel expanse of the Mackinac Bridge, crossing the phantom threshold from Lake Huron to Lake Michigan. The colossal structure loomed over our tiny boat, reminding us we were as disposable as an old wine cork.

"Will somebody just speak?" Myles finally shouted over the loud slams of lake waves against the hull. We exchanged looks, each unsure who should break the silence. Myles's story was a lot to process. Soaked from spray and already chilled by the lake-effect wind, none of us were eager to start the interrogation.

"Was the whole thing a setup?" Rollie asked. "The break-in at the antechamber?"

"And were you using us all along to get your hands on it?" continued Shively.

Myles stared ahead, his gaze fixed on the churning waters as he weighed his response. "Yep to both," he finally said, his voice barely audible.

"What did you say?" Rollie called out, struggling to hear over a loud gust.

Myles shouted back, "I said yep to both! I was looking for a way out of a crappy situation. I knew a billionaire was sniffing around the island, and the antechamber sounded promising. Did I know we'd find something valuable? Hell no! But I dig holes for a living. As it turned out, luck was on our side."

"You mean luck was on *your* side," I yelled over the wind, pointing at him.

"Don't sweat the semantics," Myles replied, giving me a dismissive look that made me feel small.

"Still don't get it, guys? It's what people like me do. We use. We lie. Essentially, at our core, we suck." This was the moment I truly recognized just how talented Myles was because suddenly, I had the urge to comfort him. To defend him. It was ridiculous! Defend him from what? We didn't snake the chalice. He did! We didn't lie to friends.

We weren't on the run from rabid old coots from Sarasota. He was!

"Okay, he continued. "You guys want some history? I got some. And it's all true." He continued to shout as the boat's hull battered the waves. "At eighteen, I was on a fast track to being the third alcoholic janitor in the Fordham family line. Other than my all-league status as a class-C high school quarterback, mopping up piss was all I had to talk about. That's before I dropped out my senior year to join the family business: Washout Janitorial and Son. And yes, that's a joke."

He turned to Shively. "How's that for a family legacy, One-Shot? At least your great-great-great-great grandfather carried a musket. Mine carried a goddamn mop."

"That's a sad tale, Myles," Shively shot back. "But genetics doesn't give you a pass to lie and steal."

Myles considered that and shook his head. "Well, I did both anyway. And I was minutes away from leaving this quaint little chunk of limestone forever. He held his thumb and forefinger close together. "I was this close to escaping with my lack of morals intact." He pointed at me. "But last night, some teenage stowaway guilted me into submission, drowned me, saved me, and now?" He gestured to himself with amazement.

Rollie and Shively turned to me like baffled Labradors. Rollie leaned in, eyes wide. "You drowned him?" he whispered.

"Not exactly," I whispered back. "Well, sort of. It's a long story."

Myles continued. "Against every instinct in my lying, rotted, termite-infested soul, I'm heading to Beaver Island, of all places … with you freaks! Acknowledging all my wicked ways. Leading yet another idiotic adventure full of

bad choices, no plan, and a fifty-fifty chance of imprison-
ment!" He shook his head. "I really am nuts!"

"How do we know this little speech isn't just another
one of your scams?" Rollie asked. "That this next heist
isn't just another angle you're playing?"

"You don't!" He aimed his finger at Rollie. "But that's
what makes it all so goddamn exciting. Admit it. You're
vibrating right now!"

He was right. I was most certainly vibrating. And I'd
bet a week's pay, so were Shively and Rollie.

"I mean, look at us. We're storming the beaches of
Beaver Island to steal back Marquette's chalice. Marquette!
The coolest Frenchie since Joan of Arc! And look at what
we're wearing!"

"Dammit!" He slammed his fist on the console. "I
WISH IT WAS A SCAM! Unfortunately for me, you
weirdos made me care about this island, which, frankly, is a
liability in my profession. But even if it were a scam, deep
down, it wouldn't change a thing. I've got a sneaky suspi-
cion you three would still be right here with me."

He gestured broadly to the expanse of Lake Michigan,
the horizon stretching endlessly, a perfect line where sky
met water. The revving of the Mercury 65 outboard filled
the air. He turned to us, and to this day, I remember the
mad gleam in his eye. "Because this, my misfit musketeers,
is living!"

Unconsciously, we all followed his hand to the ever-
approaching horizon. Forty miles away was Beaver Island
and whatever insanity awaited us at Feagler's fake fort. For
the one-hundredth time during that strange summer of
1984, we all knew, deep down, that Myles was right.

This. Was. Living.

CHAPTER 34

Whiskey Point

The Whaler's hull skidded onto the sand at Beaver Island's Whiskey Point, a gritty hiss followed by a crunch against the shoreline's driftwood-and-rock stew. Our invasion wasn't exactly D-Day in scope, and we had the advantage of not being shot at by Nazis hidden in bunkers when we hit the beach.

We hopped out and yanked the boat ashore, securing it with a rope around a leaning cedar on a sandy ridge. Thankfully Whiskey Point was deserted. In our Colonial Army costumes, we must have made for an odd sight piling off the boat. I recalled my many wind sprints from the Tea Room back to Wildcliffe in my food-streaked pirate shirt and knickers just weeks ago to avoid this kind of humiliation.

Was that really just weeks ago? I'd lived a lifetime since that day in Dr. Trumbull's office in June, lying to his face and scoring the weirdest, most interesting job I'd ever had. And now I was standing on a beach on Beaver Island dressed in a Colonial Army uniform.

Whiskey Point was a far cry from the bustling, cottage-dotted shore of Mackinac, where yachts bobbed, hulls gleaming like new tennis shoes in a mall store window. Beaver Island was untamed and wild, the sandy stretch dotted with sharp rocks and twisted, bleached driftwood that looked like gnarled, arthritic hands. A gust of wind, smelling faintly of fish guts, swept through the trees. The only other sound was the rhythmic diesel engine of a distant departing car ferry on the horizon. We stood like tin soldiers taking in the view.

"You fellas looking for the fort?" The voice was gruff, a little amused, cutting through a cacophony of squawking gulls. In unison, we swiveled to see an old man lounging on a straining lawn chair, the once-bright colors faded to a dull, weather-beaten stew.

Turned out Whiskey Point wasn't deserted.

Next to him sat a mini-cooler that looked like it had been hauling beer since Prohibition. He wore a fishing hat, oversized polarized sunglasses, and a yellow, plaid short-sleeved shirt. His slack-lined fishing pole was jammed in the sand, neglected.

"You got yer coordinates wrong if yer plannin' some sorta half-assed invasion. The new fort's six miles from here. And it's not fully built yet. More like a ..." He paused, tilting his head and shielding his eyes with one hand, searching for the word just beyond the horizon.

"A stockade?" volunteered Shively.

"A stockade! That's it. Whatta you, some sorta historian?"

"Actually, I am," said Shively, eager to elaborate on his colossally boring skill set. Thankfully, the fisherman wasn't interested and barreled ahead with his own story.

The old man's face contorted, he sneezed twice, sucked in snot, then spit it out.

"Sorry, my hay fever's actin' up. Anyhow, where was I?

Oh yeah. They ain't startin' construction on Fort Feagler in earnest 'til fall. That's what they're calling it in town. *Fort Feagler.* But the official name is Fort Beaver, which is even dumber, if you ask me—which nobody ever does. Fort Beaver sounds like some sorta frontier strip bar, not a tourist draw."

I glanced at the clearing sky, where the sun was beginning to blaze through the clouds. "Six miles" was all I heard. The heat was rising, and the prospect of trudging six miles through one of Feagler's pizza ovens, clad in a wool coat, narrow costume boots, and tricorn hat, was far from appealing.

"Can you point us in the right direction?" I asked.

The old fisherman grunted and stood. I could hear his knees cracking from ten feet away as he eased to a standing position. Empty beer cans rattled in the cooler as he folded his chair.

"I'll do one better. Consider it my good deed for a bad day of fishing, seeing as all I caught was a piss-poor beer buzz. I'll walk ya. Might as well head back to the shack for a spam and egg sandwich. The old battle-axe probably wonders if I've gotten myself lost again." He winked, grimaced in pain, revealing a chipped tooth, and gathered his fishing pole. "C'mon, let's get her movin'.""

The four of us shared worried glances. This was not a mission that needed extra company, especially not a chatty old fisherman six beers deep. "There's no need for that, sir," Shively interjected. "We can figure it … umm …" The protest halted as the man pulled down his polarized sunglasses and froze Shively solid in an icy blue tractor beam.

His lips tightened before he spoke. "Said I'd walk ya."

"Boys, let's help our local guide with his gear," Myles interjected, his eyes sharp and assessing. Rollie jammed the lawn chair between the straps of his backpack. It stuck out at odd angles, but it held.

"Lemme get that for ya," continued Myles, relieving the fisherman of his cooler and handing me the fishing pole to carry. He knew instinctively what the rest of us were too slow to grasp. The fisherman was not a human being. He was a dog. Specifically, a guard dog. He'd probably been planted on this patch of Whiskey Point for decades, squinting eyes guarding his slice of island paradise against any strange invasions from the soft underbelly.

Then we pulled up.

He jerked his head toward an overgrown two-track vanishing into the woods. "It's that way." We all began to walk. "By the way, name's Danny O'Dell. My people been on this island since the potato famine, whenever the hell that was."

"It was approximately between 1845 and 1852," said Shively.

O'Dell nodded and grunted, profoundly disinterested. We walked about 50 more yards, and then he stopped abruptly. We all stumbled to a stop with him, colliding like dominoes. He turned and gave us a long, calculating look, his eyes narrowing. "You know. It's just kinda now occurrin' to me. Somethin' weird about this whole situation. Why the hell did you fellas roll in on a speedboat on the wrong end of the island?"

"Nothing weird," said Shively, a touch too eagerly. "We're working at Fort Beaver. Guide training."

"Right. Gotta nail down the ol' spiel," Rollie said, fidgeting with his backpack straps. "Muskets, cannons. You know, the works." He paused, the silence stretching like a rubber band, before raising his two fingers, and adding weakly, "Scouts honor."

O'Dell's eyes, already skeptical slits, somehow narrowed

even further. Rollie's childish "scouts honor" hung in the air like a neon sign blinking *BULLSHIT*. You could almost hear the gears turning in O'Dell's head as the last shred of his credulity snapped.

"I've been sittin' at that spot over there for most of my life. I've caught some big fish. I even saw a few ships go down. That's some brutal water out there in a storm. But this is a first. Four strangers pull up on Whiskey Point in a Boston Whaler six miles from Fort Feagler, dressed like George Washington's nitwit cousins, and tell me they're here for a job. 'Why wouldn't they take the ferry?' my mind says. 'Why are they already in costume?' my mind says. Makes zero sense to me. *Zero*."

He stepped closer, years of weathered politeness falling away. His lips curled back, revealing stained teeth. "Here's the deal. Either you spill the whole truth about why you're really here, or we swing by the cop shop. My nephew is the chief, which would be impossible to imagine if you knew my nephew when he was twelve years old. He was incredibly dumb. But the boy got smart. Went away to Central Michigan. Learned some stuff. Now, he runs the show. My cousin Lily is the head of the chamber. My aunt Lorraine is the head librarian. I could go on."

He looked straight at Myles. "You sensin' any patterns here, Mustache Mike?"

"Yes, sir," said Myles. "You own this island."

O'Dell smiled as he considered Myles's blunt appraisal. "Maybe a touch overblown, how you just made it sound. But fine, let's go with it."

"You're dug in," Myles continued.

"Like a tick."

The distant sound of waves crashing against the shore and the calls of seagulls filled the air as reality settled in. We had inadvertently allowed ourselves to be nabbed before the caper was even kicked off by an old fisherman with lousy knees named Danny O'Dell.

"Okay," Myles leaned in, a conspiratorial glint in his eye. "You caught us, Mr. O'Dell. We'll tell you the real story." Myles pointed toward the two-track. "It's long and a little complicated, so what do you say we walk and talk?"

O'Dell nodded gamely, and we began our trek into the steaming summer forest.

After thirty minutes and three miles, we had laid out the backstory to Danny O'Dell. Each of us took turns recounting the saga of Marquette's chalice with the polished cadence of Trumbull-trained fort guides. Looking back, we delivered the story flawlessly, passing the storytelling baton without a fumble. We skipped over Myles's involvement and focused on how Feagler had legally swiped Marquette's chalice, Michigan's own Holy Grail. Feagler's plan to make it the centerpiece of a tourist mecca included high-end shopping and even had the governor's support during his presidential campaign. The state economy's decline made the timing worse for Mackinac Island. In short, we were there to snatch the chalice and take it back to Mackinac Island. Dressed in our costumes, we drove a speedboat forty miles to Beaver Island and pulled it up on the beach, where we were greeted by Mr. Danny O'Dell.

"So there ya have it," said Rollie. "Pretty straightforward."

O'Dell shot Rollie a look like he was legally insane—Pretty straightforward?—but he remained quiet, and for a while, the only sound was our boots stomping down the two-track. We had passed what appeared to be the "downtown" of Beaver Island, so it seemed O'Dell had no intention of leading us to the police station to meet his nephew.

We were starting to feel safe.

Finally, he spoke. "Okay. You got me. That's a story." He picked something out of his ear, inspected it, and then flicked it into the woods.

"Now I got one. Ever hear of King Stromberg?" He glanced at Shively, the historian among us. "You must've come across that name in your studies."

"King Stromberg," Shively nodded. "He led a group of religious followers to Beaver Island and declared himself king in 1850. Quite possibly the only self-proclaimed king in American history."

"Yup. That's the guy," O'Dell chuckled, adjusting his hat. "And if you really know your history, you know his reign didn't last long. The locals, mostly Irish immigrants, were none too thrilled to have a king on Beaver Island, especially since they'd just fled their own island to get away from that kinda stuff. Kings and whatnot." He kicked at a rock, sending it skittering. "Let's just say Stromberg's dreams of royalty were abruptly ended." He aimed a finger gun at his temple and pulled the trigger. "With bullets."

O'Dell stopped and leaned back, wiping sweat with an ancient rag. "Now, them were more violent times. Don't get me wrong. These days, nobody on Beaver messes with guns 'cept come deer season when the woods sound like goddamn Iwo Jima. And I would know. I was there. 13th Marine Regiment." He looked away for an instant, scanning the horizon. "Lemme tell ya. That was a shitty week."

Then he was back, shifting his weight from one foot to the other.

"But this Feagler character," he said, his voice dropping lower. "Kinda makes me think of Stromberg. Come to crown himself king of this rock. Big ideas about turning this place into some historical whatsit." He gestured broadly to the landscape around them. "Nothing but a stampede of bulldozers, and swarms of camera crews, you ask me. Not that anybody ever does. A fort on Beaver Island? Makes no sense. That's like buildin' a rollercoaster in a loonie bin. It just ain't needed. You ask me, the man's lookin' to fence us out. Make Beaver into his private kingdom, just like King Stromberg."

He spat to the side, and then turned a squint toward the direction of Mackinac Island. "Now, don't get me wrong. Mackinac's got its charms. I took the grandkids last summer, and we ate ourselves silly on fudge till we were near sick. But Beaver Island? It's different. Quiet. We don't need some fairy-tale fortress or high-end *bo-teeks.*" He stopped. "Look at this." He gestured to his slightly frayed but perfectly serviceable plaid shirt. "Bought this at the D&C in town fifteen years ago, and it's flawless."

He paused and looked us over. "So. You maniacs think there's even a tiny chance that returning this cup to Mackinac Island might help keep things quiet around here?"

We traded doubtful looks. We weren't even sure where we were. But since no one else seemed eager to take responsibility for such a far-fetched promise, I jumped in.

"Yes, sir. There's definitely a tiny chance."

"Very tiny," added Myles.

"Very tiny," O'Dell repeated, his eyes scanning the sky. Then he turned to us. "I'll take them odds." He rubbed his jaw. "Tell ya what. That Boston Whaler you hauled up on shore earlier? It's probably a lot safer docked. I would hate to see some delinquents untie it from that tree for a laugh and let it drift away. Seen it happen. I know a small slip. A quick walk from Fort Beaver." He smiled with the subtlety of the Joker. "Or a quick run from Fort Beaver ... should the occasion arise."

"I'll have my guy Kenny bring your boat around and dock it for now," he said, a mischievous glint in his eye. "Especially since you boys went through the effort to spin such a fascinatin' yarn."

We reached a clearing. Just beyond, new construction loomed. Myles fished out the Whaler ignition key with the Mickey Mouse keychain from a pocket in his soldier's jacket and handed it to O'Dell.

"I live just down the trail there," he said, pointing to a distant clearing where a modest, tidy two-story house peeked through the trees. "I'll take my gear off your hands and hoof it from here." He gathered his cooler, chair, and rod from us, strapping everything onto his back until he resembled the world's oldest Beaver Island sherpa.

"Welp," he gave us a quick nod. "Guess I'll see ya. Best of luck."

He shook his head as if to say, *Ain't this just the weirdest day ever,* and then he strode off toward a weeded trail marked by a rusty mailbox, empties rattling in his cooler.

CHAPTER 35

Taking Fort Beaver

We finally crested the ridge overlooking the much-discussed-but-never-before-seen Fort Beaver. Sweat drenched the undersides of our wool overcoats, and a vapor of guide funk followed us like a floating high school locker room. My limbs ached like I'd marched for days, and my ankle-boot-entombed feet screamed in protest. Images of actual soldiers flashed behind my eyelids like scenes on a movie screen. I felt ridiculously soft, knowing that real Colonial Army soldiers marched for months, dodging musket balls and dysentery. Me? I was ready to wave the white flag at the threat of foot blisters and body odor.

From our elevated vantage point, Fort Beaver unfolded like a planned village. The main entrance was impressive, a twenty-foot-high wooden stockade flanked by American, British, and French flags. Despite its total phoniness—there had never been a fort on Beaver Island—the attraction was admittedly shaping up to be an enticing draw, even with its wooden bones exposed. Like a movie set in pre-production, weeks before the stars arrived, the area hummed with action. A rhythmic clang of hammering echoed in the blacksmith's shop. Workmen rolled a rack of faux animal skins through the open gate of a faux fur-trading post. Cannons lined a platform—ten in total. Redcoat soldiers marched across a massive parade ground, their boots thudding in unison.

Feagler's intentions were crystal clear. He'd thrown a mountain of cash at this project and aimed his firepower straight at Mackinac Island and all the Wawa-golfing ingrates who lived there. A web of dirt roads hinted at a burgeoning upscale shopping district outside Fort Beaver's walls. It was all there, just like that irritating TV special we'd been forced to endure at the Pink Pony.

They called it a "soft opening"—a sneak peek to stir excitement. Judging by the lines at the ticket booth, it was working.

"How do we get in?" I asked, eyeing the entrance where families shuffled forward like sheep under a sign that read *Limited Time Opening Special.* Who knew a forgotten chalice from the sixteenth century could draw such a crowd?

"Through the turnstiles," Myles said, a gleeful madness in his eyes. "Look at us." He gestured to our uniforms. "If anyone belongs in this nuthouse, it's us."

"So we just walk in and take it?" I asked, suddenly realizing how absurd our non-existent plan sounded.

"Replace it," Rollie corrected. "With this sweet baby right here." He knocked on the backpack, producing a metallic clunk from within.

I blinked. In our frantic ride to Beaver Island, we'd overlooked one crucial detail: a plan. It was just one of many loose ends in that day's absurd itinerary.

Myles looked my way, raising an eyebrow. "A little late for cold feet. Unless, of course, you got a better idea."

He knew damn well I didn't.

In a flash, I saw my future unfold in vibrant technicolor. All four of us handcuffed and paraded down Beaver Island's Main Street like common criminals and then shipped in shackles back to Mackinac. The humiliation on my parents' faces. The whispering and judging stares from everyone who knew me on the Island. This wasn't just some infantile prank—this was theft on a grand scale. Stealing a religious artifact? *Sacrilege!*

I could hear the gossip. *They say he also stole Jane Seymour's dress … I never trusted that kid … I always knew he'd end up in the slammer … his whole family is weird … I heard they let him run wild … I heard he worshipped Satan!* I visualized the *Island Gazette* headlines:

"Jack McGuinn: Thief!"
Or worse:
"Grandson of Ceremonial Mayor Destroys Family Legacy"

The headline would accompany a close-up shot of a glistening tear rolling slowly down Gramp's ruddy cheek. Dockporter? Fat chance. After this caper, I'd be lucky to be tossing baggage at Detroit Metro Airport. My brain sizzled with hot shame, and I hadn't even done anything wrong yet.

But hold on a second. Wasn't this precisely the kind of crazy stunt I was born for? My penchant for righteous insanity might've gathered some dust over the years, but it still lurked beneath the surface. This was the same wild spark that had driven me to play detective on a cold case murder before I'd even hit puberty. The same reckless courage that had me swapping witty banter with Jane Seymour—a literal film goddess—during the whirlwind *Somewhere in Time* summer. The same audacity that had me out-handshaking Christopher Reeve—Superman himself—on the Wildcliffe front porch.

That was me!

I used to be wild. Audacious. Fearless. But two and a half summers of schlepping dishes had turned me into a soft, mushy mess. A wilting salad left out in the sun. A poofy, stained, sweaty pirate shirt flapping in the wind.

An involuntary grin crept across my face.

As we neared the frontier-style ticket booth, a sea of young faces turned our way, lighting up at the sight of four soldiers looking like they'd returned from battle marching toward them. Kids swarmed us like bees, desperate for any distraction from the endless line and scorching heat. A few girls wrinkled their noses at our ripe aroma and backed away in disgust, but most were too fired up to care. We stopped, posing for photos, shaking hands, and adding a touch of Mickey Mouse mascot magic to the "soft opening" at Fort Beaver.

Our autograph session went on far too long.

Myles leaned in, his words masked by a fake smile and clenched teeth. "Time to wrap it up, ladies," he whispered, eyes flicking toward the chalice room. We broke away from our impromptu photo shoot and threaded through the crowd, strolling like VIPs through the ticket booth turnstiles.

Inside the walls, Fort Beaver buzzed. Construction workers hammered nails and sawed wood for the ever-growing stockade, hustling to meet deadlines. Fife and drum music streamed through a state-of-the-art sound system, hidden speakers discreetly mounted in the trees, enveloping the place in a weirdly authentic colonial ambiance. Tourists, many clutching single slices of Corleone's pizza, wandered through the completed attractions, faces plastered with broad, dazed smiles. Even in this unfinished state, Fort Beaver gleamed—a sort of Main Street Disneyland version of colonial-era Michigan.

I hated it.

Shively nudged Myles and pointed toward a large, birchbark-covered chapel adorned with religious iconography. A faux-aged and weathered sign read, *Chapel of Marquette's Chalice.*

Inside the chapel, the vibe was hushed and respectful. The faint scent of piped-in incense wafted, blending with the earthy smell of old wood and flowers, creating a soothing yet utterly fake atmosphere. Detailed murals depicted a serene Father Marquette sharing communion with his favorite chalice, surrounded by curious Native American faces.

The artwork was striking, but all I could think about was how Feagler had managed to crank out the paintings so fast. Shipped them in from some sweatshop in China, maybe? Two factories down from the ParTees sweatshop? We maneuvered through the crowds.

And there it was.

At the center of the room, encircled by a frontier-style wooden stanchion accented with ornate silver ornaments, the former penny cup at the Wawa bar gleamed with a newfound brilliance. Reborn. An array of theatrical spotlights illuminated the chalice. The slow, solemn rotation of the relic held the crowd in a trance. Nobody spoke.

"Now what?" I whispered to Myles.

"No idea." Myles scanned the captivated crowd, shaking his head. "We've got a full house. There's no way we can just—"

Rollie's voice shattered the silence. "Esteemed guests," he bellowed, "We stand here in the shadow of France's greatest king!" He turned to Shively, hissing, "Which king was it?"

Shively smiled and stepped up. "The Sun King! Louis XIV! It was under his reign that Father Marquette undertook his voyage from France to New France, the land we now call the United States of America!"

Rollie nodded sagely. "Indeed! And so, we now perform the ancient Chalice Rotation Ritual—a tradition older than French cheese." His voice morphed into a bizarre hybrid of Shakespeare and Pepé Le Pew. Myles and I bit our lips so hard that we nearly drew blood, desperately avoiding eye contact.

Rollie continued. "To ensure this sacred chalice basks in the sun's glory, we must have a moment of solitude. The sacred object will be rotated eight degrees to line up with …" he seemed to be struggling for a finish. "With the sun!" Rollie nodded with a flourish, pleased with his obvious but effective improv save.

Confusion spread through the assembled tourists. A small voice said, "But we're, like, inside. There's, like, no sun. Plus, it's, like, already rotating."

A perfectly reasonable observation.

"Shush, Bobby!" admonished what I could only assume was Bobby's mom.

"What, ma?" said Bobby. "I'm just saying."

Myles seized the moment, gesturing grandly toward the chapel's double doors. "So, if everyone could kindly exit the chalice room for just three minutes, we will execute the sacred eight-degree rotation and reopen the room shortly after.

Incredibly, it worked. The crowd looked around and obediently shuffled out. Even the workmen finishing the ornate cornices headed out, dutifully setting down their hammers and power tools. We waited silently, perfectly still, as the crowd exited the chapel. A seven-year-old boy with a doubtful expression—probably Bobby—was the last to leave, fixing Shively with a slightly demented sneer. We pushed the faux-aged oak doors shut with a definitive click.

Myles had been stuffing his right fist into his mouth to stifle a laugh, and Rollie now bent over, hands on knees, hyperventilating with hushed hysterics. "Where did I come up with that stupid accent!?"

"Quiet!" Shively shot a finger to his lips. "Get to work!"

We approached the display, our earlier hysterics fading as we faced the chalice.

The weight of history descended upon us like a fog. Images flashed through my mind: this simple piece of metal, forged by skilled French hands, sanctified by a bishop's touch, carried across vast oceans and winding rivers. I could almost see it raised high by a curious, brave explorer of faith, a world away from everything he knew.

Father Jacques Marquette.

Under the chapel's soft lights, it seemed to pulse with energy. It whispered of faith, adventure, and human perseverance. The silence in the chapel deepened, enveloping us all in a bubble where time stood still.

What was happening?

"Okay," Myles broke the spell. "I'm starting to feel guilty, and I'm not even Catholic."

"Your guilt has nothing to do with not being Catholic, Myles," whispered Shively. "It's because you're shady."

Myles nodded. "You make an excellent point. Grab it, and let's go."

Rollie unzipped his backpack and produced a tarnished chalice-like cup roughly the same size. His hands shook as he swapped the actual chalice for the tarnished one. The switch was seamless, almost practiced, despite the tension in the air.

"Where'd you get that thing?" I asked, trying to steady my nerves.

"A buddy of mine, a dockporter at the Murray, found it in the hotel basement this morning. Perfect, right?" Rollie said, his voice shaky as he swapped the chalice with the tarnished cup.

I examined it closely. "Couldn't you have at least buffed this thing up?"

"Didn't have time for Goddard's Silver Polish," Rollie muttered, carefully placing the cup. "I think I did okay, considering I didn't know about this stupid plan until this morning. With these colored lights, no one will notice until we're on the Whaler."

"Goddard's what?" I asked.

"Silver polish," Rollie said. "For antique silverware. My aunt loves the stuff. She's always polishing things around her house. It's like an obsession for her. One time, she—"

"Who cares about friggin' silver polish, you dolts! Let's go!" Myles hissed

Shively pushed open the double doors. The waiting crowd surged forward. Rollie called out a rushed spiel, "Hear ye, hear ye! Father Marquette's most holy chalice has successfully undergone the sacred eight-degree rotation in accordance with the courtly traditions of Louis XIV. It awaits your pious viewing. Thank you for your patience!"

We bobbed and weaved upstream through the crowd like four unnerved salmon, desperately trying to maintain a nonchalant stroll. Once outside the chapel, we race-walked straight toward the entrance gate, our backpack radiating a blend of faith, metal, heat, and crime.

We'd just stolen back Father Jacques Marquette's chalice.

CHAPTER 36

The Escape

Behind us, a young voice blared through the propped-open chapel doors like a shrill, runty siren.

Little Bobby.

"Hey, ma! This stupid cup's a gyp!" His previously cute, curious, lilting tone had morphed into a tantrum-laced shriek. The four of us whipped around in unison as Bobby charged out, Toughskins covering little legs in furious motion, his cherubic face now contorted into a mask of red fury. He pointed a chubby little finger directly at us.

"Those smelly soldiers stole the French priest's cup!" he yelled. Every head on the parade ground swung around to look.

Myles muttered under his breath, "I knew that little creep was trouble."

"Would it be too obvious if we started running?" asked Shively, a fake actor's grin pasted on his face.

Myles glanced nervously over his shoulder and nodded. "For now, walk fast. Then we can reevaluate." We picked up the pace, occasionally waving at tourists and shooting forced, guide-like smiles. Just four sweaty soldiers with a chalice-shaped backpack race-walking toward the exit. Nothing to see here, folks.

That's when another voice halted us in our tracks.

"Jack, right? What are you doing on Beaver Island?"

That voice. Haughty. Theatrical. Collegiate. Where did I know it from?

I spun around. It was Derek the Bluecoat.

Only now, he was Derek the Redcoat.

The hammy, mushroom-dosing, shit-canned-from-Fort Mackinac Yale thespian stood flanked by Devon, Craig, and the other guy, all adorned in British colonial attire, far more refined than our sweat-and-lake-soaked uniforms, with the exception that the upper right chest area of each redcoat hosted a Corleone's Pizza logo. I remembered seeing these guys on the TV news special report at the Pink Pony, but it had slipped my mind that they were now working at Fort Beaver.

"Oh, hey there, guys," I stammered. "Um. Long time." Derek's gaze sharpened as he looked at me. "Weren't you a busboy at the Tea Room?" he asked, an eyebrow cocked suspiciously.

"Yeah, that was me," I said, cornered. "Busboy turned guide!" I added as I hammily displayed my military attire. "Who'd've thought!"

"A guide … *where?*" Devon asked, leaning and sniffing me.

The words tumbled out. "Fort Macki—" Mid-word, I realized my fatal slip and course-corrected, morphing "Mackinac" into a desperate "Fort, *Mmmmmaaaaaaan.* The fort. Man."

"Which fort?" asked Craig, advancing slowly.

"This fort! Fort Beaver!" Myles interjected with a grin.

"Where else? Best fort ever, right?" He extended his hand in a sweeping gesture. "We're the latest recruits." Now it was his turn to stumble. "I'm Allen … Camel … fjord."

"Allen Camelfjord?" said Derek. The Redcoat guides exchanged glances.

"It's Norwegian-Saudi. Great to meet you guys!" Myles continued, firmly shaking each of their hands, locking eyes as if sealing a real estate deal in Sarasota.

"We're training," Rollie said. "We start today. Training."

Shively nodded. "Yup. Training!"

We seemed to be fixated on that word. Training.

"Yup. Good ol' training. It starts today," I said. We traded looks, now all nodding.

Derek stepped closer. "We didn't hear anything about training new guides, and we'd know." He tilted his head sideways like a lousy TV cop puzzling through new evidence that just didn't add up. He pushed his hat back an inch and looked down on us. I'd forgotten how tall Derek was.

Bobby's voice cut through the tension. "Mommy! I saw it. The thingy on the cup says *Murray Hotel Employee of the Year, 1962*. It's a *fake!*"

We shot Rollie a withering sideways look, which he deftly dodged. *Employee of the Year?*

Derek glanced toward the sound of the pubescent banshee and then eyed Rollie's backpack, his eyes narrowing into a squint. He pointed at the bag, but before he could get a word out, Myles bolted. "Run!" he yelled, lowering his shoulder and bowling over Devon like a fullback. I heard an airy *oooohh* as the Redcoat dropped to the dirt like a bag of oats falling off the back of a trailer.

We sprinted toward the exit and didn't wait to discover what might happen next. While galloping past a group of tourists, I caught a glimpse of a news crew, likely covering the "soft opening," oblivious to the action movie unfolding fifteen feet from their camera lens. Shively, Myles, and I weaved toward the gate, skipping and spinning around tourists like Barry Sanders heading for the Lions' end zone.

Bobby's shrill voice called out, "It's those soldiers in the blue coats! They stole the chalice!"

The Fort Beaver Redcoat guides were now on high alert, scanning the grounds with predatory eyes. Devon was back upright on his shiny British jackboots, dusting himself off and rehearsing for the role of psychopathic angel of death.

Rollie lagged, his face a mask of fear, as if realizing for the first time in his witty life he might just be headed for an ass-kicking or worse—jail. His expression screamed a silent plea: leave me alone; I'm just the writer! As he ran, he glanced terrified over his shoulder, the backpack slipping low. His foot caught the edge of a Corleone's Pizza banner that had come loose and was draped across the walkway, and he went down with a fleshy thud. The backpack catapulted, the unmistakable sound of metal clunking as it hit the ground and rolled.

Just another dent in the 300-year odyssey of Marquette's chalice, carefully carried by Marquette himself, blessed by God, transported across the turbulent Atlantic, and then paddled in a birch bark canoe from Alabama to Mackinac Island before America was even named. It had served gallons of holy wine—a beacon of peace and enlightenment.

And now, here we were, the world's most inept rescue team, scrambling frantically around a fake fort in our fake uniforms like sugar-buzzed children at a Halloween candy scramble. I imagined the statue of Father Marquette in the park, shaking its head in disappointment. The chalice had endured centuries of reverence, only to end up with us.

With a shocking burst of speed, Myles whipped around, his boots tearing through the grass as he sprinted back to Rollie. He snatched up the backpack in one fluid motion without breaking stride while Rollie scrambled to his feet.

"Get out of here, Shartz! And try not to trip over your own two feet this time!" he shouted.

As the Fort Beaver Redcoats closed in, Myles pulled off a slick head fake, momentarily throwing them off his trail. The video crew's camera swiveled, trying to keep up with the judo-quick maneuver.

"Go deep, busboy!" Myles bellowed across the chaos. I hit the gas, spotting a clear lane to the exit. Years of watching football on the couch with a bag of Doritos and a six-pack of Mountain Dew had prepared me for this very moment.

Going deep was in my DNA.

I watched with awe as Myles slid the chalice from the backpack as he ran. He yelled defiantly across the parade ground, "Remember when I said I was an all-league quarterback!? Well, that one was actually true!" Then he lofted the chalice with everything he had.

To this day, I have no idea how he got a proper grip on the polished and buffed cup, but he did, and it was the most magnificent spiral I've ever witnessed. NFL Films, in their finest hour, couldn't have filmed a better pass. The fact that Myles was decked out like Andrew Jackson on a three-day bender made it all the more impressive. I gazed in awe as the chalice arced gracefully across the sky, blocking the sun for a split second. I could almost hear the rousing classical music as it rotated counterclockwise toward me in cinematic slow motion. For a fleeting second,

I braced for the crack of broken fingers as the metal goblet met my hands. I shut my eyes and waited, resolved to take the pain.

But it didn't hurt at all.

Instead, the chalice glided perfectly between my outstretched hands like a key in a lock with such precision that there was no time for admiration. Myles Fordham: conman, liar, charmer, and driver of the Boston Whaler, could *ball.*

I took off with the chalice securely under my arm, not looking back. Rollie, a hand on his hat and fueled by some new magical reserve in his tank, was hot on my heels. Shively was already through the gate. We darted through the crowd, prompting a clamor of reactions—shrieks, gasps, and even some cheers—as onlookers mistook our frantic escape for some well-choreographed reenactment called the Swiping of Marquette's Chalice.

Behind us, Myles's voice boomed. "Make for the Whaler! Don't wait for me! I'll catch up ju—"

—ooph!

The second bone-crunching tackle of the day silenced him. I risked a glance back. Rollie was gaining, galloping like a graceful rhino, but Myles lay writhing in the dust as two Redcoats stood over him. One began kicking him in the ribs. Brutal. But I kept going, as instructed. We hurtled through the exit lane while a female news reporter's giddy voice attempted a play-by-play. I'm pretty sure she was the same teased-out blonde I saw on TV that night at the Pink Pony.

"Did you get that?" I heard her call out.

A cameraman with a shiny head and a press pass around his neck responded.

"Oh yeah, I got it," he said, grinning like the Cheshire Cat.

O'Dell had kept his word. He'd moved the boat to a makeshift but sturdy wooden dock just a stone's throw from Fort Beaver's parking area, perfectly positioned for a quick escape. Under the seat cushion, my fingers brushed against the cold metal of the Whaler's keys. My breaths came in short, heavy gasps as I stole glances toward the sandy ridge that concealed our view of the fort.

Shively and Rollie hastily untied the lines while I wrapped the chalice in one of Myles's old beach towels and stowed it in a storage compartment. The Whaler was ready to go. With a twist of my wrist, its motor roared to life.

"We can't just leave him here!" said Rollie. I glanced at the guys, just as bewildered as they were.

"You heard him. He said not to wait!" It felt impossibly wrong to leave Myles behind. He was our leader. Corrupt, dishonest, and shady, but our leader.

But we had the chalice.

"WAIT!" a voice screamed out.

We looked toward the ridge just as Myles launched himself over it. From my vantage point, it was like watching a fresh powder skier who caught a lousy edge— limbs flailing, sand flying, head up, then down. Then up again. I hadn't appreciated how steep the sandy slope was until I witnessed Myles's spellbinding, slow-motion spill. He slid to a stop at the bottom, barely recognizable.

"Myles!" Rollie shouted, hopping onto the dock and sprinting toward Myles, who was staggering like a veteran fresh from the Battle of Camden. Blood dripped from his nose, his shirt was torn, and his jacket had vanished. Yet, oddly, his hat remained on his head. Despite the bloodied grin and the noticeable gap where a tooth—or perhaps a few—used to be, Myles laughed maniacally.

Rollie sprinted to his side, meeting him halfway to the boat, and all but lifted him to the Whaler. "Let's get the hell outta here, boys!" he groaned. "Those bastards are nuts!"

I threw off the final line as Rollie plopped Myles down in the stern with Shively's help. He landed in a heap and howled in pain.

"OUCH! Christ, I think those animals broke my rib!" He flopped across the deck like a wounded seal, dragging his battered body on his elbows to a compartment on the side of the boat. With a grimace, he pulled out an unopened bottle of rum, rolled over on his back, twisted off the cap with the teeth he had left, and took a long swig.

"Full throttle, you bastards! Glory, rum, and lovely ladies await us all on Mackinac Island! Except you, busboy. You're too young."

I shoved the throttle forward just as an angry mob appeared, silhouetted, atop the ridge. Their yells were drowned out by the roar of a well-tuned Mercury 65 outboard kicking to life and taking us home.

When we burst into Dr. Trumbull's office, I was out front, and Shively, Rollie, and a particularly ragged Myles followed, gripping what was left of his bottle of rum like Long John Silver.

Trumbull paused, his pen hovering mid-air. A stack of what looked like financial paperwork was strewn across his desk. And for an instant, he appeared almost grateful for a respite from the gloomy task of cutting costs. When his eyes landed on Myles, they widened, and he seemed to segue into a new series of mental calculations: torn clothes, a face that had seen far better, less bloody days, yet still somehow managing to wear that tricorn like a badge of honor.

Dr. Trumbull's expression shifted from shock to something bordering on amused disbelief. He didn't say a thing for several moments.

Then: "Something tells me I don't want to know," he said, setting down his pen.

"You're right," Myles grunted as he wobbled slowly back and forth in place. "But with all due respect, Doc, you're about to."

He nodded at Rollie, who wordlessly placed a hunk of something wrapped in a beach towel on the desk and carefully unwrapped it. It caught the light of Dr. Trumbull's brass lamp and gleamed with power. It looked, if possible, even more impressive than it had earlier at Fort Beaver on its elegant, phony Broadway platform.

Trumbull stared at the chalice, and then at us, his expression unreadable. "I caught a snippet of a scuffle on the news," he said. "It seems Fort Beaver had some excitement today. Some guides got into a fight, of all things. Or maybe it was a football game. It was difficult to tell."

"Maybe a little of both," Myles grinned. "Football's a very violent game."

Dr. Trumbull looked down at his paperwork. "But you gentlemen wouldn't know anything about that, would you?"

"News to us," grinned Rollie. Dr. Trumbull let the obvious reference pass.

I gestured to the chalice. "So, should we just ... leave this here?" It sat on the desk, under the lamp light like a two-foot-tall question mark.

Dr. Trumbull leaned back, eyes calculating factors. A

human abacus. He began flipping his pen in a series of spins. The pen became a blur of motion, then landed neatly between his fingers, his eyes never leaving the chalice. He repeated the motion, eyes narrowing in thought, each flip as precise as the last. It was mesmerizing, but I tried not to stare. Who knew Dr. Trumbull was a world-class pen flipper? With a final flourish, he caught the pen mid-air, stopped it cold, and tapped it thoughtfully against his chin.

Finally, he nodded, having come to some conclusion. "Who have you spoken to about this … item?"

"Nobody," said Shively. "Well, nobody but you. Maybe we should …" He trailed off as Dr. Trumbull raised his hand.

"Leave it here. Until we figure out the next … logical step."

Trumbull turned back to his mountain of paperwork.

"Close the door on your way out," he added, not glancing up. Dismissed, we stumbled out, pulling the door shut behind us. And as we stepped into the cool night air, I heard the door lock click behind us.

CHAPTER 37

The Redemption of Luther Shively

The Fort's parade grounds hummed excitedly as the crowd waited behind a rope barrier, eyeing our cobbled-together stage. Rollie and Shively's wild-eyed week of manic preparation had resulted in a curious hybrid of colonial authenticity and high school theater. A weathered table next to mismatched wooden chairs, a pair of flagpoles behind a flimsy mock jail cell. A row of Charleville muskets on a rack. A cannon. A pistol on the table. It was simple but oddly powerful.

Myles and I had read the pages just a few days before, but I recognized the potential between the lines.

It was good.

I hung back, tugging at my starchy trousers, which never seemed to fit quite right, no matter how many times Mom had altered them. Still pinching and bunching in all the wrong places. At least today, I had boxers on.

I'd triple-checked.

Mom, Big Jack, Beth, Gramps, Cassie, her dad—Governor Belkin, and what felt like the entire island population hovered. As I scanned the crowd, I picked out more familiar faces. Smitty was joking with Rick the shit-sweeper. On a different hill, Gordon snuggled with Sandy Storsen-Viking. In a brainy, tweed little huddle stood the Shively clan. This was the event nobody wanted to miss. Why? Nobody knew for sure. Maybe it was because a new reenactment show hadn't been presented since the '60s, but it had to be more than that.

Then a knot formed in my gut. We'd built our small-town fame on absurdity and slapstick—would the crowd riot when hit with today's show? I caught Rollie's eye, his determined nod steadying me. Too late now.

Time to stick the landing.

Still, I grabbed another scan. Trina was in her usual spot, sitting on her folding chair like a queen holding court to ghosts. She wore a frayed but oddly beautiful purple dress. Her usual array of costume jewelry glittered, a mix of faux pearls and tarnished silver.

Dr. Trumbull's usually stoic demeanor was transformed. Gone was the skeptical squint and resting woe-is-me face; instead, his eyes gleamed. He'd approved Rollie and Shively's script, and he knew exactly what was about to unfold. We'd put him through hell that summer, pushing him to the screaming limits of his patience and professionalism. Yet here he was, bouncing on his heels. Giddy. Did he know something we didn't, or was it just good, old-fashioned Stockholm syndrome?

Remarkably, Dr. Trumbull had kept his mouth shut about the theft of the chalice. I'd spent more than a few sleepless nights waiting for Chief of Police Richter to knock on the Wildcliffe door accompanied by a grim-faced FBI agent with some choice questions about my knowledge of certain missing religious artifacts. I mean, we'd made the evening news! The brutal Chalice-ball game at Fort Beaver was the talk of northern Michigan for at least a day or two. Yet, miraculously, not a single face had been identified. The cocky chrome-domed cameraman, too caught up in the excitement of Myles's magnificent pass, had apparently forgotten how to zoom in.

As days passed, my paranoia gave way to cautious relief. It seemed our luck hadn't run out yet. Had the Governor intervened on our behalf? That summer, anything seemed possible.

Rollie stepped forward, his stance firming into something almost militaristic. His round face grew chiseled, as if carved from limestone. His usual loosey-goosey "I wrote that!" comedy vibe was gone, and his voice boomed.

"Welcome to Fort Mackinac's hallowed grounds! Gather close!" The crowd dutifully shuffled in, kicking up freshly cut grass. I caught Rollie stealing a glance at Cassie, who stood with her father and a gaggle of bigwigs in pastel Ralph Lauren shirts with flipped-up collars. She flashed him an adorable double thumbs-up. He nodded back without breaking a smile. Today was *his* turn to take charge, and he looked ready.

"Ladies and gentlemen," Rollie began, "this summer, our little troupe of crazies has played fast and loose with the facts and smashed all rules of decorum. We've turned these hallowed parade grounds into our personal prankster's paradise!"

He pointed to the Governor with a sly smile. "We've spun more nonsense than a Governor's campaign speech to the Teamsters Union." The crowd laughed as Belkin, grinning sheepishly, raised his hands in mock surrender.

Rollie continued. "But today, we tell a new story. Today, we undo a century and a half of *MYTH!* This has it all—friendship, ambition, and betrayal." He waited for a moment. "Today, we tell … *THE TRUTH!*"

The crowd hushed. Myles and Shively straightened up and took their positions around the wooden table.

I stepped forward, practically yelling to reach the farthest edges of the crowd. "Act One: A Friendship Forged!"

Rollie picked it up. "The year was 1805. Luther Shively and Armand Duval, two young officers with dreams of glory and adventure, forged a bond. They were comrades, with a mutual respect, even when they were—"

"—keep it simple, Private Shartz," I jumped in, sticking to the script. "They were pals!" The crowd chuckled. "Duval was French. His military dad had teamed up with John Paul Jones during the Revolutionary War and felt his son should get some of that famous American grit. So, he shipped the kid to Detroit to serve in the Army. But Armand Duval? He wasn't much of a soldier. He had the soul of an artist. Words and colors were his thing." I shrugged. "He was ... well, French."

Rollie nodded with a smile and gestured to me. "What he said." Rollie then pointed to Shively and Myles at the table. "See for yourself."

Shively, playing Luther, hunched over a wooden table littered with maps, looked every bit the earnest officer plotting his next move. Myles as Duval, sprawled lazily in his chair, feet propped up, casually twirling an ornate pistol as if it were a toy. Luther shot him a glance of barely concealed worry.

"Duval, focus! These are serious times. Napoleon's just crowned himself Emperor, Europe's a bonfire, and America's on the brink of another war with England. We could be called into action any second. We can't afford to be... distracted."

Myles played Duval as the nonchalant Frenchman and shrugged, oozing indifference and affecting a slight French accent. "Eh, wars come and go, my friend. What matters is wine, women, and song." Raising his eyebrows to the crowd, Duval whispered with a glint, "... but mostly women. Besides, what use are artists in war? Perhaps I could write them into surrender? Paint a flag? *C'est la vie.*"

Rollie continued."As the years marched on, Luther's military career ascended. Honors and commendations culminated in his posting as commander of this very Fort. Out of loyalty and friendship, he brought Duval to serve as his aide-de-camp."

My turn. "Luther's star rose. Duval remained in his friend's shadow and started to change. A growing resentment? An ember of jealousy? The year was now 1812, and a fire was lit."

I gestured to the table. "*Operation Stormbreaker* is complete," said Luther, almost to himself. "Even without the high ground, we can defend against attack." He turned away.

Duval stood and raised the ornate revolver, taking aim at the back of Luther's head. The crowd drew a collective breath as Duval's thumb pulled back the hammer, and his finger tightened on the trigger.

The boom never came. Instead, a hollow *click* echoed, followed by a collective gasp that eased into laughter. The crowd had flinched, and now they chuckled at their shared moment.

I stepped forward. "I'm sure our friend Duval was just messing around. Or was he?" I winked at the audience. "Act Two: Discovering Marquette's Chalice!"

Rollie continued: "Once stationed at Fort Mackinac, destiny led Luther to an amazing discovery."

Luther opened a worn wooden box on the table, and he lifted out the chalice, holding it at eye level. His voice was low, but it carried across the hushed crowd. "It had been gathering dust in storage since the Fort's construction in 1781. Hidden in plain sight all this time."

Luther turned to face the audience, the chalice gleaming in the sunlight. "Marquette's chalice," he said simply. The crowd inched forward, straining to see.

"A whispered legend finally made real," I said. "The holiest of holies, right here on Mackinac."

Rollie picked up the thread. "Luther saw beyond the silver. A historian, a man of faith, he recognized its true worth." His voice lowered. "To him, it wasn't just a relic. It was a chance to bridge the gaps between tribes still holding Marquette's name sacred." He let the silence stretch for a moment. "Maybe even a shot at peace."

"But when he showed it to Duval," I added, "the reaction was shocking." Duval, his face contorting into a mask of rage, snatched the chalice from Luther, cradling it against his chest with a Gollum-like possessiveness.

"No! Marquette was *French*, a son of my homeland! Not this … *this savage wilderness!*" He squeezed the chalice tighter. "This belongs with my people, in the heart of civilization and enlightenment! Not wasted on foreign shores!" Duval paced with the chalice like a petulant child holding a toy.

I provided color commentary: "See, apparently, Duval had decided it was time to become … well, *French.*" The crowd hooted. "I'm kidding, of course. I love the French. I had a bucket of fries and a glass of Merlot just before showtime. Sorry, Mom!"

Luther straightened, jaw clenched. He locked eyes with Duval as he took the chalice from him forcefully. "My brother, I am your commanding officer. The chalice stays on Mackinac Island!"

The crowd watched as the tension between the two men crackled. Duval turned away and seethed.

I took a few more steps closer to the audience. "Act Three: The Betrayal!" The crowd hooted.

We had 'em.

Rollie hit *play* on a cassette player connected to some crappy speakers we'd mounted in the trees the night before, unleashing a barrage of distorted battle sounds. Cannons boomed, muskets fired, and the parade ground filled with the cries of soldiers caught in battle. Amid the amplified chaos, Luther grabbed a musket and pored over the map before him.

Rollie spoke. "The War of 1812 was on! However, leaders in Washington neglected to inform Luther Shively at Fort Mackinac. Six hundred British forces, fur traders, and Native Americans landed on the far side of the island in the dead of night."

I stepped in and playfully shoved Rollie aside. "In the words of Paul Revere, the British weren't coming … they were *HERE!*"

Luther's voice was sharp and urgent. "Duval! Rally the troops! Operation Stormbreaker—now!"

But Duval was already moving, a twisted grin playing on his lips. The crowd shifted uneasily. In one smooth motion, he raised the pistol and brought it down hard on Luther's skull.

Luther dropped like a stone, a soft grunt escaping as he hit the dirt. The audience gasped. Our prop pistol was foam rubber, scrounged from storage, but the way Luther went down, you'd think it was steel.

Duval's eyes panned the crowd, drinking in their shocked faces. They weren't sure if they should laugh or scream. Myles was channeling more Flagler College janitor rage than I wanted to know about, but it was working. Forget the Yale Bluecoats. *This* was method acting at its creepiest.

"With one savage blow," Rollie's voice cracked, "Luther Shively crumpled, betrayed by his own brother-in-arms."

Duval seized Luther by the boots and hauled him across the parade ground. Limp as a loose marionette, Luther bounced over every pebble on his way to our makeshift facade of a jailhouse. With a flourish, Duval lashed Luther's wrists and ankles.

"No! No!" The kids' cries echoed off the fort walls. You'd think they were watching Captain America get captured. Their excitement spread, and soon the whole crowd howled.

It was fantastic.

Rollie's voice trembled with barely contained outrage. "But folks, the betrayal cuts deeper! Duval handed over the fort to the Redcoats after a single warning shot. One measly pop of gunpowder!"

The crowd's collective gasp was like a punch to the gut.

I seized my moment, striding to center stage. "You hearing this?" I bellowed, my voice echoing off the fort walls. "Duval didn't just wave the white flag—he gift-wrapped the fort! He let history blame *Luther* for the surrender. Then, during the confusion of the surrender, he took the chalice and buried it in a field not far from this very spot."

The sounds were loud. Military music blared as Duval stashed the chalice in its box. He sprinted across the parade ground to a pre-dug hole about fifty feet away, hastily covering it with dirt.

I gestured north toward Wawa. "Duval's journal tells us he meant to return for it once things quieted down." I paused, letting the implication sink in. "Then he would be off to Paris, chalice in hand, to play the returning hero. Maybe to Napoleon himself!"

Rollie's voice hardened. "With this act of treason,

Duval sealed the fate of Fort Mackinac—and his friend. Down came the Stars and Stripes, up went the Union Jack."

As he spoke, I quickly donned a British redcoat and swapped the flags on our rickety pole.

A groan rippled through the crowd. Rollie paused, his gaze fixed on the British colors now fluttering above us.

In the makeshift brig, Luther stirred. He thrashed against the ropes, grunting and straining until they gave way. Staggering from the cell, wild-eyed and disheveled, Luther's voice rang across the grounds: "Rally the troops! Commence Operation Stormbreaker!" Shively's performance as Luther was mesmerizing.

Rollie shook his head, his voice heavy. "But it was too late. Fort Mackinac had fallen. Luther Shively, once a commander, now a prisoner—this time of the Redcoats."

Luther froze, his eyes locked on the Union Jack fluttering overhead.

I stepped forward, now in British red, and clasped the handcuffs around his wrists. As we marched offstage, I called out, "Act Four: Echoes of Honor!"

Rollie stood alone, letting the moment hang in the air. The battle sounds faded, giving way to a mournful melody.

We let it play. Maybe longer than we should have, but it was working.

Luther and Duval drifted back to center stage, standing shoulder to shoulder in silence. Their faces glistened with sweat, eyes heavy with more than just physical exhaustion. The past ten minutes had been a performance, but it went beyond that. Something had shifted.

I sensed a change I couldn't quite name. It was as if they'd walked through fire and come out the other side, altered but intact. Years later, I'd find the word for what I saw in their faces that day: *redemption.*

"The fates of the men," said Rollie, "diverged after that day. Luther Shively met his with dignity. He never breathed a word about the betrayal, shouldering the burden alone. Whether from a sense of duty, misplaced loyalty, or something else entirely, Luther bore the cross alone."

Shively stepped forward, embodying Luther one last time. "I drew my last breath in a Fort Detroit prison, killed during an American assault. History christened me 'One-Shot Shively'—the coward who surrendered Mackinac after a single warning shot." He paused, the weight of generations pressing down on his shoulders. "This damnable lie stained my family's legacy for decades to come, all because of one man's betrayal."

Damnable lie. That phrase again.

Then I took my turn, gesturing to Duval. "Duval never got to dig up the chalice he'd buried."

Duval stepped forward. "The British held me at Fort Mackinac for a year in the very same cell I'd thrown my old friend into. Then they shipped me to a prison in England, and I was never heard from again."

Duval picked up the journal and held it high. "But I did leave behind my journal," he said. Sad. Heavy. "In it, I poured out my sadness and guilt for what I had done to my friend." He paused, running a finger along the worn cover. "I also hid something else within its pages—the coordinates for the chalice, disguised in the lyrics of a poem." Duval looked out at the crowd, his eyes reflecting a mixture of shame and wonder. "The chalice was finally discovered 150 years later—this very summer—not far from where we stand."

I bit back a grin, thinking of the part we'd all silently

agreed to omit: "Behind the bar at the Wawa, stuffed full of pennies and old golf tees." I jogged to the freshly filled hole, unearthing the box and extracting the chalice. As I raised it high, sunlight glinted off its surface.

Rollie called out. "Ladies and gentlemen, this isn't just a prop. What you see before you is Marquette's actual chalice!" He paused for a beat. "Ladies and gentlemen, everything you've just heard … *is true.* Thank you!"

The crowd erupted in thunderous applause. We lined up, linked hands, and dove into an over-the-top, drama club-worthy bow. It was pure overkill, deliciously pretentious, and silly. But damn, it felt good. Years later, I'd feel that disorienting rush whenever someone praised one of my photos. The artist's mantle never sat quite right on my small-town Michigan shoulders. Praise always felt stranger than criticism.

But that day? I savored every second.

I swept my gaze across the crowd, drinking in the sea of beaming faces. Mom, Dad, and Beth were going wild, their voices hoarse from cheering. Gramps, never one to be outdone, had his patented whistle going—two fingers jammed in his mouth, unleashing a sound that could shatter glass—the shrill note cut through the din, ricocheting off the Fort walls.

At the far edge of the crowd, Trina caught my eye. She'd abandoned her usual perch on the lawn chair, standing tall and clapping with unexpected fervor. Gone was the aloof, slightly boozy queen bee act she typically wore like armor. Instead, her eyes were bright and alive with genuine excitement.

The Shively saga was island lore, a story we all knew and retold with a mix of guilt and relish. It was just too juicy to resist. And Trina? Well, she probably had her own closet full of rattling bones.

Sure, she applauded our performance—we'd nailed it, after all. But there was more to it than that. She was cheering for the Shivelys and every family that had ever weathered the storm of whispered lies and sideways glances. Her clapping was for all those who'd walked through the mud with their chins up, refusing to sink.

We linked hands once more, diving into another over-the-top bow. The crowd cheered even louder, and we basked in it shamelessly. I glanced at Shively and followed his gaze to where his family stood.

The Shively clan—eccentrics and bookworms—were going bonkers. A sea of thick glasses and sportcoats (summer heat be damned) erupting in unbridled joy. Some leaped like kids on Christmas morning, while others maintained a veneer of academic composure, offering measured nods that barely contained their elation.

One of their own had finally broken the curse.

We nudged Shively forward. He raised his hands, and a hush fell over the crowd.

"Ladies and gentlemen," his voice rang out. "172 years ago, my great-great-great-great-grandfather, Luther Shively, was branded a coward for a surrender he never ordered." He paused, drawing in a deep breath. "My name is Burt Shively, and I stand before you honored—and humbled—to share the blood of that brave and honorable man."

The crowd erupted once more. Shively stood rooted, drinking it all in.

Mackinac Island would never hear the name *One-Shot Shively* again.

CHAPTER 38

Curtain Call

That summer, we'd put on our share of shows, with more to come before the season wrapped. But none of them hit like *The Redemption of Luther Shively.* Not even close.

Most fudgies probably missed the point. To them, it was just a fascinating little diversion before they climbed into their horse-drawn carriages and clip-clopped off to their next tourist attraction. But for islanders? It was seismic. The tale of Luther Shively's Fort Mackinac surrender at the outbreak of the War of 1812 was as much a part of Mackinac fabric as the smell of horse crap and fudge or the noon siren.

It was Truth. Set in limestone.

And we'd just taken a sledgehammer to it.

Ten minutes. That's all it took to rewrite a century and a half of history. Add Marquette's chalice into the mix, and it wasn't just a show but a blockbuster double feature that left jaws on the parade ground and minds blown.

Moments after it was over, we dropped all pretense and waded into the crowd like rock stars, soaking up back pats, handshakes, and hugs. It was a huge break from protocol, but Dr. Trumbull was there watching the whole thing, wearing a wide, satisfied grin.

Each of us found our pocket of adoration. Rollie was swept up in a bold and full-of-heat hug from Cassie. Two Secret Service types in dark blue suits instinctively moved toward them but backed off with an approving nod from their boss, the Governor. He leaned in and whispered a few words to Rollie, his expression warm. Without knowing the details, I sensed that the Michigan government-funded spigot of cash was about to be redirected from Fort Beaver right back to Fort Mackinac. Cassie had softened the beaches, as the soldiers say, and we'd stuck the landing. Whatever political behind-the-scenes moves had been made didn't matter now. We had the Governor on our side and the chalice in our possession. Nine-tenths of the law, just like Cassie said.

Shively moved toward Dr. Trumbull, who enveloped him in a monster embrace. Better than anyone, Dr. Trumbull grasped the significance of what had just transpired. As a historian, he recognized that we'd made history— righting a wrong and setting the record straight in one fell swoop.

Then Shively stumbled into the waiting arms of his clan. The eccentric, brilliant, and historically cursed Shivelys engulfed him. For a century and a half, they'd been ridiculed. Now, in just ten beautiful minutes, one of their own had wiped it away.

The McGuinns swarmed me, radiating pride. Mom's eyes were saucers, still processing that her son could act. Big Jack's handshake was firm, while Gramps dissolved into unexpected giggles. Beth, our co-conspirator from the start, shot me a knowing grin and a head shake that whispered, Ya did it again, ya little shit.

A raspy voice cut through the buzz of high spirits and back-slapping. "Come here, young Jack McGuinn." I spun around to find Trina sitting in her lawn chair a few yards away, peering up at me through the folds of a floppy straw hat adorned with fake lilacs. Black eyeliner smudged the corners of her eyes.

"I've roamed around this Fort since the twenties, if you can believe that. I've been watching reenactments just as long. What you boys did today beats all. Took me to another place."

I steadied her by the hand as she struggled to her feet. Her jewelry jangled, and her sun-faded purple dress and yellow feather boa caught a gust of wind. She continued:

"You know, I always suspected the Luther Shively story was a buncha crap. Gave up after one shot? Come on! No soldier worth his salt would do that." She edged in closer. "Seeing you scoundrels sort it out was something else." She reached up and patted me gently on the face a few times. "And I don't even wanna know how you ended up with that chalice."

"Well, it's a long story," I said, trying on a bit of that aw-shucks modesty for size. It didn't fit, and Trina knew it.

"Maybe someday you'll tell me the real story." She paused as if considering whether she should go on, and then she did. "So, what are your plans for next summer? Coming back to the Fort?"

"I'm thinking about it." The truth was, I hadn't thought about much the past few days beyond remembering my lines and not getting arrested for stealing a precious artifact.

"Well, that's a shame," she said. "But I'm sure Dr. Trumbull will be happy to have you back." She secured her fluttering boa and moved toward the exit ramp with the rest of the crowd.

I called up to her. "Why? Why is it a shame?"

She stopped short but didn't turn around. "Well, it just so happens a dockporter position opened up at the Wibho for next summer."

My knees weakened.

She turned around. Her eyelashes fluttered, and she studied me as if for the first time. "You're still a little scrawny. But you can put on a show." Then she turned curiously toward the McGuinn camp. "Besides," she added, "your Gramps thinks you're ready."

She pushed a lock of her hair, now shot through with gray, behind her ear—a simple move that somehow took years off her. I noticed the silver bracelet jangling down her age-pocked arm, catching the sun. It was a small chain with three or four charms.

Saint Ignace, Michigan.

She hid the bracelets, so I gave her one as a thank you.

Across the commotion of the parade ground, Gramps's gaze met mine, edged with the slyest of smiles—my wingman.

As Trina headed off, I heard a voice behind me.

"Great show, Jack." I turned to see Jenna Bonnet. She was wearing her costume and looked like a frontiersman's dream. "Truthfully? I almost cried. You guys really brought it home."

We brought it home alright.

Her smile wasn't the usual allusive Mona Lisa trace. This was ... different. She hovered, giving off an energy I'd never felt. Was I imagining things? Probably. But with summer's clock ticking down, I filed it away for further investigation. I pulled out the Boyish Grin grenade and pulled the pin.

This time, for real. She smiled back. This time, she didn't break away.

"Jenna, quick favor?" I thrust my Kodak Instamatic into her hands. My eyes scanned the crowd, gesturing to the team. "Guides! Huddle up!"

The guys scrambled around me, elbowing for prime spots. I squinted at the light and the backdrop, shuffled our formation, and then nodded to Jenna. We puffed out our chests, aiming for tough. My eyes landed on the set.

"Wait!" I said.

Soon, we each clutched our muskets, completing the look.

"That's more like it!" Jenna grinned, framing the shot.

Just as her finger hovered over the button, we cracked. Laughter erupted as she clicked off two.

"Classic. You lunatics still can't hold it together." She passed the camera back, eyes twinkling. "Bet that's a keeper."

Later, studying the photo, I saw beyond our grins. Exhaustion mingled with joy. We stood united, not by battle, but by experience.

By living.

Jenna called it. It was a keeper.

Later that night, after we'd shed our costumes, I walked to the North Sally Port with Myles in a worn cowboy shirt, and, for reasons known only to him, his tricorn hat. It was an odd ensemble, but he made it work. As we walked, he informed me he was leaving for good. This time, he'd done things by the book. Trumbull had already found a replacement—an eager intern ready to take over for the fall season, someone who knew the cannons, muskets, and stories as well as we did.

It hurt, so I skipped the crap. "Myles," I said, stopping

under the shadow of the white wall. "You have to do the right thing."

He flashed his infuriating, irresistible grin. "And what does our resident sixteen-year-old consider 'right?'"

It was a fair question. Our summer had been an instruction manual on blurring the lines between good and … not-so-good. The once-clear waters of morality were murky now.

"Turn yourself in? Give the old coots their money back? I dunno."

I *didn't* know.

He squinted into the darkening sky as if contemplating Life's Big Mysteries, but I doubted he was. "Yeah. I suppose I could give the old *coots* their money back—as you call them." He looked at me, playing the moralist. "I prefer retirees, by the way," he said. Then he chucked me on the shoulder to make it clear he wasn't actually playing the moralist, and continued.

"Thanks to the Pizza King, I can afford it and still have some cash to spare. Feagler can't touch me legally— I earned that money fair and square and got him his cup." He paused and shrugged. "Now granted, we stole it *back*, but if our luck holds, he'll never connect the dots."

He exhaled slowly, considering. "But turn myself in? Boy, that's a stretch." He fixed me with a look that was equal parts amusement and affection. "Tell you what. For you … I'll think about it." He gave my shoulder another chuck, this time gentler.

My guess was he wasn't going to "think about it." Not that day. Not ever. But I believed him about the coots— sorry, *retirees*—getting their money back. Myles had his own code, as indecipherable as it might be to the rest of the world.

He looked towards the south. "Hey, we made some history this summer, didn't we, busboy?"

I nodded, the beginnings of something that felt like a lump forming in my throat. I turned away.

His voice lowered. "Listen, this embarrassing little moment we're sharing here?"

"Yeah?" I answered.

"It's about as close to a sincere goodbye as I've ever given in my life. So take care. Keep taking pictures. They're good."

He turned and walked away under the South Sally Port's arch, his silhouette framed in shadows with the tricorn hat atop his head.

I called out to him. "That hat. It's State Park property."

"It was a gift," he called back, raising his hand to adjust the tilt to a jaunty angle. Was it true? With Myles, who knew, but picturing Dr. Trumbull gifting the hat wasn't a stretch. He was as captivated by Myles as the rest of us were, even if he tried to hide it.

Besides, what's a tricorn hat or two between friends?

***

Here is what I know about the players, performers, and portrayers from that summer of 1984:

Bert Shively graduated with a master's in history and eventually landed a job as a curator at the Smithsonian. He also wrote a few books, one of which was about Luther Shively. I heard it sold well. I have a signed copy on my shelf.

Rollie Shartz, the jumbo writer with the goofball grin, snagged a job as a writer for *Saturday Night Live.* Rumor has it he wrote up the first "Church Lady" skit for Dana

Carvey. I can't confirm, but it's a hell of a story, so it's the one I tell.

Governor Belkin never became president, but he clung to his governorship for another term and loosened the purse strings for Fort Mackinac. I heard his daughter Cassie ended up out west in Silicon Valley, CEO of some tech giant. That doesn't surprise me one bit.

After losing the chalice and his chummy relationship with the governor, Feagler had a meltdown, sued Beaver Island, and was run out of town by the locals before Fort Beaver could officially open.

Perhaps knowing Stromberg's story, Feagler vanished from public view, although his pizza empire is stronger than ever. In fact, I just ordered a few pies last Thursday for the Tigers game. They deliver to the Island from St. Ignace, but not in 22 minutes or less. It's cold when it arrives, but it's just as good that way.

Marquette's chalice sits in a place of honor at Fort Mackinac. Sometimes, I head up the ramp to the South Sally Port, buy a ticket, and just look at it. It's still got power.

I never heard from Myles again. But in my head, he's living the good life on some key in Florida. Maybe sitting on a quiet beach with a tan wife, looking out on his 44-foot Viking. And wearing a tricorn hat.

Me? The following summer, I took Trina's offer and became the youngest dockporter ever.

But that's a whole different book.

Back at Rogue's Gallery, the story was finally over.

They waited, giving the old man all the time he needed to soak it in. Jack had started in Marquette Park, but that first day ran short. The old man had grown tired, his eyelids drooping as dusk settled in. So Jack took his time, milking the opportunity to spend more time with him. Over the next three days, they'd meet in the park at noon, the old man settling comfortably in the grass while Jack talked and gestured animatedly, his kids tossing a frisbee with his old dockporter pals. Later, they'd relocated to Rogues Gallery, where the ambiance shifted to the busy but intimate confines of the gallery.

It was here on the third night that Jack finally finished. Despite the late hour, the place buzzed. Chairs arranged in a semi-circle around the central exhibit were all occupied. Candlelight created an ambient glow. There was still plenty of wine and beer, and the dockporter gang laughed in small, rowdy groups, choking down the cold cuts Erin had laid out. No one was in a hurry to leave. All that was missing was a boombox playing "The Boys Are Back in Town" by *Thin Lizzy*.

Tonight, it was "Chet Baker Sings," and that worked, too.

The old man remained silent, his eyes fixed on a large photograph on the wall. It was a shot of a group of dock-porters, captured in a rare moment when they seemed both timeless and eternally young. The kind of photo that made you wonder if they had any idea how good they had it. Jack loved the image. It was the first of his that Erin had ever loved, all those years ago, when everything was simpler.

Erin glanced at Jack, but they remained respectfully quiet, waiting, giving the old man space to process.

Finally, he spoke, his voice a soft rasp. "A fine yarn. A bit long … but fine," he said, looking up and nodding. "I always wondered how Marquette's chalice ended up on Mackinac Island. I'd heard all kinds of versions, but I'm going with yours. You and your friends stole it."

He chuckled softly, a deep, warm sound as if recalling an inside joke. Then, he grew quiet again. Erin noticed a flicker of unease on his face. "Is something wrong?" she asked.

"Not wrong," the old man replied. "But there are a few things you didn't get quite right."

Erin pointed to Jack, smiling. "Talk to this guy. It was all before my time."

Jack leaned in, intrigued. "What did I miss?"

The old man settled deeper into his chair. "Well, according to what I heard," he began, leaning forward as if sharing a secret, "Feagler didn't fade away. Yes, he gave up on the Fort Beaver project and had a few tough years 'in the wilderness,' as the writers like to say. You got that part right. He vanished to sort things out."

He chuckled softly. "Some say it was the chalice itself. Feagler wasn't exactly a religious man unless you count the worship of cheese, pepperoni, and profits. But word is, something about that cup got to him. Maybe it was the weight of history, or some lingering trace of Marquette's faith. Who knows? But a man like Feagler could've fought harder to keep control of the chalice if he wanted to. Fight it in the courts. Call the cops. Who knows? Those rich bastards are a little nutty when they want to be. But he didn't. He let it go. And when he let it go, he let many things go."

He paused, gaze distant. "Maybe, after three centuries, the cup still had a bit of magic left. But what do I know? But rumor is, he came out of it stronger. Guess in many ways, he was just getting started."

Jack and Erin exchanged glances.

"I'd heard he was a recluse," said Jack. "Nobody ever hears from him anymore. I had no idea he did anything."

"Not many do," the old man said. "Maybe that's the point."

"So. What did he do?" asked Erin.

"He founded three hospitals, funded a kids' cancer research charity, and set up camps for the disabled. He even funded a few projects right here on the island. On the island! Imagine that! After all that bitterness. He never put his name on a single project, but that wasn't his aim anymore. He didn't want to be known, not for pizza, not for forts, not for chalices. Being a king wasn't his calling anymore. But eventually—this is the best part—he ended up on a throne after all."

"A throne. I knew it!" said Jack. "Don't tell me. He built some obnoxious billionaire mansion in Grosse Pointe. Ended up all alone, doing 10,000-piece puzzles and burning cash in a big fireplace to keep warm."

The old man shook his head. "Nothing that strange." He wheeled closer, lowering his voice conspiratorially. "See, now we're weaving a little woo-woo into the story, but what the hell. It's late." He touched the side of his nose.

"See, it was a different kind of throne. It had damn near everything he didn't know he needed. Took him anywhere he wanted to go. All over the world. He saw places and things that would blow your mind. India. Egypt. The Amazon. He even traced Marquette's route in a canoe!" He looked back at the gallery, but his eyes were somewhere else, shining now.

He snapped back to the present as if waking from a dream and glanced at Edna, who hopped up. He suddenly looked very, very tired.

"Let's head back to the WibHo, woman. The old man's beat. Been listening too hard. Maybe we can order a pizza from Corleone's, like the boy said. They deliver from … what did you call it again? Swingin' Iggie?"

I'm fifty-something, and he calls me a boy.

I'm really starting to adore this man, thought Jack.

"If you want Corleone's, it's too late," said Jack. "The last boat was two hours ago. But there's Sarducci's Pizza on Main, and it's not too bad."

He waved it off. "Nah. I'm a Corleone's man. I love the deep dish. It's fine. I'll just have a few Oreos and a Scotch and call it a night."

As Jack watched them roll towards the door and out into the island night, he called out. "Thank you, sir. It was great meeting you." Erin hesitated, then added, half-jokingly, "I wish we could hear more about that magic throne. It sounds intriguing."

The old man raised a hand, and Edna stopped. They remained in the doorway.

"Funny you should say that. I've seen it, actually!" His eyes lit up like a kid on Christmas morning. "It's impressive. Drink holder, heated seat, fast-charging batteries, even customizable controls."

His bushy eyebrows danced as a sly grin crept across his weathered face. He gave his wheelchair's armrest a couple of pats. "And would you believe it? It's got wheels." As Edna began to push him forward, he called back, his voice carried on a chuckle, "It's better than authentic!"

And then he was gone. Better than authentic?

Jack turned to Erin, finding her frozen in place, jaw slack with disbelief. "It can't be," she breathed, barely audible.

Jack shook his head slowly. "It is," he said.

The next part, they said together.

"Feagler."

OTHER BOOKS

THE DOCKPORTER

In the summer of 1989, Jack McGuinn, a Mackinac Island dockporter, takes on a high-stakes luggage-hauling bet that could save the island from overdevelopment. With his crew of misfits and an Irish cellist named Erin, Jack discovers hidden strengths in this coming-of-age tale. A 2021 Michigan Notable Books Selection.

SOMEWHERE IN CRIME

In the summer of 1979, paperboy Jack McGuinn's world flips when Hollywood descends on Mackinac Island to film *Somewhere in Time*. As movie mania grips the island and his family life crumbles, Jack and his metalhead frenemy Blaze chase a cold-case murder. Their goal: save Jack's family amidst the chaos of a classic film production.

Join our Facebook Group:

https://www.facebook.com/groups/mackinacdockporter

Join our Substack:

https://davemcveigh.substack.com/

We want to thank all the history buffs—both professional and amateur—who tolerate our take on an island we love. Your passion for preserving Mackinac's history is inspiring. Whether you're a lifelong resident, a frequent visitor, or someone discovering Mackinac Island for the first time through our book, we hope you enjoyed this misadventure as much as we did creating it.

Forgive us for making it a little insane, but by now, you know it's kinda what we do.

Jim and I met as dockporters years ago. That story has been told in another book, available if you wish to explore that era of Jack McGuinn's life. This book, however, delves into a different facet of Mackinac's history.

But before the dockporter era, we both worked at Fort Mackinac. Jim was a guide, gaining intimate knowledge of the Charleville musket and tasting gunpowder after ripping open cartridges with his teeth. I was a busboy at the Tea Room under then-owner Jan Sposito's fantastic tutelage. My mother, Kate McVeigh, headed PR for the Mackinac Island State Park, allowing me to meet amazing historians like David Armour, Eugene Peterson, Phil Porter, and many more.

Being immersed in Mackinac Island's history was a gift for us both. While we took huge liberties with history in this book (Marquette's chalice isn't actually at the Fort, so don't look for it), we chose this theme out of love. The island's history provided fertile ground for storytelling.

For those interested in Mackinac's true stories, we recommend books like *Fort Mackinac: A History* by David Armour, *Mackinac Island: Its History in Pictures* by Eugene Peterson, and *The Grand Hotel: Mackinac Island's Crown Jewel* by Phil Porter. These offer windows into the island's genuine history, often stranger than fiction. There are many more.

Mackinac Island is more than a place; it's a living, breathing narrative that continues to evolve. We're grateful to contribute our twisted little chapter to its ongoing story and look forward to more stories to come.

We hope to see you on the island, perhaps at the Tea Room or Fort Mackinac, sharing stories and making new history.

- Dave and Jim
  July, 2024

ACKNOWLEDGMENTS

From Dave: To my wife Mardy and daughter Kelly: Thank you for indulging my pursuit of these stories when I could have been mastering Mahjong with you. To my amazing siblings, whose calls keep me tethered to America across the miles. To my late parents, who instilled in me both a passion for history and a touch of lunacy—the perfect recipe for creating this book. To Jim, for fighting the good fight.

From Jim: To Dave McVeigh: You provided me the opportunity to bring ink to life, to collaborate, to write. To my kids, Anna, Charlie, and Grace, who keep my life lit with an unending fire of love and smiles. And to my entire family, the foundation of who I am. To the teachers in my life who made the difference. I know who you are, and will remember you forever —thank you. And to my friends. All is well no matter where we are. Because.

From both of us: To Janie Barnewell and the crew at the Island Bookstore for their unwavering support. To Dan Riney, proofreader extraordinaire—seriously, hire this guy! To all our beta readers: your help meant more than you know. To Phil Porter, for setting the history bar sky-high. And to the real MIDPA boys, whose stories inspire us to keep writing and give us the perfect excuse to return to the island for yet another unforgettable ride. On it goes!

ABOUT THE AUTHORS

Dave McVeigh is a creative director, marketer, and business owner living in Cebu, Philippines, with his wife, Mardy, and daughter Kelly. He's worked on film and television campaigns for Disney Channel, HBO, Warner Bros, Nike, and more. A University of Michigan graduate, he is Michigan-born and raised and spent 23 summers on Mackinac Island, where he specialized in stone-skipping, dish-shlepping, bike-riding, and fudge consumption. He also hauled luggage in the basket of his bike, where he formed friendships that grow stronger every year.

Jim Bolone grew up in Detroit's east side, the youngest of seven, whose father was a Detroit big band leader, and his mother an artist. He attended the Detroit Public Schools, then on to earn a B.A. in English from Wayne State University. Jim worked on Mackinac Island for nine summers, eight of them as a dockporter, and one as a tour guide/historical interpreter at Fort Mackinac. Currently, Jim is a junior high creative writing teacher and currently lives in Northwest Ohio.

Misguided is the third novel in the *Mackinac Island Novel* Series.